The Greenwood Shady

Elizabeth Cadell

The Friendly Publishing
thefriendlypublishing.com

This book is a work of fiction. Names, locals, business, organizations, and incidents are products of the author's imagination or are used fictitiously. Any resemblance to actual events, locals, or persons, living or dead, is entirely coincidental.

Copyright © 1951 by Elizabeth Cadell
This edition, Copyright © 2016 by the heirs of Elizabeth Cadell
"About the Author" Copyright © 2016 by Janet Reynolds
Cover art by Aparna Bera
All rights reserved.

No part of this book may be reproduced in any form or by any electronic or mechanical means, including information storage and retrieval systems, without written permission from the author, except for the use of brief quotations in a book review.

Chapter One

The River Starr begins its course as an insignificant trickle in Berkshire. It flows south-west, explores a corner of Wiltshire and, with an impetuous rush, washes across the border into Hampshire. After flowing steadily southward for more than thirty miles, it makes another excursion into Wiltshire, sweeps round in a wide horseshoe turn, tumbles into Dorset and makes for the sea.

The land enclosed within this horseshoe—an area of some hundred acres—is thickly wooded. At the sides of the horseshoe's open end stand the towns of Easton and Weston, both rapidly expanding and closing the four-mile gap between them. A traveller driving from one town to the other along the broad highway sees nothing of the woodland stretching between him and the curving river. If he is unobservant, he also fails to notice the narrow by-pass which, wandering out of the main road without a sign, comes back to it with equal nonchalance a mile or so farther on. Even those who see it seldom follow it, for it gives no promise of leading anywhere, and looks, instead, likely to narrow and end in a ploughed field.

It is a road well worth following, however, for shortly after leaving the highway it dips and enters the thick greenwood. In another half-mile it enters a clearing in which nestles the hamlet of Deepwood.

The local guide-book does not describe Deepwood adequately. It observes that it is astonishing to find, midway between two progressive towns, a cluster of tiny cottages set amid trees. It describes the cottages as thatched, old-world and quaint, gives a photograph of the inn—the smallest in England—with its historic sign: the King's Men. It supplies the dimensions of the tiny schoolhouse and the village shop. But there it ends, urging the tourist to go and see for himself.

The tourist goes, and is transported from the sober realities of everyday straight on to a stage set for a scene featuring "Snow White and the Seven Dwarfs." He inspects the properties timidly and finds them all real—the little well, the rustic bench outside the inn, the tiny green wicker gates, the flower-lined paths and rose-hung doorways. Stooping low he peeps into the shop—and sees Grandma du Cane seated behind the counter looking like Miss Matty Jenkins and selling the shop's only wares: photographs of its exterior. He stands in the lacy pattern of sunlight coming through the trees and counts the cottages—seven, with the inn making eight. Eight of them...straight out of Grimm or Andersen. Charmed, bemused, he goes slowly away from this fairy-tale spot, and follows the road as it rises again out of the wood and leads him back to reality.

The inhabitants of Deepwood—thirty-eight in number—

The Greenwood Shady

scarcely lived up to their surroundings. Grandma du Cane counted the day's takings and spent them each evening at the King's Men. Mrs. Jenner charged tourists threepence a time to fill a bucket at the Wishing Well, thereby ensuring herself a steady water supply and a steady income. Landlord Robbins presented a beaming, rubicund front to tourists and a sour visage to his wife, who presented him with an even sourer one in return. Old Grand-dad Robbins was sometimes taken out and propped up in a picturesque attitude on the bench, with a crooked stick by his side and a mug of beer at his elbow, but his language when the mug was not refilled regularly was so unfit for the lady tourists' ears that he was put back again in the back parlour, where he sat happily regarding his favourite possession—a pewter mug, which he had won in a beer-drinking contest in his youth. He had made a special bracket for it on the wall—a somewhat rickety perch, from which the mug was often dislodged.

The seven scholars who trooped out of the school-house were also shockingly out of keeping with the scene. They were lusty little boys—Mrs. Sprule, who was at once headmistress and staff—had agreed to take boys or girls, but not mixed. She taught them their alphabet and their two, three and four times tables, and then passed them on to the grammar school at Weston for polishing. Classes were from nine to twelve, and dismissed with a roar and a rush that lifted the thatch from the roof and knocked old Grand-dad Robbins' pewter mug spinning off its perch.

Deepwood knew its tourist value, and held out stubbornly and successfully against modernisation. Gas and electricity passed it by; main water was scorned and main drainage spurned. By-passing the cottages, these amenities went through the big iron gates behind the village, and found a welcome in Deepwood House and its Lodge.

The iron gates were ugly, but imposing, and were surmounted by two figures which resembled seahorses. Looking at this entrance, and the sweep of drive beyond, strangers went forward with the expectation of coming upon a handsome pile—a Chatsworth or a Blenheim. Once inside the gates, however, the illusion was soon dispelled; the Lodge was a larger edition of Deepwood's fairy-tale cottages, and Deepwood House, two hundred yards farther on, looked as though several thatched cottages had come into violent collision and remained inextricably mixed. Chimneys stood up at odd angles; windows appeared under the thatch, half obscured, like a Guardsman peering from beneath his bearskin. Artists sketching the building took away a faithful picture of it and gained international reputations as surrealists.

Deepwood House, with the Lodge, the iron gates and the wooded acres within the horseshoe, had been bought some twenty years earlier by Alexander Stirling, a man about whom nothing was known except that he was rich and wicked. In quite what way he was wicked, nobody in Deepwood could have specified, for he committed no local crimes, but it was understood that his frequent visits to London were spent in

The Greenwood Shady

shady dealings. Deepwood had not long to endure this unpopular squire, for he died shortly after his arrival, leaving the Lodge to his wife and the House and land to his brother, Mark.

Mrs. Stirling moved to the Lodge, and it was at first feared that Mark Stirling would take up his residence at the House. Mark, said Deepwood, was as shady as his brother had been, and they wanted none of him. Mark, however, sold Deepwood House to an architect, who divided it into four flats and sold them outright, together with their gardens.

At the Lodge, Elinor Stirling lived for some time alone. Though she was less than thirty when her husband died, she made few attempts to join the society of Easton or Weston, and stayed at the Lodge, seldom going away, and too shy to make many friends. She sometimes visited or entertained the tenants of the four flats, but made no close contacts.

As the years passed, the towns of Easton and Weston grew steadily, but Deepwood remained a retreat. The town mothers, after some unfortunate attempts, gave up the idea of using the woods as a free recreation park. The sudden dips and hummocks wreaked havoc on pram wheels; children wandering away were found again only with the aid of a posse; the banks of the river were toboggan slopes fatal to non-swimmers. Loving couples were equally discouraged: the woods were deep, but damp; they were dark, but unromantic, and the paths of error were pitted with rabbit-holes.

Deepwood sometimes wondered whether Elinor Stirling would marry again, but came to the conclusion that her first experience had made her bitter, and no wonder.

This—like most of Deepwood's conclusions—was inaccurate. Though her marriage had not been a success, there had been nothing about it to embitter her except, perhaps, her own regret at not having taken the advice of her relations. They had all disliked Alexander Stirling, and had begged her not to marry him. But Elinor was twenty-five—an age at which she felt that she should be capable of making up her own mind and, further, nobody had been able to put forward any definite objection to Alexander Stirling. They distrusted him, they spoke of him as shady, there were rumours in the City and whispers in drawing-rooms; but there was nothing more tangible. And Elinor married him.

It had not lasted long. Whatever feeling brought them together died quickly and painlessly; Alexander Stirling spent more and more time in London and less at Deepwood, but there had been no talk of separation or divorce. There had been no scandal. There was so little between them that there had been scarcely disagreement. At his death, Elinor had felt regret, but hardly knew what she regretted. He had gone, and with him went her youth and girlish hopes. She was scarcely more lonely in widowhood than she had been as a wife, and she found, after a time, that she was happy.

When she was about thirty-five she received a letter from a relation whom she knew as Cousin Clarry. Cousin Clarry's name was Mabel Clarence, but as there were already, among Elinor's numerous connections, an Aunt Mabel and a Cous-

The Greenwood Shady

in Mabel, Miss Clarence had come to be known as Cousin Clarry. She had written a somewhat curt letter, asking whether Elinor could put her up for a week.

Together with this letter came one from Aunt Edwina Clarence. This was longer, and couched in mysterious terms. It warned Elinor that she must be *very careful,* as C.C. was obviously *looking for a home.* Since dear Uncle H.'s death, C.C. had taken herself, *with her luggage,* to Aunt B., Uncle and Aunt W. and even to poor Cousin G. If Elinor did not take care, C.C. would settle herself on her *for ever.* The writer's only purpose, said a postscript, was to *warn* her.

Elinor, having thought over these two epistles, sent Cousin Clarry a carefully worded reply, inviting her for a week. Posting the letter, she tried to recall what she knew of her, and remembered only that she was about sixty, of enormous bulk and something of an oddity.

Cousin Clarry wrote to say that she would arrive on the twenty-third. On the twenty-first there arrived two shabby suit-cases, a leather trunk with a curved top, two heavy wooden cases, a cello-case and a sewing-machine. On these articles, which had with great difficulty been carried up the little stairway and placed round the walls of one of the spare bedrooms, Elinor had been asked to pay the sum of one pound four shillings and eightpence. She had not begrudged the money—Cousin Clarry, she knew, was not well off—but she could not help wondering why anybody coming for a week's visit should find it necessary to bring a sewing-machine. Reflecting upon the matter, she remembered the letter of warning, and recalled that Uncle Herbert, with whom Cousin Clarry had always lived, and whom she had looked after, had died about four months ago. She was probably without a home, but it would surely, in such a case, be better to store her heavy luggage until she found somewhere to settle. It must be very expensive to have to pay all that....Well, perhaps, thought Elinor, remembering the one pound four shillings and eightpence from her own purse, perhaps it didn't work out so expensive, after all.

Cousin Clarry arrived, looking larger than ever. She was of average height, but her great bulk made her appear almost as broad as she was long. She wore a voluminous tweed cloak, which Elinor remembered having seen on Aunt Winifred twenty years ago. Her hat was of the kind known as a straw boater, and was affixed by a piece of black elastic to the back of her collar. Her sparse grey hair grew in a wild and uneven fringe in front and in bunchy tufts behind, and looked as though she cut it herself without the aid of a glass—-which afterwards proved to be the case. Her gigantic feet were encased in men's shoes—Cousin Clarry had long ago given up waiting in the Ladies' Department-while assistants mounted ladders and turned out warehouses for the more improbable sizes; she now marched into the adjoining salon and demanded, and got at once, a man-size nine.

On the second day of her visit, Cousin Clarry looked thoughtfully at Elinor's attempt at baked fish, and offered to

The Greenwood Shady

do the cooking. The next day there appeared on the table food of a kind which Elinor had seen in magazines and which she had imagined to be the result of trick photography. Washing the plates after lunch, she heard sounds upstairs, and knew that Cousin Clarry was unpacking the large, old-fashioned trunk. After cooking a dinner consisting of a fairy soufflé and a transfigured trifle, she unpacked one of the wooden cases, which turned out to be full of books. Elinor, helping next day with the unpacking of the second case, saw Cousin Clarry lifting hideous pieces of china out of it and placing them tenderly about the room.

Elinor went for a long walk and thought the matter over. In spite of the signs of permanency, she knew that Cousin Clarry was waiting for a word; she knew, moreover, that at a word the books would be put back and the china re-packed without hesitation. Cousin Clarry was ready to move on. Move on where? Elinor wondered. There could not be many relations left who would receive her and risk having her *for ever*. Walking slowly homewards, Elinor thought of the ungainly figure; the soft, fleshy face with its pendulous chins and the scarecrow fringe; the low, booming voice and the downright speech; the un-tuneful, wobbling performances on the cello. It added up to an unattractive total, but Elinor, reviewing the past week, found, to her surprise, that she had enjoyed every moment of it. She could not imagine what it would be like to come downstairs to a kitchen in which there was no large figure in a tweed skirt and Russian tunic. She had seen Cousin

Clarry in the straw boater and Uncle Herbert's old grey trilby, but there was still the black Homburg and the hunting bowler. She had heard her waver through Handel's Largo on the cello, but there still remained a pile of sheet-music to be listened to. Life had suddenly become full of entrancing possibilities. The reactions of Deepwood's residents to the first sight of Cousin Clarry had been more than rewarding, but there were several on whom the blow was yet to fall. The days promised to be amusing and the evenings companionable. Life with Cousin Clarry...life without Cousin Clarry.

There could be no comparison. Walking swiftly homeward, Elinor went into the kitchen and invited her to extend her visit indefinitely. Cousin Clarry turned a peculiar shade of yellow, fumbled inside the Russian tunic for a handkerchief, failed to find it and sniffed.

"About the housekeeping," she said. "I'll take it over. I do better on my own."

Thereafter Elinor confined herself to the housework, while Cousin Clarry became the queen of the kitchen. Every morning of the week, armed with two string bags, shielded by Aunt Winifred's cloak and crowned with the trilby, she went into Easton to do the shopping. Before the tradesmen had recovered from the shock and decided that she was a Bertram Mills escapee, Cousin Clarry knew their full names and history, and was using both. She was soon recognised as unique, and the string bags became symbols of unique service.

When plenty turned to shortage, it was some time before

The Greenwood Shady

Elinor—who was not observant—noticed that she was unable to echo the complaints of other women on the difficulty of obtaining supplies. The string bags came back each morning as swollen as ever, and there seemed to be no appreciable difference in the size or content of dishes placed on the table. The string bags were not the only source of supply: she knew that mysterious parcels came occasionally to the back door, brought in cars, on bicycles and even in prams. Cousin Clarry took in the parcels and paid spot cash, but it was impossible to suspect black-market activities over a package on which the sum of three and fourpence halfpenny had changed hands. Nor was it likely that the bearers—some of whom included leading and respected tradesmen of Easton—would involve themselves in anything of the kind. Elinor asked direct questions, and got no satisfactory answers, and decided at last that Cousin Clarry must be using her intimate knowledge of the tradesmen's private lives to levy some form of blackmail.

About three years after Cousin Clarry's arrival, Elinor had a visit from her husband's nephew, the young Mark Stirling. She had not seen him for some years, for his business was in East Africa, and he was seldom in England. He was on leave, and came to Deepwood to save his father one of the periodical visits he paid on affairs connected with the Deepwood property.

Elinor received him coolly; she did not like him, and she was expecting a visit from her niece, Joanna Clarence. She and Joanna got on well, and it was a pity that their pleasure was to be spoilt by the presence of the unwelcome Mark.

Joanna came, and before the week had ended Elinor saw—too late—what was happening. The possibility of the two falling in love had never once crossed her mind—she was too deeply rooted in her dislike of the Stirlings to imagine for a moment that Joanna could care for one of them. She had forgotten that Joanna was less prejudiced—that she could, like herself, be swept off her feet....

As in Elinor's own case, pleas and arguments proved useless. Joanna, like Elinor, demanded more than vague warnings, and there was nothing more to give. There was nothing but rumour, dislike, shrinking; there were no facts. Joanna was younger than Elinor had been—she was only twenty, but she was a product of a generation that decided for itself. She listened to Elinor and went on with her preparations; she married Mark in London, and sailed almost immediately with him for East Africa. Elinor was left to hope that things might be different, that Joanna would find more happiness than she herself had done.

Cousin Clarry took the affair philosophically. What was done, was done, and divorce could undo it. There were lions in Africa, and Mark often hunted them; anything could happen. If the lions failed, there were elephants and rhinoceroses; there were tropical diseases and the Victoria Falls. You heard terrible things about white cargo and black magic, and the only thing to do was to hope.

And in the meantime, there was the shopping to do.

Chapter Two

Cousin Clarry's coming had an unexpected result: it brought Elinor into contact with the tenants of Deepwood House. Her previous knowledge of them had been slight, but Cousin Clarry's ceaseless investigations brought to light their interests and incomes, their fancies and failings. Like Deepwood village, she wanted to know everything, and had no false pride about the source of information.

The House and the Lodge stood in full view of one another and, to add to Cousin Clarry's pleasure, there were two windows in the kitchen—one overlooking the drive and the other commanding an unrivalled view of the House and its gardens. The gardens had—after consultation among the tenants—been merged into one, and the care of the whole given into the hands of Mrs. Fleury, who lived in one of the ground-floor flats. She accepted the charge gracefully, confident in her position as the only one in the neighbourhood who could not only pronounce *eschscholtzia*, but who also knew what it meant. She agreed to engage the gardeners and supply the flats with flowers and vegetables.

She and her husband, Colonel Fleury, were an elderly

couple with an only child, Francesca, who had made a surprise appearance late in her parents' union, and who was now twenty-one. Mrs. Fleury was a tall, elegant woman with a well-preserved figure and good dress-sense; she sat on several committees in Weston, played bridge and organised most of the fetes and bazaars which took place during the year. Colonel Fleury was as tall and as trim as his wife, and collected clocks—there were fourteen in the flat, and visitors were shown the water clock, the Clepsydra worked by a drum, the lamp clock, the ormulo clock, both grandfathers and four impulse dials controlled by a central master clock and working in unison. Musical friends found the tick-tock, tick-tock hypnotic, and ate their dinner or played their cards in strict time.

Francesca Fleury was a product of England's best pre-preparatory, preparatory and public schools. On her reports the words ' helpful ' and 'co-operative' had occurred regularly, and when she emerged, her parents felt that the money spent on her education had been well repaid. Francesca danced well, spoke prettily, played good tennis and golf; she dressed well and made-up to a point just short of sophistication. Everybody, when she was eighteen, said that she would be married within the year, and she undoubtedly had numerous admirers among the young men of the district.

But Colonel and Mrs. Fleury, like the kings in the fairy tales, set a steep course for suitors—a course far too difficult for the young gentlemen of Easton and Weston, whose ideas on wooing were clear and well-defined: a few dances, a few cinemas, some practised petting and—when everything was fixed up—a word to the parents. There was nothing in their syllabus about sitting through a dreary dinner and learning that Lachenalia should never be trusted in the open ground and that the concentric minute-hand had not been introduced until about 1670. The treatment cooled the most ardent of Francesca's swains, and at twenty-one she had fewer and fewer young men bidding her good night in the drawing-room and being seen by the Colonel to their cars.

Opposite the Fleurys on the ground floor lived a retired couple, Mr. and Mrs. Warren. Mr. Warren was a short, sturdy Yorkshireman, hearty and jovial and devoted to his wife—she had been delicate when they married forty years ago, and he still regarded her as a tender plant. Mr. Warren had been in business in Easton; he had made a comfortable fortune as a chemist and had given generous donations to the town's charities; many park benches, bus shelters, creches and reading-rooms bore his name. He had intended to retire to his native county, but when the time for retirement came both he and his wife had elected to remain within reach of old friends at Easton.

Between the Fleurys and the Warrens there was politeness, but nothing warmer. Mr. Warren and his wife, childless themselves, had a warm feeling for Francesca, which she returned, but Colonel Fleury nursed a strange delusion that a colonel was better than a chemist, and there could be no point of contact between Mrs. Fleury, who had studied Lieder, and

Mrs. Warren, whose favourite tune was "MacNamara's Band."

The tenants above Mr. and Mrs. Warren were abroad and their flat advertised to be let, but above the Fleurys lived the fourth tenant, the Honourable Georgina Finck, who, until Cousin Clarry's arrival, had held chief place in Deepwood's private museum of curios. She was a well-made, handsome woman nearing forty, whose charms could fairly be described as luscious. She was of independent means and independent views, the strongest of which was that, after centuries of being kept down, women were at last free to lead men's lives. They were free to live and free to love. She refused to marry, and said that she would take love where she found it. Deepwood came to the conclusion that she found it abroad, for she went away on frequent trips and returned with foreign-looking gentlemen whose habits were as odd as their appearance. The most spectacular to date had been the Russian who walked in the garden by night, singing so lustily that Grand-dad Robbins' mug had twice fallen off its perch and he had been obliged to get out of bed each time to replace it.

Georgina kept a manservant, Curzon, who was large and discreet and had hair which stood up on his head—a fact which the village thought not to be wondered at. Both Georgina and Curzon looked quite unsuitable in a rural setting, and both would have preferred to live in London or Paris, but Georgina had chosen Deepwood because it was near enough to her home to enable her to keep an eye on her father, who, though over seventy, was showing unmistakable signs of remarrying.

Since this would not have suited Georgina at all, she had stationed herself near enough to be kept informed of any affairs at Cheddarborough Castle that looked like developing dangerously. Georgina had frequently had to put an end to an affair of her own in order to hurry away and put an end to one of her father's.

Cousin Clarry's interest in the tenants was two-fold: to her love of collecting information was added a feeling that they were living in a house which she still regarded as family property. She was disappointed at Elinor's lack of interest in what had once been her home.

"Don't you want to see it more often?" she asked.

"Well, no—why should I?" asked Elinor. "It's not as though I'd ever been very happy in it. I used to like watching the workmen while it was being converted—I never understood how they could make all that jumble of rooms into four flats."

"What became of all your furniture?"

"It wasn't mine," pointed out Elinor. "It was Alexander's."

"Well, yours or his," said Cousin Clarry, with the irritation she showed when anybody contradicted her. "What happened to it?"

"Well, when Alexander died, Mark told me to take what I wanted, and I suppose the rest was sold."

"Sold? But he couldn't sell your furniture—your own furniture. What became of that sideboard that Aunt Mary gave you? I've never seen it anywhere here. And there was that tallboy of Uncle Jim's, and that dresser. What happened to those?"

"Those were sold while Alexander was alive—he never really liked them."

"And did you give him leave to sell our property?" demanded Cousin Clarry.

Her voice was deep and a little hoarse, and she used her jaw in an odd, fish-like way. When she was surprised or angry it fell open and worked up and down until Cousin Clarry found the words she wanted.

"I never knew what Alexander did," said Elinor. "He used to do something first, and tell me he'd done it afterwards. I never knew where he was, or what he was doing, or whether he was disposing of his property, or mine, or somebody else's. So there isn't much point, Cousin Clarry darling, in bringing up Uncle Jim's tallboy."

Cousin Clarry, for once, did not pursue the point. She loved Elinor, and she had learned a great deal about her during the past five or six years. She had known little of her at the time of her marriage; she had shared the family's regret at her marrying a man about whom nobody knew anything good, but she decided that Elinor had done it to get away from home. Many girls married to get away from home—she would have done, too, if anybody had given her a chance. Elinor was not a good subject for an inquisitor, and Cousin Clarry's facts had been hardly won, but she knew by now that Elinor's unhappiness and regret had been great.

Cousin Clarry had never seen Alexander Stirling, but she had once or twice met his brother, Mark. He had come down on one of his unheralded visits a few months after Joanna's marriage, but Cousin Clarry had seen little of him. She had been practising her cello when he arrived—it was winter, when, instead of lighting a fire in her bedroom, she practised in the warm kitchen. Mark had come late, and was gone by morning, but there was no suggestion that the cello had hurried him away. He had been once or twice since, and soon after the conversation regarding the furniture he paid his last visit.

It was a breezy spring morning. Elinor was across at the House, and Cousin Clarry, hearing a car stop at the front door of the Lodge, went through the hall with her peculiar gait—half stride, half shamble—and found Mark Stirling paying his taxi fare. The driver put two suit-cases in the hall, touched his hat and left. Mark stood without moving, and Cousin Clarry, after one glance at his face, let her greeting go unuttered. Taking him by the arm, she steered him towards the drawing-room.

"Easy now," she said. "Easy. There's no hurry. In here. This chair, now—there."

Mark Stirling lowered himself into it and leaned back with his eyes closed. Cousin Clarry piled logs on the fire, fetched brandy and put it by his side; then, hearing Elinor, went into the hall.

"Whose taxi was that?" asked Elinor.

"Mark's. He's in there, and he's ill," said Cousin Clarry. "I'm going to ring up the doctor.—Can't I get that nice young Doctor Beale, Elinor, instead of the old dodderer?"

Elinor hesitated.

"No," she said at last. "He knows the old one, and he'd prefer to have him."

The old doctor, hobbling painfully downstairs from the bedroom in which Mark was now settled, had little to say.

"If there's anyone you ought to let know..." he said.

Cousin Clarry saw him out, and came back to find Elinor staring out of the drawing-room window.

"Is there anyone?" she asked. "Only young Mark, I suppose."

"That's all," agreed Elinor, without turning.

"Well, what'll you do? Cable?"

"I can't cable," said Elinor. "I don't know where he is."

"Don't know where he is?" Cousin Clarry's voice went from a boom to a squeak. "But you told me only the other day that he's in that place with the hyphens—Dar-es...Dar-es..."

"Dar-es-Salaam." Elinor turned, and Cousin Clarry saw that she was looking very pale. "He was, but he isn't there now."

"Well, you can cable to Joanna," said Cousin Clarry. "You must know where she is."

"Joanna," said Elinor, "is on her way home."

"Way home? When did you hear that?"

Elinor walked over to the table and picked up the morning's letters. Extracting a bulky one, she slipped it out of its envelope and re-read portions of it. Five pages—six, counted Cousin Clarry, wishing with all her heart that she could know what was in them. Six closely written sheets in Joanna's handwriting—there couldn't be all that going on in Dar-es-whatever. The letter at Christmas had been a brief, one-page affair. Six sheets looked like an outpouring...and she was on her way home....

"I suppose," she said, after some thought, "I suppose she's left him."

"Yes."

"Well, what did you expect?" asked Cousin Clarry. "They don't stay together nowadays once there's any hitch. I suppose she's found out what he is; and it's about time, too—they've been married three years and two—no, three months. You can find out a lot in that time."

"I don't see quite what I can do about letting him know—Mark, I mean," said Elinor. "I can send a letter to Joanna at Port Said, and if his father gets worse, she'll have to cable him from here."

"What," asked Cousin Clarry, "are you going to tell her?"

"I'll say what the doctor said," replied Elinor. "I'll tell her that the end isn't far off."

Chapter Three

May in the Red Sea. The *Candallia*, 10,000 tons, homeward bound from East African ports, was making fourteen knots on a sea that had the shine and smoothness of a dining-table. The passengers sat or lay about listlessly, a look of endurance on their faces, and only one thought in their minds—that soon they would be out of this inferno. Suez lay ahead; the Canal, and beyond it the blessed breezes of the Mediterranean. In the meantime there was nothing to be done but drink long, cooling draughts and endure the heat and the children.

The *Candallia* carried only one class of passenger; cabins cost more or less according to their position and degree of comfort, but the decks and lounges were common to all. There was not a great deal of space—the promenade deck afforded room for games and dancing, and a canvas swimming-bath had been rigged on the aft well-deck. Below was a narrow strip of deck skirting the cabins, and this was understood to be the place where children should play. The Company, however, had fixed no definite rules; it was a matter left to the mothers' good feeling, but on this trip it would have been impossible for even the best feeling to have found room on the lower deck for the numbers of children aboard. Nobody could remember having travelled with so many prams and play-pens; the promenade deck, a place where the childless could usually be expected to enjoy reasonable quiet, was a scene of juvenile chaos. Little girls opened shops and post-offices on the deck-tennis courts; the quoit-buckets were filled with sand with which toddlers made mud-pies. The less energetic little boys laid tortuous railway-lines that tripped up unwary passers-by; the more lively dragged noisy toys up and down the deck, organised races and shouted encouragement to the entrants. As the ship entered the Red Sea and the life of the adults flagged, tireless children, their cotton clothes sweat-drenched and sticking to them, threaded their way in and out among their recumbent elders, leaving a poison trail of hate.

There were ninety children on board, and it was agreed that they had to be somewhere. A committee had been formed to engage them in quiet and useful group activity, but it was found impossible to impose discipline on group members who had spent most of their lives imposing discipline on their devoted African bodyguards. The committee was disbanded; short of pushing the children overboard, there was nothing to be done but endure and wish that every child on board was like Julian Hume.

Julian Hume was seven, blue-eyed, fair-haired and the only child on board with an unblemished reputation. He sat all day at his father's feet, reading or sketching—he had a remarkable talent for drawing birds and beasts. The passengers patted him on the head and congratulated his father, who tried to look pleased—but he found it difficult, for he himself at Julian's age had been the terror of the countryside, and he would have given a great deal to see in Julian something of the old spirit. Perhaps the English air would have an enlivening effect; in the meantime, Willy Hume leaned back in his deck chair and closed his eyes tranquilly.

This tranquillity was an essential part of his character, but he had an exterior designed to mislead strangers. He was forty-six; tall and fair, with a thin, lined face and corrugations on his brow that made people think that care sat heavily upon him. In fact, care never sat upon him at all; Willy had shoulders which shrugged off worry.

He had left England some years earlier to try his hand at farming in Africa, and had taken out a wife, but both farming and matrimony had met with an equal lack of success. His wife had left him—he had been greatly relieved, and bore her no grudge, but he could not understand how she could abandon Julian. She had subsequently married an American, and was now a Mrs. Tonkers of Yonkers, which Willy considered sufficient retribution.

The farm was sold; Willy was on his way home, and with him was Strone Heriot, a life-long friend, who had come out on a visit and had cancelled his air passage in order to travel home with Willy on the *Candallia*.

The sun beat down mercilessly; the breeze that blew along the deck was almost worse than the heat in the cabins below.

The woman on the deck-chair next to Willy's gave a long sigh of despair.

"I believe I'm on fire," she said.

This statement, which might have roused Willy's interest in any other latitude, merely caused him to turn his eyes on her in sympathy.

"Stick it," he urged. "Suez soon, and then the first thing you know, you'll be down in the baggage-room stuffing all your cottons in and getting all your woollies out."

"Don't talk about woollies," she begged. "I—"

There was a crash of breaking glass behind the chairs, and she closed her eyes.

"Tommy?" she asked, fearfully.

Willy screwed his head round to investigate.

"I'm afraid so," he said. "And Tommy's victim legging it down the deck to complain to the purser or the captain, or both."

Tommy's mother leaned back in her chair.

"As long as nobody comes complaining to me," she said, "I don't mind." She glanced over the back of her chair at her son and, looking beyond him, saw something else that held her attention for some moments. Turning back, she glanced at Willy with her eyebrows raised.

"Willy."

"Mrs. Denwood?"

"When you turned round," said Mrs. Denwood, "I suppose you saw what I saw?"

"Hm?"

"Don't pretend. They're both standing there, as large as life, and you've only got to look at his face to see how far gone he is. Look at them—go on."

Willy turned and glanced in the direction indicated. A man was standing on the deck looking down at a girl. She was bent over a play-pen, trying to persuade the occupant that climbing over the side was a hazardous undertaking. The man beside her stood still, watching; after a few moments she raised her head and looked up at him. Willy Hume turned back to find Mrs. Denwood's eyes fixed on him.

"Your friend," she said significantly, "is heading for trouble."

Willy looked more worried than ever, and spoke in his soft, placid voice.

"Everybody on a journey," he said, "always has a little affair."

"Given the opportunity," agreed Mrs. Denwood. "But this hasn't been a good trip for couples. Children, children everywhere—even up on the boat-deck at night. Besides, Strone Heriot doesn't strike me as the kind of man who has affairs, even on board. And if he is, I think you ought to give him a hint that he couldn't have picked on a worse partner than Mrs. Stirling.—Now, could he?"

"She's a nice girl," said Willy slowly. "And she's lonely

The Greenwood Shady

and unhappy. And anyway, it'll soon be over. England, home and—rations. And porters. One of them'll cart Joanna's luggage *this* way, and another'll whisk Strone's trunks *that* way, and that'll be the end. Never the twain shall meet."

"I hope you're right. It isn't my affair," said Mrs. Denwood, "but I've known you for a good many years, Willy Hume, and I know you're not a man who takes anything seriously. You got Strone Heriot out on this visit, and if he walks into trouble, it'll only be because you're too lackadaisical to give him a word of warning. I've watched the business ever since it began."

"How exactly *did* it begin?" inquired Willy.

Mrs. Denwood put her arms behind her head and spoke slowly.

"She was looking after those awful twins while their mother was feeding the baby—they were crawling along the corridor near the cabin, and I saw Strone Heriot trip over one of them and tread on the other. Joanna picked up one of them, and just as I came along he was picking up the other and looking at Joanna in a curious sort of way—you can never mistake the signs."

"Then *that*" said Willy, "must have been why he was so staggered when we walked into her when she was keeping an eye on the Harris infants. He must have been trying to work out how she could have four children all in arms. He asked me how many she had, and I explained that she hadn't any, and that she was just giving a bit of assistance here and there to overwrought mothers. Next time I saw him she was holding one Harris and he was holding the other. And ever since then—But he's not making much progress, you know. She's doing all she can to choke him off."

"So far, yes. But what woman," asked Mrs. Denwood, "could hold out long against Strone Heriot?"

Willy lay back in his deck chair, eyes closed, pondering the question. How long could a woman hold out against Strone?

Strone Heriot was an actor, moderately but steadily successful. Dark, reliable-looking, somewhat stockily built, he invariably played the steady character on whom the hero—or heroine—could rely. His detractors said that he had never acted anything but Strone Heriot, but he appeared in countless plays and films, and gave always the same satisfying performance. He was unmarried, and his name had never been linked with any woman's.

How much, Willy wondered, was he affected now? It was a pity he had picked on Joanna Stirling. There was nothing to be said against Joanna, but—well—it was a pity.

He passed the two that evening, when the deck was comparatively empty and the temperature a degree or two lower. He came up to them in time to hear Joanna's words of excuse and to see her make her escape. He joined Strone, propped himself up with his elbows on the rail and looked down at the beautiful phosphorescent effects in the water.

"Hello, Willy."

The Greenwood Shady

"Just look down there," invited Willy. "Almost makes me feel it's worth putting up with the Red Sea, just to see"

"You know," broke in Strone, "I'm not doing very well."

Willy twisted round on one elbow.

"Well, no—I can see that," he acknowledged. "Can't say I'm sorry, you know, old boy."

Willy called most people 'old boy', but there was nothing hearty in the title; it was delivered gently and affectionately in Willy's soft voice.

"What've you all got against her?" asked Strone. "You, Mrs. Denwood—everybody. There's some sort of prejudice against her and—"

"Prejudice? You're wrong—you're quite wrong, Strone, old boy." Willy's voice, slightly shocked, came through the darkness. "Nobody's got anything against Joanna. On the contrary, everybody likes her very much, and everybody's only too anxious to help her. Everybody's always been sorry for her—she's so young, for one thing. She couldn't have been more than twenty when she came out. Everybody's tried to help her, but she doesn't give them half a chance. People knew what she was up against, and they could have done quite a lot for her, if she'd let them—but she wouldn't. She always kept herself to herself, which I think was a mistake. There's no point in shutting yourself away where friends can't get at you. She never, to my mind, got the proper spirit of life out there. You've got to mix, and when you do, you find that most people are pretty decent and pretty helpful. But Joanna—for these three years—has just kept to herself."

"I know," said Strone. "Willy—"

There was a pause.

"Well?" asked Willy.

"What exactly is there—I mean, what exactly is wrong with—with her—with Stirling?"

"Mark Stirling?" Willy brought out the name slowly and thoughtfully, and appeared to ponder for some time. "Well, nothing, in a way," he said at last. "That is, he's an ordinarily good-looking fellow, pleasant to look at; but there's just—"

"Women?"

"No, not women. And not drink either. That's perhaps why we all find him so repulsive. He's not one of these unsteady characters who go under through weakness—you can feel sorry for those, but there's nothing about Stirling you can feel sorry for. The man's just—"

"Well?"

"Well, he's just a dirty crook, that's all," said Willy in the same gentle voice. "If you were to ask anybody just what he'd got his fingers in, or just where he makes his money, they couldn't tell you. But you hear rumours of a crooked deal now and then, and you know Stirling's in it. You learn about something that makes the Englishman's name stink out there, and you're pretty sure he wasn't far away. I think he's been watched by the authorities for years, but he never involves himself so closely that they can pin anything on him. But there's *some-*

thing. He wasn't around when you were there, but if he had been, you'd have seen at once what it's difficult to put into words—the antipathy people felt for him. He'd come into the Club, and not a soul would say a word to him. Nobody wanted anything to do with him; nobody ever asked him anywhere. People felt sorry for his wife, but, as you see, she isn't a girl you can do much for. I mean, she isn't the co-operative type, is she, old boy?"

Willy's unstressed tones ceased, and he was silent for some time. When he next spoke, it was on a different topic, as though he had said all that could be said on the subject of Mark Stirling.

"Would you say," he asked, "that Julian was a bit of a sissy?"

Strone roused himself with a start.

"Julian? Don't be a fool," he said. "Just because he doesn't pull the ship apart, like Tommy Denwood—"

"He sits and draws pretty pictures," said Willy sadly. "And he's got fair, curly hair and blue eyes. It all adds up to a very sinister total. Perhaps it's because he was called Julian. I wanted him to be George, like my father, but his mother said No. If I'd known she was going to leave me with the baby, I might have taken a firmer line. Mine wasn't what you might call a successful marriage," he ended musingly. "It's a tricky business, Strone, and that's why I want you to be careful."

"It's a funny thing," said Strone, in slow and puzzled tones. "I've got a feeling—why, I don't know, but it's a strong one—that I've come across Mrs. Stirling before. I couldn't have done, or I'd have remembered her—but I could swear I'd come across the name. Not just casually, but in some closer way."

"It's a fairly common name," commented Willy. "It's a place-name too, and it's also a castle. And a battle. You run into it frequently."

"Yes. But all the same, when I first heard the name Mark Stirling, it rang a bell. Odd, isn't it?"

Willy made no reply. The mattresses were being brought up for those who were to sleep on deck, and some of the women were appearing in what Willy considered delightfully cool night attire.

"Get an eyeful, will you, Strone?" he murmured. "We'd better go across to the men's side, even if it is too hot for passion."

The ship reached Suez and steamed through the Canal. At Port Said, Strone realised that he had made virtually no progress with Joanna Stirling since they had met. She was calm, friendly—and elusive.

He went down to the purser's office and collected his mail. Sorting it idly, he threw the less interesting correspondence into his cabin in passing, and went up on deck to read his personal letters. He stood for a moment looking round at the few passengers who were not ashore; they seemed strange and unfamiliar in warm clothes, and the children's feet, once bare and pattering along the decks, looked heavy and fettered in woollen socks and lace-up shoes. The stewards were no longer in white; the deck-chairs were clustered on the sunny side of the deck and covered with travelling-rugs.

In a far corner Strone espied the form of Joanna Stirling, and he made his way towards her. He drew a chair close to hers and lowered himself into it.

"Letters," he said. "Did you get yours? Yes, I see you did."

There were two or three opened letters in Joanna's hand. She looked at them and nodded slowly.

"Yes, I got them."

"Ah. Good news, I trust," said Strone lightly.

There was no reply. Turning to look at her, Strone found her staring thoughtfully across at the waterfront.

"Not *bad* news," he said, with a touch of anxiety.

Joanna's gaze was still ahead.

"Well, in a way," she said. "At least, someone's dying. My father-in-law."

"Oh. And is he," asked Strone, feeling his way, "are you—"

"I scarcely know him," said Joanna. "But he's my aunt's brother-in-law. It sounds a little like a French grammar, I suppose—the father of my husband is the brother-in-law of my aunt. But he is."

"And it's on *her* account," suggested Strone, "that you're worried?"

"No, not on her account," said Joanna. "She doesn't—

they don't—" She paused and began again: "I was going there when I got home. And now things will be—well, not quite as I planned them, that's all."

"Where does she live?" asked Strone.

"Wiltshire."

Wiltshire....Mark Stirling... Strone frowned in an effort to follow the slender thread of memory, and then abandoned it.

"I don't know much about Wiltshire," he said.

"I don't, either," said Joanna. "At least, I never lived there. I only went down to visit relations—the aunt I spoke of, and a cousin." A smile touched her lips. "Cousin Clarry," she ended, the name seeming to bring amusing memories.

Strone felt as he sometimes did when a Press photographer, without warning, flashed a bulb in his face. He realised dimly that Joanna had risen and was murmuring the now familiar excuses. She had moved away. Before she had gone four paces, Strone was after her.

"Mrs. Stirling!"

She went on. He had no means of telling whether she had heard, but he did not call out again. Instead, he took two or three long strides, grasped her arm and led her firmly to the rail.

"Just a moment," he said, and there was a change in his voice that she could not fail to notice.

"If you'll excuse me," she began, with a slight frown.

"Not this time," said Strone. "I've known, ever since I

heard your name, that there was something—I couldn't make out quite what—but there was some sort of connection. Well, there is."

"Connection?"

"The very word," said Strone. His voice and manner were, for the first time in their relationship, firm and assured. One hand rested on the rail; with the other he still held her arm. They looked at one another, oblivious to the constant coming and going on deck, deaf to the shouts of the Arab boatmen clustering round the ship's side and offering their wares, blind to the sun-drenched port behind them. It was the first time Joanna's eyes had ever rested on him for more than a few seconds; she looked at his square brown face, firm jaw and pleasant mouth, while she waited for his explanation.

"Over there "—Strone jerked his chin at the deckchairs they had just left—"over there you mentioned a Cousin Clarry, didn't you?"

"Yes."

"And you laughed as you said her name. Right?"

"I may have done."

"You did. Well, I've got a Cousin Clarry, and my Cousin Clarry's enough to make a—enough to make anyone laugh. As long as she's broad, extraordinary hair, extraordinary feet, extraordinary clothes, voice down here—boom boom boom—and a magnificent cook. That's *my* Cousin Clarry. Is that yours, too?"

"In every detail," said Joanna. "But—"

"All right. Then we're related." Strone's manner became quieter; he released her arm and turned her round to face the rail.

"Where exactly does the relationship come in?" asked Joanna.

"Well, we'll see. Clarry, naturally, is a Clarence. She—"

"My name was Clarence," said Joanna. "And Aunt Elinor—"

Strone banged a triumphant fist on the broad wooden rail.

"*That's* it!" he exclaimed. "I've got it now! Elinor Clarence—*she* married a man called Stirling. I *knew* I'd come across the name somewhere before."

"Do you know Aunt Elinor?"

"No. At least, I may have met her when I was young—I can't remember. But I come in on the other side. Cousin Clarry lived with an Uncle Herbert once. Remember?"

"Yes."

"All right. Now, Uncle Herbert's name was Clarence, but he had a sister called Aunt Winifred, who—"

"I don't—"

"Well, it doesn't matter—just follow me. Aunt Winifred began life as a Clarence and married a man who had a sister who married a Heriot. And that's where *I* come in. We're not related, you and I, but we're connected—I hope I've got it right. Anyhow, we both own Cousin Clarry, and she went down to Wiltshire to live with—"

"With Aunt Elinor—yes."

There was silence. Strone felt as though he had dropped ten long and troubled years. She was married; her husband was a crook; she was unhappy. But she was no longer an elusive stranger who could slip away when the ship reached England. He had the means of reaching her; at this moment he felt that he had almost the right. Dear, thrice dear Cousin Clarry, whom he hadn't thought of for years and had regarded hitherto as a prize exhibit in a museum of odd relations—dear Cousin Clarry, who had bounded into first place in his affections, to whom he would henceforth cling, to whom he would shortly write....

He pulled himself together and came back to the present. In a quiet, almost uninterested tone, he asked Joanna a question.

"In your letter, did they—do they say when your father-in-law—do they say how long he'll last?"

Joanna stared across at the sunny streets.

"No. But they say that the end isn't far off."

Chapter Four

Mrs. Fleury boarded the Deepwood bus at its Weston terminus and took her place on one of the rear seats which faced sideways. The bus was empty and, though darkness was falling, not yet lit—the bus company saw no reason to waste electricity on the least profitable route in the neighbourhood.

The withered old conductor assigned to the Deepwood run clambered on to the platform with difficulty, and the bus jerked into motion. Mrs. Fleury paid her fare and sat half dreaming, half dozing. It had been a troublesome committee meeting in Weston, but she had carried all her points. The Spring Fete was to take place soon and Georgina was not to be on the committee. A detestable woman, Georgina, but if one didn't cultivate her, it would be said that one was prudish....

Gardeners. Yes, that was a trouble. The gardens had been without attention for over a week, but nobody had answered the advertisements, either at Easton or Weston. It was shocking that gardeners could turn down a cottage and two pounds a week in order to earn more by casual labour....Perhaps Mrs. Stirling would be able to suggest somebody for the gardener's job....No, not Mrs. Stirling—of course not. Not just now.

The Greenwood Shady

Her brother-in-law sinking fast, they said, and wouldn't last the night. Well, one couldn't be sorry—Mark Stirling was a wicked old man, even though nobody could quite put a finger on his crimes. Not drink; not women—some sort of shady dealing. Well, he would have to answer for it all soon.

At this point Mrs. Fleury saw, to her surprise, that there was another passenger in the bus. She felt a slight shock—she had not heard the vehicle stop and she had not noticed anybody getting on.

The old conductor was struggling with the same sense of wonder. Dang funny thing—he must have pushed the bell in his sleep. And given the old buffer his ticket in a dream, for all he remembered. It all came of eating sardines with his tea—they didn't agree with him, not really. Fancy missing a buffer of that size getting on the bus. Must weigh fifteen stone. Sixteen. Almost as big as that Miss Clarence. And a funny-looking customer—might be a gentleman, might be anyone. Couldn't remember hearing his voice when he asked for his ticket....Funny.

Mrs. Fleury's reactions were somewhat similar, though differently phrased. She could study the other passenger freely, for he sat opposite to her, with his hat pulled over his eyes, as though dozing. His clothes sat loosely upon him and, like the conductor, Mrs. Fleury found him difficult to place. She looked at him with a vague feeling of uneasiness and turned to open a window, for the bus seemed suddenly to have become intolerably hot.

If they could have seen his companion, who sat beside him, Mrs. Fleury would have felt still more uneasy and the conductor would have abjured sardines for ever. For the second passenger was a thin, undersized individual, with light-coloured eyes and an expression of faint disdain. He was dressed from head to hoof in close-fitting black; his head was covered with a black cap, through which protruded two small horns. He carried a small pitchfork and was having a little difficulty in arranging his forked tail on the seat of the bus. After trying it this way and that, he curled it up beside him and, leaning back, subjected Mrs. Fleury to a stare of calm appraisement. Once or twice he turned to his companion as though about to make a comment, but appeared to think better of it.

The bus turned off the main road and bumped over the uneven surface leading to Deepwood. Mrs. Fleury loosened her coat and drew a difficult breath. The weather had changed very suddenly—when she had got on the bus at Weston she had felt almost chilly. Now she was almost stifled; but they would soon be there.

The bus negotiated a difficult turn, bumped into Deepwood and set its passengers down at the iron gates. Mrs. Fleury got out, and was surprised to feel the coolness of the air. She walked with unusual haste along the drive, and was relieved to see the lights of Deepwood House before her.

The bus drove slowly away, and the large stranger, waiting until he could be certain of not being overheard, addressed his companion.

The Greenwood Shady

"This must be the place," he said.

"S'pose so. Deepwood, I 'eard 'im say."

The big man looked down with distaste at the meagre, black-clad form. A Cockney! He shuddered. If there was one form of mangled English which he detested more than another, it was that. On the last assignment, he remembered, he had been sent out with a Welshman, and had been forced to endure his whining, sing-song intonation for almost eight hours. And now this pert, sparrow-like Londoner. Stepney or Bethnal Green—one or the other. Once more he was to listen to English—beautiful English—maltreated and debased. He himself, he reflected with pride, could boast of faultless delivery. His voice and accent were alike perfect...and he was tied to an undersized Cockney and doomed to listen to his nasal mispronunciations for the next ten or twelve hours.

The smaller man knew he was being inspected, and in turn sized up his companion. Big, but not much good—he had dropped from the second grade to the fourth in his last two assignments. Plenty of ability, they said, but lazy. No go; liked to sit and do nothing. This couldn't be much of a job, or they would have put on someone more efficient. Well...

"Won't be long," he said, reading the big man's thoughts.

"No. Have you got the instructions?"

The small man took from somewhere on his person a scroll and, after peering at it, pronounced that it was too dark to see.

"Well, we'll go under a light. Follow me, and we'll stand under one of the windows of that Lodge over there. Deepwood Lodge—that must be the place."

The two walked to the Lodge and stood together under the light streaming from the kitchen. Within, they could see Cousin Clarry busy with saucepans. The small man looked at her and whistled.

"Coo! Bigger'n you, she is—look!"

"Quiet!" hissed the big man. "Do you want to rouse the entire populace?"

"Populace? There ain't much populace that I can see. Those cottages over there an—'"

"Go on—read!"

"Well, there ain't much to read. There's the date—May the fifteenth."

"That's tomorrow. Go on."

"There's the name—Mark Stirling."

"What else?"

"There's the time. Five in the morning. Five sharp on the morning of May the fifteenth, it says. And there's the address—Deepwood Lodge in the county of Wiltshire. Well, that's all easy enough."

"True." The big man took the scroll and rolled it up. "Well, that's all."

"'Tain't all. I saw what it says, orl right."

"I said that's all," repeated the big man coldly. "The in-

The Greenwood Shady

structions, and nothing more."

"Oh yes, there was! Assignment Fourth Grade, it says. An' it's the first time I've gone out on a Fourth Grade, I can tell you. The last time I—"

"I'm not interested in your reminiscences, thank you. You can keep them to yourself. In fact, you can keep yourself to yourself altogether. For the moment, all we have to do is wait until five o'clock in the morning, and the best thing to do is find a comfortable spot in the woods over there and wait."

The Cockney swung his tail to and fro in obvious discontent.

"There's lots we can do," he pointed out, "between this and then. We could—"

"Am I," demanded the other, "in charge of this expedition, or are you?"

"Well, o' course—you are. But wot I'm saying is—"

"There's nothing for you to say," said his companion. "We shall wait in the woods. I'm not going to do any more than I have to. Come along."

He turned and walked across the drive, striking into the wood and following one of its narrow paths.

They reached a clearing, and the big man stopped and looked about him.

"This seems a comfortable spot," he said. "We'll stay here until morning."

He sat down on the ground with his back resting against

a tree; the small man stretched himself out full length beside him, staring up at the portion of sky above them. They talked now and then, pausing always to listen to the distant sound of the chimes carried by the breeze from the clock on the Easton Town Hall.

"Eleven," grunted the big man.

"I s'pose that clock keeps English summer time?" surmised the other. "Wouldn't 'alf be awkward if we got the 'ole affair an hour wrong."

"You don't imagine, do you, that they don't go to the trouble of adjusting the clocks?"

"Orl right, orl right—there's no need to be 'uffy. I on'y asked. Keep your 'air on, Mr. what do you call yourself?"

"I always," said the big man, "use the same name. Frobisher. It's easy to remember, and the most earnest attempts to misuse it are defeated. Even you could say it without effort."

"Fro-bish-er. Frobisher. Yes, I see wot you mean. It comes easy. If you want to call me anything, I—"

"I don't."

"Well, orl right. But if you did, you could call me Telemachus. I've allus—"

"Tele-*machus*? Tele-*machus*?" Frobisher's voice was almost choked with scorn. "Tele-machus? Why, you undersized little absurdity, you can't even pronounce it. The name is Te-*lemma*-cus."

"Te-*lemma*-cus. Fancy! I never dreamt!"

The Greenwood Shady

"And did you ever hear of a Cockney—and one your size, to boot—being named Telemachus?"

"P'raps not. But he and I—me and Te-lemma-cus—we 'ad the same job, in a way. Did you ever sing that song—you know—

'My mother kept a boarding-'ouse *Hullabaloobalay*'

—that one?"

"I know it."

"Well, my mother did—see? Kept a boarding-'ouse, I mean. An' my ole man used to 'ave to go on long voyages, same as 'is father—Telemachus's father, I mean. An' it was my job to keep the men away from my ma. That's wot Telemachus did—I read it."

"The Household Homer. And so," said Frobisher, "you saw yourself as the son of Odysseus?"

Telemachus made no reply and, as the silence grew prolonged, Frobisher turned and looked in his direction. There was nothing to be seen in the gloom but the faint white tip of Telemachus's nose, dimly outlined. He was murmuring to himself, but Frobisher could not hear what he was saying.

"What are you mumbling?" he asked at last.

"I ain't mumbling," said Telemachus. "I'm looking. Up there."

Frobisher glanced up.

"Star-gazing?" he asked in surprise.

"Yes. I've missed 'em," said Telemachus simply. "I used

49

to like looking at 'em more'n anything else—that, and reading about them Greeks—They're bright tonight, ain't they? Can you see Capella and Cepheus and Cassiopeia and—"

"Aa-ah!" Forbisher put his hands to his ears and moaned. "Your pro-nun-ci-ation!"

"Well, never mind 'ow I *say* 'em. Can you *see* 'em?"

Frobisher looked up, rather at a loss; stars were not his strong point.

"I can see the Pole Star," he said. "And anybody can pick out Ursa Major and Ursa Minor."

"Well, yes;

> ' *If you 'ud like to know the stars*
> *And learn the where and 'ow*
> *First you must look and find the Pole,*
> *An' arter that the Plough* ',"

quoted Telemachus. "That's 'ow my 'ole man made me learn it. An' 'e told me the names of the seven stars o' the Plough. You know 'em?"

"Of course I know them. Everybody knows them. Dubhe, Merak...Phad.. Phad...Phad..."

"Well, go on."

"Megrez..."

"'Sright. Megrez, Alioth, Mizar and Benetnasch. 'Ow's me pronunciation?"

"Appalling."

The Greenwood Shady

"That Mizar one's a sort of double one—'e's got a little feller near 'im called Alcor. My ole man told me it was so faint, Alcor, that it used to be used as an eye test. Used to stand out at night, I did, starin' up and tryin' to see Alcor.—Can you see Cassiopeia?"

"No."

"Well, go on," urged Telemachus. "Take a squint."

Frobisher, interested in spite of himself, screwed up his eyes and scanned the heavens.

"I don't see—"

Telemachus gathered himself up, rose with a little bound and placed himself in line behind his pupil.

Pointing with his pitchfork, elucidating, he spent the hours of the night brushing up Frobisher's astronomy. When the first faint light of morning began to dim the radiance of the stars, they had followed several of them in their courses. When there was nothing more to be seen, Telemachus stretched, yawned hugely and rose to his feet.

"It's about time," he said. "We'll go along by the river, and get to the Lodge just on five."

They walked slowly. The air was keen, and Telemachus shivered once or twice. The bird-songs were beginning, and Frobisher paused and put out a hand to check his companion.

"Ssh! Did you hear that?" he asked softly.

"'Ear what?"

"Oh, quiet, *quiet*" breathed Frobisher angrily. "Listen,

can't you? Don't you know bird-songs?"

"Bird-songs?"

"There it is again—listen." There seemed to Telemachus to be a confused medley of cheeps and twitters, but Frobisher's ears were more attuned. A little bored, Telemachus looked at the river and, forgetting himself in his excitement, poked his companion with his pitchfork.

"Quick—look!" he hissed.

"Listen to me," said Frobisher, swinging round and speaking with cold fury. "If you jab at me with that—"

"Look!" said Telemachus, pointing. "Little ducks."

"Little ducks? Little *ducks*? Have you never heard of moorhens?"

"Moorhens? Is that wot they are are? Pretty little things, ain't they?" said Telemachus.

Frobisher put out a hand and took a step forward.

"Wait a minute," he said softly. "I'm not quite sure, but I think there's a nest in those low branches overhanging the water there. Follow me—and be *quiet,* you understand?"

Telemachus followed quietly, and soon, with the utmost caution, Frobisher leaned down, parted the low branches, and beckoned his companion closer. Peering, Telemachus saw a nest made of reeds, grass-lined. Following the pointing finger, he saw others, looking like miniature islands, floating near the bank.

Straightening, they walked up the bank and stood for a

few moments.

"The chicks are beautiful—really beautiful," remarked Mr. Frobisher. "Fluffy little black balls—poor little things!"

"Why pore little?"

"They're hounded—to the death, most of them. Rats, herons, otters—they all—"

He stopped abruptly and stared at Telemachus, his face blanching. Telemachus stared back, aghast. Each tried to speak, but it was Telemachus who finally brought out the words.

"The...the clock!" he muttered frenziedly. "It struck—it—"

"The quarter." Frobisher's voice held the calmness of despair. "A quarter past five." He stood without moving for a moment, and then began an ungainly lope up the banks, calling to his companion: "Come on—we might still be in time. Come on—*hurry!*"

They reached the front door of the Lodge to find the old doctor's limousine—some said it was as old as the doctor—standing before it. The young chauffeur, bored, sleepy, was slumped in the driving-seat. He looked at Frobisher with no curiosity—the servants, he supposed, were all up. Frobisher seemed about to ask a question, when a light was put on in the hall and the door opened. The doctor came out and a trim nurse closed the door behind him. As the doctor was stepping into the car, Frobisher started forward.

"Excuse me....Mr. Stirling...?"

"Gone," said the doctor. "Five o'clock exactly."

Chapter Five

Though Mark Stirling had been so little at Deepwood and was so little missed, his death seemed to cause some kind of stir. The funeral took place in London; the nurse went away and things became normal once more, yet Deepwood, in settling down, found that there had been some changes. The young Mrs. Stirling was home, and it was understood that her husband was to arrive in six weeks. Miss Clarence was back at her cello. Georgina had been entertaining a foreign-looking man from Joppa, which was discovered, to everybody's surprise, to be a place near Edinburgh. She had taken him away, and Curzon said that she was going to Spain for a week. There was still no tenant in the empty flat, but Mrs. Fleury had at last succeeded in getting a gardener—a man named Frobisher, who had come out from Weston with her in the bus on the evening before Mr. Stirling's death.

Frobisher was regarded as an odd customer, but it was agreed that Mrs. Fleury had had little choice. Deepwood waited for him to appear at the King's Men, where they could inspect him at leisure, but he stayed in the grounds of the House and made no attempt to speak to anybody outside the iron

The Greenwood Shady

gates. He lived in the gardener's cottage and appeared to have weak eyes, for he kept his hat pulled low over them and never removed it. It was said that he had been heard talking to himself, and Mrs. Fleury was of the opinion that he had come down in the world—his accents were those of a gentleman, but he seemed anxious to avoid notice.

Telemachus found this avoidance of society a great setback. The relations between the two were not cordial—it would never be established whether it was looking at Cassiopeia or the moorhen's nest which had brought about the disaster of missing their appointment, but it was certain that between one and the other, they had come close to ruin. Frobisher, sitting in his favourite secluded spot by the old boarded-up well near the tool-shed, frequently expressed his bitterness.

"O.K., O.K., O.K., let's share the blame," said Telemachus at last. "It was my fault and it was your fault. Can't say fairer than that, can I?"

"Yes, you can. You can admit that if I hadn't—by the merest chance—found out that he wasn't the only Mark Stirling, we shouldn't be sitting here now with a chance of retrieving our position."

"But six weeks..." pointed out Telemachus. "D'you mean we're going to do nothin' but sit 'ere for six weeks?"

"You'll have more opportunity for sitting than I shall. When I'm being watched I shall have to go through some gardening motions."

"But w'y *gardening*?" asked Telemachus. "If it comes to

that, wot did you 'ave to take a job at all for? We could've 'ung about for six weeks, couldn't we?"

"*You* could. You forget," pointed out Frobisher, "that we're not quite similarly placed. Nobody can see you, so you can do all the hanging about you please, but can you see me hanging about for six weeks without arousing comment?"

"Well....But w'y *gardening*?"

"For the simple reason that they wanted a gardener. And for the further reason that that inexpressibly silly woman, Mrs. Fleury, mistook me for an applicant for the gardener's job. Do I look like a gardener?"

"Can't say you do."

"Precisely; yet she engaged me as one."

"All those long words she keeps using—all those long flower-names—do you understand 'em?"

"Do I look as though I understand them?"

"Yes, you sort of do."

"Then that's all that matters."

"But it's *work*," pointed out Telemachus. "Wot I mean is, she'll expect to see some kind o' results, won't she?"

"Very likely," admitted Frobisher calmly. "But gardening—as I hope to demonstrate to you during the next few weeks—is a thing at which you can do a great deal, or at which you can do nothing. Furthermore, while you're doing nothing, you can appear to be busy. And in a garden like this there are nooks and crannies, shrubberies and shelters behind which—"

The Greenwood Shady

"I get you."

"So I shall pass the time in the garden, and nobody will be in the least suspicious. And—"

"Not goin' to be very exciting, is it?" commented Telemachus. "Aren't you going to do—well, a bit here and there on the side, as you might say?"

"No." Frobisher's tone was firm. "Mark Stirling will be here in six weeks; if we're careful, nobody need ever know that he isn't the one that was on that scroll. Until he comes, we do nothing—except gardening."

"I'm going to git awfully tired of flowers," groaned Telemachus. "Nice bit of excitement for me, I don't think. Six weeks of takin' it easy!—An' an other thing," he said. "'Ow do we explain being six weeks late on this job?"

"We can say that we didn't notice the date.—Incidentally, have you got that scroll?"

Telemachus produced it, and Frobisher glanced at it uneasily.

"We shall have to get rid of it," he said. "But we shall have to be careful—if one smallest fragment got into anybody's hands—"

"We can tear it up," suggested Telemachus. "Pity this well's all boarded up—we could've shoved—"

Frobisher had risen and was examining the boards.

"They're more or less rotten," he said. "If you and I gave it a pull here and there we could—"

It took some time to wrench away the boards, but it was done at last, and Telemachus tore the scroll into small pieces and dropped them down the well. There was a pause, and then a curious shuffling noise, and he looked at Frobisher in surprise.

"I 'eard something," he said. "Did you?"

"No."

"Well, there's somethin' down there."

"Any amount, I should say," said Frobisher. "Rats and spiders."

Telemachus peered down the well.

"Big rat, from the sound," he commented uneasily.

He replaced the boarding carelessly and followed Frobisher across the lawn.

"Six weeks," he muttered. "Flowers'n fruit'n vegetables..."

Behind them, the boards that Telemachus had replaced lifted slowly. A hand appeared and pushed the boards apart; an arm followed, and then a head—a handsome head which turned from side to side in an effort to locate the speakers who had so lately conversed at the well's mouth.

"Gone!" muttered a disappointed voice. "Gone, damme!"

In her bed at the Lodge, Joanna Stirling put out a hand, pushed back the bedclothes and yawned noisily. Slipping out of bed, she put on a dressing-gown and went in the direction of the bathroom, pausing as she heard the sound of splashing.

The Greenwood Shady

"Is that you, Aunt Ellie?" she called.

"Yes. I won't be long."

"It's all right—take your time."

Joanna went back and propped herself up comfortably against her pillows. When Elinor came in she was half dreaming, half dozing, a smile touching her lips.

"Sorry if I've been ages," said Elinor. "But I weighed myself, and I was so stunned that I had to take time to recover."

"And what stunned you?" demanded Cousin Clarry, looking in on her way downstairs.

"My weight. I shall have to start slimming. I've been eating all the things you've been cooking to fatten Joanna up—and they've fattened me up too. Cousin Clarry, I've got to diet."

"And let me catch you," said Cousin Clarry. "Let me see you ruining your health going without good food and nourishment. Look at Joanna, now—look at her cheeks. They've filled out and she looks twice as well as she did when she arrived looking like a scarecrow. There's room for improvement yet. An egg-nogg in the middle of the morning and a drink of milk before you sleep—that's the thing. Diet!" she muttered, going out. "Rubbishy theories."

Elinor went over and sat on Joanna's bed. In the morning light, without make-up, the resemblance between the two was very strong. Joanna's hair, fair and curling, had a brightness which Elinor's had lost, but their eyes—brown and set at an attractive slant—their small noses and wide mouths were alike. There was less resemblance in their way of speaking, for Joanna spoke quickly and Elinor with a little hesitation; but it was in their expressions that the greatest difference was to be found. Elinor looked what she was—a woman a little unsure of herself. Joanna's expression, without being over-confident, showed that her mind was fully made up about most matters.

The sun streamed into the room, and Elinor, putting out a slippered foot, wriggled it in the warmth of a sun-patch on the rug. Joanna, lying across the bed, watched her idly.

"It's warm," she remarked. "I hadn't remembered that England could be so warm. Is this a heatwave?"

"I think so; but it's rather a long one," said Elinor. "This is the second week of this hot weather. Personally, I find it a bit too much; all I want to do in heat like this is just to sit about and enjoy it."

"Wouldn't you say," observed Joanna, "that Cousin Clarry, carrying all those tons, would wilt? But she doesn't: she stays in that steaming kitchen looking quite unmelted—or perhaps some of the tons *have* melted, only we don't notice? Aunt Ellie, do you like her?"

"Who—Cousin Clarry?" Elinor gave an amazed laugh. "Like her? Good heavens, Joanna! I can't imagine how I ever lived without her! She's...well, I can't launch into a description—it would take all the morning."

"Has she got any money of her own?"

"I haven't any idea," said Elinor. "For a woman who goes to such lengths to find out everybody else's business, she's remarkably close about her own. Uncle Herbert left her nothing—I know that. And she seems to be the repository—depository?—for the old clothes of all the old aunts. She opens the bundles they send her, chooses what she wants and takes the rest down to the almhouses at Easton. I give her a cheque for the house-keeping expenses. What she does with it I never inquire. She hasn't been away on a visit or a holiday since she came here. I suggested it once, and a queer look came over her face—as though she was frightened that I was asking her to go. It upset me so much that I've never mentioned anything like that again."

"Did she know Uncle Alexander?"

"No."

There was a pause. Joanna lay still, staring absently at Elinor. Presently she put a question.

"Aunt Ellie, why didn't you ever...divorce him?"

Elinor took a little time to answer.

"I don't quite know," she said at last. "Partly, I think, because divorce was regarded by my generation as something rather fatal. Nowadays it's so common that you have to be careful when you talk to people—I mean you find that the wife isn't the one a man had last year, or the children are the wife's by another husband, or something of that sort. But when I was married, and for some time after, a divorce was still a—a breaking up. People didn't think it disgraceful any more, but they did think it a very, very last resort. And then, for a divorce you must have some cause for complaint—unfaithfulness or cruelty or desertion, things like that—and I had nothing of that kind to bring forward. If Alexander had ever fallen in love with another woman, or if I had ever met anyone I cared for, we might have discussed divorce; but as it was, we just left it."

Joanna rolled over and raised herself on her folded arms, looking at Elinor with an intent gaze.

"Aunt Ellie, what happened, exactly? I mean—did you love him?"

"When I married him, yes—very much. I knew very little about men—girls didn't then. I met him on a train. There was a slight accident as we ran into Waterloo—-nothing much, but I got a cut on my head, and he took me home. It went on from there. Everybody, without exception, objected; everybody disliked him. I couldn't see why: nobody could give any sound reason or any proof that he wasn't what I thought him; all they knew amounted to rumours—he was thought to be this and that. And of course, I didn't listen, just as you didn't listen when you fell in love with Mark. We were married, and we came down to Deepwood. It was a terrible old house, but I loved the grounds and the river and the village—I still do. For a few months he stayed down here, and we were happy. Then he went up to London more and more. I never knew anything about his business and I never asked—I suppose that sounds incredible to a modern wife"

"No, it doesn't—not to me, anyhow. Go on."

The Greenwood Shady

"Well, gradually I began to realise that he wasn't—well, that he was...crooked. I used to read things in the papers—unsavoury cases of fraud or blackmail—and the police were always trying to find all those who were implicated, but never did. I don't suppose Alexander was in all of them, but I know—I *know* he was in some. And he began to look different—furtive, in a way. You couldn't, after some time, look at him and say that he was a straight person. But still there was nothing—no facts—to go on. After those first months there was no more feeling. He used to come home, for a rest or a change, I think; but he never made any...demands. I got his room ready, gave him his meals and soon he went away again."

"It's funny," said Joanna thoughtfully, "how we both fell for the same type."

"No, it isn't funny," said Elinor.

"We both fell in love with the first one that came along, I suppose," said Joanna. "Well, you did try to warn me, if you remember."

"Yes, I tried.—Were you unhappy, Joanna?" Joanna pulled absently at the fluff on a blanket.

"Yes," she said. "It was all over long before I sent you that letter. You see, I went right into it: we sailed for Africa almost as soon as we were married, and there it was—isolation. You've never been abroad, Aunt Ellie, so you don't know how differently you grow to look at things like nationality. Here at home you spend half your time avoiding people and hoping you never set eyes on them again; but when you get far away, with thousands and thousands of miles of strange land all round you, you discover that it means an awful lot to meet people who—who talk the language and who remember the same smells—like hawthorn—and the same sights—Oxford Circus and London buses and primroses and snowdrops and Christmas decorations and mowing lawns and Wimbledon and point-to-points and a bad Channel crossing and a three-day fog in London and the clans marching past at a Gathering and—and—oh, all of it! I left it all behind, quite regardless, and went out with a total stranger, practically, and found that at the very sight of him people held their noses. They did, Aunt Ellie, they did! When we walked in, people walked out. People waited until he was out of the way, up-country, and then invited me out alone. Men never talked to him—they looked at a point somewhere above his head and stepped round him, and women looked through him and talked through him. All round us people lived and hunted and shot and played games and rode and did all those sort of hearty things they do out there—lions crop up in the conversation just like that, and shooting, and safari—and there it all went on, and we were marooned in the middle of it, like castaways in the Pacific."

Her voice had risen and she was doing great damage to the pile on the blanket, but Elinor made no attempt to check her. She wished that she could have found the same release when things had gone wrong in her own marriage. She waited until Joanna ended, and then sat in silence for some time.

"Feeling better?" she asked at last.

The Greenwood Shady

"Heaps better," said Joanna, a little shakily. "I wanted to do that the minute I arrived and stepped inside the hall, but—well, there were other things. So it had to be bottled up for a bit longer."

"Joanna, have you any—plans?"

"Yes," said Joanna. "I want to divorce him."

"Does he know?"

"I think so. At least, he knows I'm not going back. I don't think he minds. You ought to understand that better than anyone else, Aunt Ellie. Whatever it is he does, it keeps him absorbed and—detached. He never gets mixed up with women, white or black, as far as anyone knows, and he doesn't drink. I suppose if I'd been in England I wouldn't have felt so—so cut-off; but as it was....After I wrote to tell you I was coming home, I booked my passage and wrote to Mark—he was up-country—and told him when I was sailing. He didn't reply, and he didn't come back before I left, so I concluded that we were just—separating. When I got your letter at Port Said I wrote to him and told him the news; and then when I arrived there was his cable saying he was arriving in six weeks.—Will he have to come here, Aunt Ellie?"

"I think so. There's a good deal for him to fix up."

"Did his father leave him everything?"

"Not everything. I get a reasonable income and this house. Mark gets the rest: not Deepwood House, of course, because that was sold some time ago, but he gets all the land behind—

with Easton and Weston coming so near, he'd get a very good price if he wanted to sell."

There was silence for a time. Elinor was longing to ask a question, but had to summon a little courage.

"Joanna," she brought out at last, "I was wondering—"

"Well?"

"Is there—anyone else?"

Joanna slipped off the bed, walked to the window and stared out over the woods.

"Yes, Aunt Ellie," she said. "There is."

Chapter Six

One morning, soon after Joanna's arrival, the post brought two letters—one to Elinor, the other to Cousin Clarry. A glance at the contents made both of them anxious to sit down and read them carefully, but visitors were seen coming up the drive, and soon Mr. and Mrs. Warren were in the drawing-room making Joanna's acquaintance.

Mr. Warren's smile was broader than usual, for Georgina, whom he detested, was away. Mrs. Warren sat beside him on the sofa, fat and placid and, as usual, taking no part in the conversation beyond a word interpolated here and there when she considered her husband was going off the subject.

Mr. Warren looked at Joanna with the frank approval he extended to all pretty girls, pulled down his waistcoat and congratulated her on her appearance.

"You're looking a treat," he assured her. "You're looking more like. Ah got a look at you when you drove in that first day, and Ah said to Ada here, Ah said, Ada love,' Ah said, 'that girl looks as though some of Miss Clarry's cooking wouldn't do her any harm.' And Ah said, 'That girl's the spitting image of her aunt, Mrs. Stirling.' And so you are. Same colouring, same eyes, same eyebrows, same sort of—"

"You're like your aunt," summed up Ada.

"Yes, you are that," said Mr. Warren. "Well, now, how're you settling down, eh? Did you have a good voyage, now? Ah thought of you once or twice on that boat, Ah did, and Ah remembered all our trips to the Cont'nent in the old days. We used to get about, Ada here and me. Ah used to do my share of parleyvooing across the Channel, and—"

"Booloin," defined Ada.

"Yes, that was it," said Mr. Warren, unruffled. "And now Ah don't feel quite so ready to leave home and see the world—Well, Miss Joanna, and how do you like Miss Clarry's fancy cakes, eh? Ah'm a great admirer of your Cousin Clarry's, Ah am. She says Ah come after the fancy cakes, but don't you believe her. Though last time Ah was here, mind you, and they'd just come out of the oven, piping hot, Ah took three of them, and Ah was punished, Ah can tell you. When Ah went home, Ah felt just as though—"

"Wind," diagnosed Ada.

"Well, p'raps, and p'raps not," said Mr. Warren. "Now look, Miss Joanna, we came in—Ada and me—to see what you'd say to coming along to the Fete tomorrow—eh?"

"Fete?" repeated Joanna, at a loss.

"It's called the Spring Fete, and it takes place every year at Weston," explained Elinor. "It's more of an exhibition—people exhibit the work they've done during the winter: needlework, knitting, rugmaking and so on. And there's a Flower Competition arranged by Mrs. Fleury. She gets it up and—"

"—and she wins all the prizes," put in Mr. Warren. "Rum co-in-ci-dence, eh?"

"Don't be wicked now," said Cousin Clarry.

"Wicked? Four years she's got it up, and four years she's scooped the prizes," declared Mr. Warren. "Ah don't say she doesn't win them fairly, but Ah do say she ought to step down and let someone else have a go. Look at Miss Clarry's roses that she grows in that little bit of garden of hers out there— why can't they give *her* the Cups, for a change?—Are you showing any this year, Miss Clarry?"

"Of course I am," said Cousin Clarry. "If they haven't dried up, that is. Did you ever see the House gardens looking so brown?"

"It's all this heat," said Mr. Warren. "Perhaps this new gardener chap can do something. He's big enough. They say he's not all he ought to be in the top story. He—"

"Daft," said Ada.

"Who says so?" asked Cousin Clarry.

"They all say so," said Mr. Warren. "He talks away to himself by the dozen."

"Well, that might be the heat, too," said Elinor. "Perhaps it upsets him."

"It might at that," acknowledged Mr. Warren. "When Ah was a young chap, Ah never minded whether it blew hot or cold, but now that—"

"Fete!" said Ada.

"Eh? Oh—Fete. Well, Miss Joanna, how about it? Will you come?"

Joanna sent a look of appeal towards Elinor, but it was Cousin Clarry who came to the rescue.

"It's kind of you, but she's not up to meeting all those strangers yet," she said. "If you'll let me come in with you, I'd be glad of a lift."

"And we'll be glad to take you. Ah gave old bus a good wash yesterday, and tinkered her up a bit, so there's quite likely to be a—"

"Half-past three," said Ada.

"That'll suit me very well," said Cousin Clarry, sweeping them out. She returned to the drawingroom and looked round for her glasses. "Now I can read my letter," she said. "A nice couple that, Joanna. No need for Mrs. F. to look down her nose—I'd rather have good, solid Easton tradesmen than some of that arty Weston lot. That Ada's a nice girl."

"She's hardly a girl!" protested Elinor.

"She's my age," said Cousin Clarry, putting on her glasses and peering over the top of them. "Have you anything to say?"

"Nothing," said Elinor.

"Good. Then all be quiet and let me read this letter again. It's a garbled bit of composition. Who's yours from, Elinor? Anyone I know? No, don't tell me now—it'll only confuse me

The Greenwood Shady

more."

She held her letter at arm's length, drew it nearer to focus it, settled her glasses firmly on her nose, got the focus correctly adjusted and read the letter with an accompanying mumble.

"Yes...yes, that's right enough...yes. Aunt Winifred, yes. Yes...yes, Uncle Herbert, first cousin, second cousin...."

Elinor, defeated, put down her own letter until the mumbling stopped. Looking up, she saw to her surprise that Joanna's eyes were fixed intently on Cousin Clarry, and that her cheeks wore an unusual flush. Cousin Clarry put the letter down on her lap with a final grunt.

"Can't make head or tail," she said. "All I can make out is that he's fishing for an invitation; but, if so, why not just *ask*? Why all this family tree and cousin this and that? He could say, in plain English, ' I'm a relation,' and leave the branches for another time."

"Who?" inquired Elinor.

"Name of Heriot—an actor. At least, he says he's an actor, but I can't say I ever heard of a Heriot. Half the people you meet now tell you they're actors, but you can never find a sight or sign of them on any stage. Did you ever hear of this Heriot?"

"There's a Strone Heriot," said Elinor. "Is that the one? He's quite well known."

"Strone?" Cousin Clarry peered once more. "Is that what it's meant to be? Looks to me like Stone or Bone."

"Did you say he wanted to come and stay?" asked Elinor.

"Yes. He knows it isn't my house, but he says he can approach me—silly word to use, but he uses it—as a relation and ask me to present his case. Says he met Joanna on the boat." She eyed Joanna over her glasses.—"Did he meet you on the boat?"

"Yes."

"You mean you travelled together?"

"Yes."

"Then why does he present his case to me? Why doesn't he present his case to you?"

"Well, because—I mean—"

"You mean that this rigmarole, this hope of getting to know me, this picking up old threads—does he mean I'm an old thread?—all this, I take it, is my eye and Betty Martin?"

"No, it isn't. He found out—quite by chance—that you were a connection of his. And when he heard that I was coming here, he—we—thought he'd write and suggest a visit. What's wrong with that? It's a perfectly natural suggestion, and I think it's a very friendly letter."

"There's nothing friendly about it," declared Cousin Clarry. "It's plain fishing. How old is he?"

"Thirty-six."

"Then he's been related to me for thirty-six years without bothering to write. What made him so anxious to know me all of a sudden?"

The Greenwood Shady

"Me," said Joanna, abandoning pretence.

"Ah. If we go on long enough we'll get to the bottom of this. And why didn't this whoever he is write to your Aunt Elinor?"

"Well, all he wanted to do was to establish a connection," said Joanna. "He wanted you to present his case, just as he said in the letter—but he didn't know you'd present it so badly."

"Let him come, Cousin Clarry," said Elinor. "Write and offer him the bedroom at the end of the corridor, and tell him about the mice in the wainscoting."

"And when he comes here," Cousin Clarry asked Joanna, "is he going to be my visitor or yours?"

"Oh, mine. Definitely mine."

"I see. I suppose you've been having one of those boardship affairs, like your Aunt Lucy, who couldn't go across from Dover to Calais without getting entangled with one if not three entire strangers. When she brought that foreign husband of hers back from Switzerland, she arrived at Waterloo on the arm of a fair man with a fair moustache, and where was her husband?"

"Behind a dark moustache?" hazarded Joanna.

"You may joke, but I don't care to be referred to as an old thread.—Who's your letter from, Elinor? Someone else claiming relationship?"

"He doesn't claim any relationship," said Elinor. "He only asks if he can come."

"What...*another*?"

"Oh, Aunt Ellie, *who*?" asked Joanna.

Cousin Clarry raised her eyebrows.

"You mean you don't know who?"

"I honestly don't. Who, Aunt Ellie?"

Elinor glanced at the letter.

"Yours sincerely, William Hume," she read.

"William Hume?" Joanna repeated the name in bewilderment. "William *Hume*? Who's William Hume?"

"Was he on the boat, too?" asked Cousin Clarry. "If so, he didn't make much impression. Well, who *is* William Hume?"

"He says he's a friend of Strone Heriot," said Elinor. "He says he's heard that he's visiting us, and he wants to know if I can suggest any accommodation for him nearby. He's got a seven-year-old son."

"Then don't make the accommodation too near by," said Cousin Clarry. "Where's his wife?"

"He doesn't mention a wife. He just—"

"Oh, Willy *Hume*!" said Joanna suddenly. "Of course I know—yes, Willy Hume."

"Well, now that you've placed him, perhaps you can tell us where he's placed his wife," said Cousin Clarry. "Was she on the boat I—"

"No; she left him and married somebody else. He's Julian's father—Julian's a sweet little boy. And his father's nice, too, although I didn't talk to him much. He's oldish and tall and sort of willowy and—"

"When it's a man," said Cousin Clarry, "they're not willowy—they're gangling. Did he gangle after you?"

"No. He isn't the type that gangles after anybody," said Joanna. "And he only wants to come here because he and Strone—Mr. Heriot—have been friends all their lives."

"Can't he take that empty flat over at the House?" suggested Elinor. "I could give him the address of the agents and tell him what the rent is, and if he doesn't like the sound of it, he needn't come."

"Why did his wife leave him?" asked Cousin Clarry suspiciously.

"Oh, Cousin Clarry!"—Joanna's tone was amazed—"how on earth do I know? I hardly know him. I couldn't go up to him and ask him things about his wife! And I didn't want to know, anyhow. There's nothing about him you won't like—he's harmless and quiet, and so's Julian."

"For a married woman," commented Cousin Clarry, "you seem to have done a great deal of scrimmy-shenanniging on that boat."

"I didn't do any scrimmy—whatever it is," said Joanna, with some warmth. "I hardly spoke to a soul until we got to Port Said, and then Strone Heriot discovered we were more or less related, and so—"

"Ah! Port Said! That explains everything," said Cousin Clarry. "How many people were there on the boat?"

"Oh, about three hundred. Why?"

"I was just wondering how many of them would be turning up in Deepwood, that's all. Elinor, I think you'd better answer this Heriot one: it'll come better from you.—Who's that coming up the drive?"

"It's a girl—rather a pretty girl," said Joanna, glancing out.

"Francesca Fleury; you haven't met her yet," said Elinor. "Do be nice to her, Joanna. You'll like her."

"Never mind about being nice," said Cousin Clarry. "Just help her to keep hold of one of her young men. Show her how to shake off her parents."

Joanna went to the front door and brought Francesca in. The two girls, chatting, took stock of one another. Francesca admired, but could not imitate, Joanna's easy grace and informality; she remained her pretty-mannered, somewhat correct self, and Joanna wondered whether she would be heavy going. Francesca was handicapped by having to adjust her ideas, for Deepwood had come to the conclusion that young Mrs. Stirling had finished with her husband and wanted to be free, and the rumour, reaching Francesca, had led her to expect a younger edition of Georgina. She was further disconcerted by Joanna's youthful appearance, having been told by her mother that marriage—to say nothing of Africa—took its toll of a woman. She looked at Joanna with secret wonder and admiration, and Joanna eyed her with a little reserve: nice, but school-girlish; attractive, but vaguely lavender-bag.

The Greenwood Shady

"How are the preparations going for the Show tomorrow?" asked Elinor, as Francesca's visit ended.

"Oh, beautifully, thank you. Mother's going down early, as usual, and Daddy and I are following. And the gardener's going to get the flowers ready for Mother to take when she goes.—Are you coming, Mrs. Stirling?"

"I'm afraid not; but Miss Clarence will be there."

"Oh, good!" Francesca turned shyly to Joanna. "I don't know whether you'd care about it," she said, "but we'd be so pleased if you would come and have dinner tomorrow after the Show. Will you? It'll be very, very quiet."

The evening meal varied a good deal among the residents of Deepwood. The village took high tea at six and made it the last meal of the day. Mrs. Fleury provided a meagre meal at a quarter to eight, served it with ceremony and called it dinner. Mr. and Mrs. Warren, throwing out casual but warm invitations to come and take pot-luck, dispensed huge portions of heavy food with true Yorkshire hospitality. Elinor and Cousin Clarry spoke of supper and allowed guests to help with the washing-up.

Joanna, who had no wish to dine with the Fleurys, managed a smile.

"It's very kind of you," she said. "What time?"

"Oh, about half-past seven."

Joanna thanked her, saw her to the door and, returning, wrinkled her nose.

"Caught!" she said. "What'll it be like?"

"You heard what she said," replied Cousin Clarry. "Very, very quiet. You'll be able to hear the clocks ticking."

Chapter Seven

Nobody in Deepwood, waking on the calm, clear morning of the Fete, had any suspicion of the strange events that were to take place before the day ended.

Mrs. Fleury followed her usual Fete routine. The prize blooms were brought to her by the gardener and placed carefully in the car—one hired from a garage at Weston. On arriving at the Hall in which the Fete was held, she arranged the flowers on their usual stand, but at this point there occurred a dreadful hitch in the smooth progress of affairs. The flowers were no sooner arranged than they began to wilt and, in spite of Mrs. Fleury's frenzied efforts to revive them, drooped and died.

The two large Cups—for the conveyance of which Mrs. Fleury always kept the car for the return journey—were handed to the astonished Miss Clarence, amid applause more enthusiastic than tactful, and Mrs. Fleury sought in vain for somewhere to lay the blame. The gardener had handed the exhibits to her in perfect condition; the car windows had been open on the journey; she herself had been the only one to handle the flowers at the Fete. Sympathetic officials blamed the heat-wave and the undue exposure to the sun of the Deepwood gardens, but the fact remained that for the first time for years Mrs. Fleury had failed to wipe the board.

Cousin Clarry, in an attempt to soften the blow, sent the Cups back to the Lodge with Mr. and Mrs. Warren, and herself drove back with Mrs. Fleury in the hired car. Conversation was difficult, but presently Mrs. Fleury, lowering her voice in order not to be overheard by the driver, spoke in a tone of anger and bewilderment.

"I don't know why I think so," she said, "but I feel certain that that gardener has had something to do with it."

"Gardener?" echoed Cousin Clarry. "You mean the Deepwood one—the one they call Crow something?"

"Fro—Frobisher."

"But you said he gave the things to you in—"

"In perfect condition—yes. He did, but there's something—I can't put my finger on it, but there's something."

"Something about him, you mean to say?"

"Yes. In the morning, when I saw him in the garden and told him what I wanted him to let me have, I was rather hurried, and I made one or two silly slips. For example, when I meant to say gloxinia, I said nemesia."

"Now, that's a word they never used much in my day," observed Cousin Clarry. "They just used to call it loss of memory and leave it at that and—"

"*Neme*sia. And the point is this: when I *said* nemesia, I

The Greenwood Shady

wasn't looking at the nemesia."

"You weren't?"

"No. I was looking straight at the gloxinia. And—" Mrs. Fleury laid a hand on Cousin Clarry's arm "—and *the gardener was looking at the gloxinia too!*"

There was a pause, during which Cousin Clarry strove to see the point. After a time Mrs. Fleury offered some further assistance.

"You see, don't you? Why should a man who calls himself a gardener—why should he look at the gloxinia when I said nemesia? Can you answer that?"

"Well, you know how it is," said Cousin Clarry. "I point at something and call it my umbrella, and you know perfectly well it's my handbag. My godmother used to be a great one for—"

"But it happened more than once," said Mrs. Fleury.

"Well, perhaps the poor fellow's got a slight squint," suggested Cousin Clarry. "That would account for his always keeping his hat pulled down over his eyes."

"I said something to him about the cosmea seedlings," said Mrs. Fleury, "and I looked at the dianthus, and so did he—I'm quite certain he thought that the dianthus was the cosmea."

"Dear me!" said Cousin Clarry, wishing she had gone home with the Cups. "Dear me! But, as I was telling you, my god-mother was always mixing up—"

"When he came, his references were vague—extremely vague. And there was nothing in writing. Normally, I should have been far more thorough in interviewing him, but I had begun to feel that nobody would ever apply—I was ready, far too ready, to take him."

"Well, half a loaf—"

"I don't trust him. He touches his hat when he sees me, but he never lifts it from over his eyes—he must be hiding something."

"But didn't you tell me he'd come down in the world and looked respectable?"

"He speaks in the most cultured tones: he's been a gentleman or a butler—one or the other. But he talks to himself, and he doesn't know cosmea from dianthus. Doesn't that suggest something, in a way, furtive?"

"Well, call him and check his references again," suggested Cousin Clarry, noting with relief that the car was entering the iron gates. "Tell him about this afternoon—tell him you think he must have put the 'fluence on the flowers. Look how they dope race-horses just before a big event; though, now I come to think of it, it looks suspicious, since I'm the one who benefited by it. Well, don't let him prey on your mind. Go in and make yourself a nice cup of tea and lie down.—Wouldn't you like to call off this dinner thing tonight? I'll tell Joanna you've gone down with a headache and—"

"By no means. Certainly not. I'm a sportswoman, after all," said Mrs. Fleury, with a venomous look at the Cups,

The Greenwood Shady

which Mr. Warren was at that moment handing in at the Lodge door. "I can take a defeat, I hope, in the proper spirit. I shall expect Joanna at half-past seven."

Joanna found it an uncomfortable visit. Connected as she was with the Cup-winner, she felt it wiser to keep off the subject of the Fete, and searched about in her mind for safer topics. She soon found that none was required, for Colonel Fleury talked of nothing but clocks and Mrs. Fleury of nothing but bridge. The only other guest, young Doctor Beale, talked of nothing at all, but sat through dinner crumbling his bread and looking up now and then to gaze broodingly across at Francesca.

Joanna, with Cousin Clarry as an informant, knew all about Doctor Beale. He was the most persistent—almost the last remaining—of Francesca's suitors. He had wooed her in the teeth of heavy discouragement from her parents; he was said to be the only one to whom Francesca herself had shown any leaning. He was joining an uncle who had a practice in Ottawa, and was to leave England in just over a fortnight. It was easy to see, from his set, unhappy expression, that all his efforts to get Francesca to go with him had been unavailing. Joanna felt a pang of sympathy. He was about thirty, solid and sensible-looking, with unhappy brown eyes. He listened abstractedly to the conversation, and seemed unconscious of what he was eating and drinking—a fact which Joanna, prodding her tasteless fish, thought might explain why he had outstayed the rest of the suitors.

She had a moment or two alone with the young man at the end of the evening, when he roused himself and offered to escort her across the two hundred yards to the Lodge door.

"I hear you're going away soon," she said.

"Eh? Oh yes, I am," said Doctor Beale, tearing his attention away from the gravel. "Yes, I am...unfortunately."

Joanna glanced round; on one side were the iron gates and the sleeping village: on the other the deep woods. Above was a bright and unobserved half-moon. It was a lovely night and a lovely scene; it was a pity that young lovers should be unhappy. She thought of Strone Heriot—somewhat older than this man and far more imperious. He saw difficulties and strode determinedly over them. This sad young man...

"When do you go?" she asked gently.

Doctor Beale looked at her, as though sensing her sympathy.

"Friday fortnight," he said.

"And—do you think she'll go with you?"

Doctor Beale halted, ran a hand through his hair and gave voice to his desperation.

"It's hell, isn't it?" he asked.

"It's...difficult," admitted Joanna.

"Don't they *want* her to get married?" ground out the doctor. "I'm fit, I can take care of her, I can support her, and she loves me. Where's the trouble?"

"If she loves you," said Joanna, "I don't see why there

should be any."

"You've just been there, haven't you? You've sat there and talked clocks and Three Clubs, haven't you?—I don't know why I'm talking to you like this, when I never saw you before; but—well, what's a man to *do*? I know what you're going to say—get Francesca away. Yes. But how? She isn't a twentieth-century product at all, Mrs. Stirling: she thinks she oughtn't to go so far from her parents, and of course they—well, they're doing everything they can to jam things up. But Francesca can't see it."

"Have you ever had a chance to talk to her by herself?"

"Yes—no. That is, I've seen her shopping, and had a word or two; I've met her at other houses and got her into a corner; I even got her out for a walk one Sunday—but her parents fixed a time and place for meeting us. You can't rush Francesca, you know, and by the time you've worked her up to the point of being responsive—"

"I know—father and mother arrive."

"Yes. It's unbelievable," observed the doctor simply. "In these days! Why, most parents die off, to all practical purposes, as soon as a girl gets out of school—often before. But those two"—he jerked a chin backwards—"those two are in the limpet class. Nothing short of surgery could—"

"Well, if it's any comfort to you," said Joanna, pacing slowly across the remaining space to her front door—"if it's any help, all of us here are anxious to—well, we're all behind you. But what we can do, I don't quite know."

The doctor grasped her hand with painful fervour.

"You're sweet," he said, "and you've made me feel a whole heap better. If we can't do something—all of us—between us—"

He was gone, and Joanna went quietly into the house. Elinor and Cousin Clarry were in bed. She drank the hot milk from the flask in the drawing-room and came to the conclusion that Francesca, after all, was lucky to have no more serious barrier than parents between herself and love. Compared with her own situation, Francesca's was enviable....

She woke late, and on getting downstairs found Cousin Clarry back from the morning's shopping and on the point of dishing up a fragrant breakfast.

"There!" she said, transferring the contents of a frying-pan to a warm plate. "Now go along quickly with you into the dining-room. No, no, I'll bring this. Go along."

Joanna tasted some of the delicious gravy, sank her fork into a tender kidney, and then paused, looking up at Cousin Clarry with a puzzled expression.

"Kidneys!" she said.

Cousin Clarry waved a huge hand.

"Kidneys, certainly. Don't tell me that African animals don't have kidneys, now, because I know perfectly well that—"

"I don't mean that. But last night Mrs. Fleury—at supper, sorry, dinner—was moaning because she hadn't seen kidneys for four years. And look—this is the second time I've had them!"

"Well, then, eat them," advised Cousin Clarry. "They're very tender."

"They're delicious; but what I meant was, how can we get them and—"

"If you'll kindly leave the housekeeping to me," requested Cousin Clarry, "as your aunt does, and just eat what you're given, you won't fare badly, I promise you."

"No," persisted Joanna. "But *why* don't we? How do you lure all the kidneys to—"

"I don't loower anything," stated Cousin Clarry, spreading her hands, fanwise, on the table and regarding Joanna with indignation. "I haven't time to go loowering. Kidneys exist; butchers sell them; I buy them. Have you anything to say?"

"Heaps. Why can't Mrs. Fleury buy them too?"

"I don't go shopping with Mrs. Fleury, and so I can't tell you why she can or can't buy this and that. Ever since I've had to go out and do the daily shopping," said Cousin Clarry, "I've taken a strong line. 'Don't attempt,' I said to them all—'don't you attempt to palm me off.' And I stand over them and see that they don't. Your Mrs. Fleurys pick up a telephone"—Cousin Clarry picked up an imaginary one and addressed it in high, mincing tones—"'Is thart the boochah? Send me three rahtions of the best you've got, will you? Tharnk you.' And that"—Cousin Clarry rang off decisively—"that's why she doesn't loower the kidneys."

"But if they all stood over the—"

"And another thing: you will acknowledge, I hope, that I can cook?"

"Oh, Cousin Clarry, darling, never, never have I tasted—"

"Quite so. Now, take that supper dish I gave you the other night—that fricassee of veal. You enjoyed it?"

"Yum-yum...."

"And the breast of lamb and the breslau of beef and the sweetbreads with mushroom. I made them well, but it's no use expecting me to turn out dishes like that out of a piece of scrag-end of neck. Some people—and this Mrs. Fleury is one of them—don't know rump-steak from rabbit. If *she'd* had those kidneys you're eating, she'd have thrown them into some fat and served them up like pieces of old boot. Everything she cooks—everything a lot of women cook—turns out like old boot. And that's why I say: save the old boots for those that like 'em. Before you get well served you've got to know good from bad, and then they can't palm you off."

"But—but somebody's got to have—"

"Oh, yes, yes, yes! I've got to take my turn at the old boots while somebody else gets a piece of tender steak and serves it up like horse. And the same with every other kind of food."

"But—do you go and queue and—"

"Queue? *Queue?*" Cousin Clarry stared. "And let everybody see what I'm getting? *Cer*-tainly not! I know the times, and I know the places. What's more, I know the prices, and I pay 'em, and not a penny more. Now stop sitting there moralising, and eat up your good food. Mrs. Fleury will never, never turn out anything like that, no matter what good ingredients she has to start with. She's only got three flavourings: horse, whale and old boot. That's why the Colonel's kept his figure so well all these years.—And one thing more: do I eat kidneys?"

"No, you don't. I never—"

"And do I eat all the other tiddly-widdlys I cook for you and your aunt? No. I like cooking it all, but I don't like eating it. I like to stick to my egg-and-cheese affairs because they suit me better. Now, if I brought home the best for my *own* stomach, that would be a bad thing—a selfish thing. But since I'm in a sense employed by your aunt, then it's m'duty to see that I spend her money to the best advantage. And so I do. Have you anything to say?"

"No."

"Well, then, eat up."

Joanna finished it all and, urged by Cousin Clarry, took a piece of bread and wiped the last morsels from the plate.

"That's right, never waste the drip—it's the best part. Your Uncle George always used to shout his head off if they forgot to give him a piece of dry bread to mop up his bacon-fat. That was when you could get bacon, of course. Now he'd just have to do with the dry bread. Now who's that?" she muttered, as an urgent summons sounded on the front-door bell.

The caller was Mr. Warren, looking far from his bluff,

cheerful self. It was obvious that something had occurred to upset him greatly. He followed Elinor into the drawing-room and sat on a hard chair, rising again as Cousin Clarry and Joanna came into the room.

"What's the matter?" asked Cousin Clarry. "You're looking pasty this morning. I told you those Yorkshire puddings of yours were heavy. Indigestion?"

"No. It's a—well, it's a bit of an urgent matter," said Mr. Warren gravely.

"Is it a private matter, too?" asked Elinor.

"Private?" Mr. Warren considered the question with a distracted air. "Private? Well, no—that is, it won't be private for long, Ah dare say."

"Sit down," said Elinor gently. "Is your wife well?"

"No; that's just it," said Mr. Warren. "That is, she's well enough, but she's—she's had a shock."

He nodded several times, as though he found the phrase to his satisfaction. "That's it—she's had a nasty shock."

"What sort of shock?" asked Cousin Clarry.

Mr. Warren hesitated, his fat hands spread over his knees, his gaze on the carpet. After a while he looked at his three listeners.

"See here," he said. "You all—well, 'tany road, two of you know me, don't you?"

He was reassured on this point.

"Ah. And you know Ada, too. You know, anyhow, that

The Greenwood Shady

she's a sensible body—eh, and with a good head on it, too. A good Yorkshire head with no nonsense in it. Now remember that."

"We will," promised Elinor. "Go on."

"Last night," said Mr. Warren slowly, "Ada saw a ghost."

There was a dead silence. Mr. Warren looked at the three faces before him and found them all equally blank. He took out a handkerchief and wiped his brow.

"Yes," he murmured, half to himself. "Yes, Ah knew. Nobody'll believe a yarn like that."

"It's a little sudden," began Elinor uncertainly.

"Did you see the ghost, too?" asked Cousin Clarry.

"No. No, Ah didn't. Let me tell you how it all happened. We were both sleeping soundly—as we always do, Ada and me—and at about midnight Ah woke up to find her clutching my arm and shaking it. Ah sat up, and she was in a state, Ah can tell you. She couldn't speak at first, and she had me in a stew. Ah took it that she was ill, at first; but when Ah'd got her a glass of water and dosed it with a drop of brandy, she began to talk—and at first Ah thought she'd gone wrong in the head. But she's as right as any of you sitting there, and she gave me a plain, sensible account when she got herself pulled to rights. And what she told me was this: The door of the bedroom opened, and she paid no 'eed—she thought Ah might have left it unfastened. Then she saw a man come in. He walked in a bit cautious-like, she said, and stood there looking

91

round as if he'd lost something—really searching, Ada said he was. She was clutching the sheets and tried to call out to me, but she couldn't make a sound; but at last she gave a kind of choke and he saw her and—and dashed out of the room."

Mr. Warren came to an end and wiped his brow once more. Cousin Clarry was the first to speak.

"Why did you say this wouldn't be private for long?" she asked.

"If there's any talk of a ghost, then all'll get to know about it," stated Mr. Warren. "Besides, a man like me doesn't say his wife's seen a ghost and let it go at that. No. And that's why Ah've come to you"—he looked at Elinor—"this morning. Ah've got Ada in bed, and young Doctor Beale's gone over her, and he's going to keep her in bed for some time, because of the shock, like. But Ah promised her Ah'd come along to you and ask what you could tell us of whoever lived in the house before you did.—Did you ever hear any rumours that the house was haunted?"

"Haunted? Oh no! Good heavens, no!" said Elinor. "I lived in it—and when we had servants, the servants lived in it—for years, and there was never, never any—"

"Who had the place before you did?" asked Mr. Warren.

Elinor considered.

"A rather elderly couple, I think—their name...I can't remember their name, but I seem to have an idea that they inherited the house and had lived in it for some time. So that doesn't

The Greenwood Shady

sound as though they had ever—"

"True enough," admitted Mr. Warren. "But what Ah was thinking was, if you'd ever heard any story—any kind of gossip that would have given us a bit to go on—the date, the period, as you might say—"

"Date? You'd get that," said Cousin Clarry, "if your wife could describe what the ghost was wearing. His clothes would give the period better than anything else."

There was no answer. Mr. Warren's fingers performed an embarrassed tattoo on his knees.

"They would have done," he said slowly at last; "but now we come to it." He cleared his throat. "The chap—the ghost, he...well, he had none."

"None?" demanded Cousin Clarry, outraged.

"Not a clout."

"Not a—"

"And if that doesn't prove that Ada wasn't seeing double," declared Mr. Warren, "then Ah don't know what will. Ah've heard ghost tales before, and Ah've swallowed them all with a helping of salt. But they've all run to pattern—midnight, with the wind going ooo-eee-ooo"—Mr. Warren put his fingers into his mouth and, waggling them, gave a very good imitation of wind whistling eerily through trees—"that sort of thing, and no head on their shoulders, and chains clanking. Ah've had all that, and Ah dare say you have, too. So when Ada tells me that she saw a man who wasn't a man—she saw the door-knob clean through him—and when she says that he's lost something and that he had no clothes on, then Ah believe her. Ah believe her," repeated Mr. Warren, looking round with more than a touch of belligerence.

"Well, don't lose your wool," said Cousin Clarry. "We believe her too."

Mr. Warren stared at her.

"Do you believe in ghosts?" he asked in bewilderment.

"I'll give you a considered opinion," said Cousin Clarry, "when I've seen one. But this fellow certainly sounds credible to me. What could be more practical than his costume, for a heat-wave? And your wife says that he was looking for something—I would have said that perhaps he was looking for Georgina, but in that case he would have looked straight at the bed—and anyhow, she's not home yet. He bolts when he sees Mrs. Warren in her nightgown. That's understandable, too. I mean," she added hastily, "it proves what you said about this being different from the usual run. The ordinary ghost would have glided on past her—or through her—and out of the window. But this one behaves in quite a human way, and bolts. You're quite certain your wife said she could see the door-knob?"

"Ab-so-lutely. Straight through him."

"Well, then, go back and tell her that Mrs. Stirling will go in and see the house agents and ask if they know anything about the previous tenants. Tell her not to worry, and not to let that Mrs. Fleury know anything about it. Now, if *she* saw a

The Greenwood Shady

ghost," said Cousin Clarry, shepherding the visitor to the front door, "then I'd say at once it was some of that trumpery-prumpery business; but your wife's got a good hard head."

She closed the door behind him and went back to the drawing-room. Elinor looked at her.

"Joanna's just said," she remarked, "that it's odd to think of an other-worldly thing like a ghost in connection with such a down-to-earth woman as Mrs. Warren. She's so sensible."

Cousin Clarry sucked her cheeks in thoughtfully.

"You can't tell how far down sense goes," she said. "Look at your Aunt Estelle, who would have been taken for a headmistress anywhere. And you know that *she* was as empty-headed as the most frothy-looking whimsey-pimsey. No. What puzzles me is that Mrs. Warren is a fine, healthy creature who isn't given to imagining anything. And she isn't at a silly age, either."

"What's a silly age?" asked Joanna.

"Women are always having them," said Cousin Clarry. "When they're thirty they begin to feel unsettled because they're too old for the young set and too young for the old set. And when they're forty they read in books that it's an awkward age, and so they look round for something to be awkward about. And when they're fifty and more they're beginning to be sensible. So you've got a long way to go."

"Well, if Mrs. Warren is sensible, why's she seeing ghosts?"

"It might be this long spell of hot weather," suggested Elinor. "I've never known it go on as long as this, and Mrs. Warren doesn't do well in the heat."

"It's her cooking," decided Cousin Clarry. "It's having its effect at last. Do you remember what I went through, Elinor, last time we went to supper there? Do you remember what her custard tart did to me?"

"The same as your little cakes did to him, I suppose," said Joanna. "But why an *undressed* ghost."

"That," said Cousin Clarry, "we shall never know."

Chapter Eight

The gardener was lying in his favourite spot and in his favourite position—on his back on the grass behind the kitchen gardens, screened by bushes and further protected by Telemachus, who was stationed at a strategic point ready to tap with his pitchfork on the cement path if anybody came in sight. The morning was uncomfortably warm, and Telemachus, tired of his job as look-out, had plunged one end of his fork into the ground and, padding the other end with tufts of grass, was using it as a shooting-stick. His orders were to look out for anybody coming from Deepwood, so that a stir in the bushes behind him caught him unawares and caused him to lose his balance. He hit the ground and leapt up in one movement and swung round to investigate. Frobisher raised himself on one elbow and looked irritably at the black-clad figure.

"What're you staring into the rhododendrons for?" he inquired. "Nobody's going to come from *that* direction. It was probably a squirrel or a—"

He came to an abrupt stop. Telemachus had hurled himself on him and was clinging to his coat, his eyes still fixed on something in the bushes. Frobisher shook him off.

"Get off me," he said furiously, "and pull yourself together. It's easy to see you were brought up in a town—the sight of a toad or a frog sends you into a state that—"

"Not a toad. Not a f-frog," said Telemachus, getting his voice back. "But there's s-something." He rallied, gave his tail a defiant twitch and picked up his pitchfork. "Musta been seeing things," he muttered. "I—no, I wasn't, guv'nor—I wasn't seeing anything. There it—there it is again."

Frobisher turned. The bushes parted and a face appeared—an interesting face, not unhandsome, with a curly moustache and trim side-whiskers.

"I beg your pardon," he began courteously, "for this unceremonious—"

Telemachus, now completely recovered from his fright, gave a long, low whistle, and the newcomer turned to him.

"I'm afraid I startled you," he said. "But—"

"No, you didn't," denied Telemachus. "I jest slipped off me fork, that's all. I wasn't expectin' anyone *that* way."

"What do you want?" demanded Frobisher.

"My name is Vandeleur—Captain Anthony Vandeleur, of Her Majesty's—"

"Well, don't stand there bowing," interrupted Frobisher. "Come on out."

"I'm very much afraid—"

"I am not going to talk to a head sticking out of a rhododendron bush," stated Frobisher. "If you want to see me, come

The Greenwood Shady

out." The Captain stepped out hesitatingly, and Frobisher, after one glance of horror, spoke in outraged tones. "How dare you!" he said. "How dare you walk about like that in broad daylight? Get back—get back at once!"

Captain Vandeleur got back.

"And now go away," ordered Frobisher. "If anybody came round here and saw me talking to a—to an apparition without even a sheet to his back, what do you think would happen?"

"Sir," said the Captain with dignity, "I can assure you that I have done my best, but Deepwood House has changed a great deal since I was last in it, and, in my efforts to get my bearings, I lost my way and...and unfortunately entered a bedroom in which a lady was..."

"So *that*," said Frobisher slowly, "is why Doctor Beale is attending Mrs. Warren. I wondered what it was—she didn't look ill, but there was a mystery somewhere. And so it was you! You crept into a lady's bedroom and gave her the fright of her life and—"

"If I could explain" begged the Captain.

"You can save your explanations," said Frobisher, "until you've got yourself something to wear."

"But my dear sir, how can I?" protested the Captain. "I've been looking everywhere for my uniform. Ever since you let me out, I've—"

"Ever since I *what*?" inquired Frobisher in astonishment.

"Ever since you let me out. Out of the well.—Didn't you

99

know you let me out?" asked the Captain in surprise.

"Telemachus."

"Yes, Guv?"

"Find out what he's talking about," ordered Frobisher. "It sounds remarkably like Greek to me."

"I was down in the well," explained the Captain. "You were both sitting beside it and talking, and I heard you. I called out to you several times, and then, to my joy, I heard you tearing away the boards. I came out as fast as I could. You threw something down, and that made me lose my grasp for a moment or two. But when I got up, you had gone."

"So *that's* what the noise was!" said Telemachus. "You were down there!"

"Yes."

"How long?" asked Frobisher.

"Well, I hardly know," said the Captain. "What year is this?"

Telemachus told him, and the Captain began some calculations, found them too difficult and gave up.

"It was the year that the Prince Consort died," he said. "Eighteen sixty-one."

"Coo! Then you missed the wars," exclaimed Telemachus. "Then wot choo goin' round looking for your uniform for?"

The Captain's head seemed to lengthen on its stalk. He spoke with extreme hauteur.

"Sir," he said, "I missed no wars. I obtained my com-

The Greenwood Shady

mission at the age of twenty. I fought against the Ashantis at Dodowah. I served in the Crimea. I was at the siege and fall of Sebastopol. I was at the relief of Lucknow. I was—"

"Well, never mind that now," broke in Frobisher. "You can talk about sieges when you've found your clothes."

"But where are they?" asked the Captain. "When I came to this house I was wearing my uniform—I can show you the very room in which—"

"It doesn't matter about uniform," said Frobisher. "A shirt, a coat, a pair of trousers and—"

"But, my dear sir," exclaimed the Captain, aghast, "you cannot, you really cannot expect me to accompany you *without* my uniform."

It was Frobisher's turn to stare.

"Accompany me? Who," he demanded, "said anything about accompanying me?"

"But—but—I thought that's what you'd come for! For—for me."

"Then you were mistaken. We're here on a totally different mission. I had no idea you existed."

The Captain, in his agitation, left the shelter of the bushes. "But now that you *are* here, now that you've—wittingly or unwittingly—let me out, now that I've presented myself to you, there can surely be no question of leaving me behind? 'The Devil take you', he said—I heard him distinctly. 'The Devil take you.' And when I came to myself, I was in the well,

Elizabeth Cadell

and ever since then I've been waiting, waiting—"

"Ah," said Frobisher. "I begin to see. You were—so to speak—consigned to us?"

"Quite definitely. Beyond all dispute."

"In that case," said Frobisher, "you can come with us—when we go. But you can't come like that, you understand?"

"I'll do my utmost to find my—"

"Never mind your uniform. There are clothes in all those rooms—not the kind you're used to, but you'll have to accustom yourself to the change in fashions. The best thing you can do is to try the flat that Miss Finck lives in. Top floor left. She's got a manservant. He's a bit larger than you, but you can probably make some kind of adjustment. Get something of his."

"Finck? Finck with a ck?" inquired the Captain.

"That's the one. Now go and—"

"I wonder....I knew a young man once—Georgie Finck—he became Lord Cheddarborough and—"

"That's the family," said Frobisher. "Now go on—go away."

"Ain't it a small world?" Telemachus asked the bushes. "You should'a told him," he said to Frobisher, observing that the Captain had gone, "you should'a told him that Georgina was away. He'll be no end disappointed when he finds out."

Georgina, however, was no longer away. Elinor, going into Weston to see the house agent, passed the pale blue saloon with Georgina and a dark, bewhiskered gentleman, and received a friendly wave from them both.

She carried this information home to Cousin Clarry, who already knew it and was able to inform Elinor that the dark man was called Stanislaus and that he was now playing his oboe in Georgina's drawing-room. The other item of news that Elinor brought was, however, fresh. The house agent had been unable to shed any light upon previous tenants, but he had told Elinor that the gentleman to whom she had recommended the flat had wired and was going to take it for four weeks. The new tenant, with his young son, was to arrive in two days.

"Then they're all coming," commented Cousin Clarry. "They've just telephoned a telegram from that actor—my new relative. He's coming tomorrow afternoon. Can we get anyone to come up and see to that damp patch in his room?"

"I'll ring up and see," promised Elinor. "By the way, are we to mention anything to Heriot's friend—the one who's taken the flat—about the ghost?"

"No," decided Cousin Clarry. "We'll say nothing. It'll only give that little boy of his nightmares, and besides that, it may be the sort of apparition that pops out at one person and not at another. I remember when your Uncle Rory used to get the d.t's and see people running about all over the room, I used to hunt for them for hours. I was young at the time, of course—six or so—but you can't say that the beautiful women weren't there; all you can say is that Uncle Rory could see them and I couldn't.—Come and give me a hand with these sheets, Elinor, and we'll get that bed done."

Elinor helped to prepare the room, and the next day went up and gave it some finishing touches. She went downstairs to find Joanna in the drawing-room, just about to walk into Weston to meet Strone Heriot's train.

"Why walk?" she asked. "You could order a taxi and keep it to come back in."

"I want to walk," said Joanna. "I feel like walking—and there's lots of time."

Elinor looked at her. She was dressed in brown, with a small, becoming hat. Her cheeks had filled out and her eyes were bright.

"Will I do?"

"You look very nice," said Elinor cautiously. "Are you trying to make an impression?"

Joanna drew on a glove and smoothed it carefully.

"I've made one already," she said. She raised her eyes, and Elinor saw that they had grown serious. "There's a lot of trouble and muddle coming, Aunt Elbe, but I can't help it."

"Are you in love with him?" asked Elinor.

"Yes—oh yes! burst from Joanna without hesitation. "But when I knew I was beginning to like him, I tried terribly hard to—well, not to. For a long time, on board, he tried to be friendly, but I was tired and I felt rather ill and worried, and all I wanted was to get home to you, and leave Africa and everything in it miles and miles behind me. But then he discovered, in this odd way, that we were both related to Cousin Clarry, and that was, I suppose, the beginning. The awful hot weather stopped, and we were in the Mediterranean, with lovely cool breezes, and our cabins weren't like infernos any more, but nice and comfortable, and you could have your bath and dress for dinner without streaming with perspiration and sticking to all you'd got on. And in the mornings you'd go up on deck before breakfast feeling well and alive—and cold, and you'd begin to look forward to meal-times, and there were games, and all the masses of children seemed to stay in their cabins more, so that you could move about on deck, and at night there was dancing, and everything was quite different. I didn't really notice how much I was with Strone at first, and when I did notice, it was too late. I remember exactly the minute when I realised that it was too late—it was one night when I went down to the cabin to get a coat after dinner. He seemed to think I was rather a long time, so he came down and banged on the—on the sort of wall of the cabin in the corridor and called out, Where are you, Joanna?'—and I put my hand on the curtain across the doorway to walk out, and then, without warning, I just came all over queer. I stood there clutching the curtain, and he came down the little alley-way and saw me. I think I walked out and tried to look normal; but, whatever I looked like, he knew. He just took the coat from me and put it round my shoulders and said—he was behind me—he said, 'So it's happened to you, too?' I didn't say anything—we just walked up one of the sort of stairways, and when we got to the top he tucked my hand under his arm and said, 'Joanna, I love you—and you're not to worry. Everything's going to be all right.'"

She stopped, her eyes on Elinor and her mind far away, back on the dimly-lit deck looking out over the dark expanse of ocean. Coming to herself with a start, she looked at the clock on the mantelpiece and pulled the other glove on hurriedly. On an impulse, she came across and dropped a light kiss on Elinor's cheek.

"A nice revelation," she said ruefully, "from a married woman with a husband who'll be home in a few weeks. But—all that was over so long—oh, so long ago, Aunt Ellie."

"It's a pity Mark's coming home," said Elinor slowly. "Did you tell Mr. Heriot?"

"Oh, don't call him Mr. Heriot! It sounds awful! No, I didn't tell him. I thought I'd get him here safely first, and then tell him. I think he'd have come in any case—even more quickly, perhaps—but I didn't want to take any chances."

Elinor watched her go, and walked thoughtfully into the kitchen. As she reached the door she heard the sound of Cousin Clarry's cello being tuned, and paused.

"Come in, come on in," said Cousin Clarry, looking up. "I'm going to have half an hour before this actor gets here. I hope he's musical."

Elinor hoped he wasn't. The more musical he was, the less he would like the lugubrious sounds Cousin Clarry drew from the strings. Her programme never varied: three or four scales, out of tune; some wavering arpeggios, Handel's Largo

The Greenwood Shady

and a piece which she explained was the Death of the Swan. Nobody who heard it ever needed to ask what killed the swan. Cousin Clarry sat now on a hard kitchen chair, the cello between her enormous thighs, her feet planted squarely.

"I feel I'm improving," she commented with satisfaction. "Do you notice any difference in my vibrato?"

"Well, darling," said Elinor, "I never know whether you're wobbling because you mean it or because you've seen Mrs. Warren's ghost."

Cousin Clarry, unmoved, climbed carefully up a scale and down again.

"This young man of Joanna's," she said, pointing the bow suddenly at Elinor. "There's going to be trouble, isn't there? She's in love with him, of course—she bought that hat specially to go and meet him, and she leaves the bathroom smelling like a prostiwhatyoumaycallit's boudoir. Couldn't you advise her to wait till she's off with the old husband before she's on with the new? I want her to be happy; and so she will be, when she's got rid of that nasty fellow she married—but she hasn't got rid of <u>him</u> yet, and perhaps you ought to remind her. This new one looks dependable—I've been looking at pictures of him in some of those illustrated papers. The broad-built sort—she'll be able to lean on him; and he's going to get broader as he gets older, so there'll be more and more to lean on. A pity she didn't find someone like that the first time; but she was like you—neither of you smelt out that fishiness that both the Stirlings had. Now I could always size up a man—perhaps that's why I never got as far as marrying one.—And then this man who's taken the flat. What's he coming here for? Joanna, of course."

"I think you're wrong, Cousin Clarry. Joanna says that he and Mr. Heriot are lifelong friends."

"Then he's probably coming to watch the progress of the romance. One thing puts me at ease—Joanna thinks he's senile—said he was over forty in the tone you'd use if you said he was over a hundred and forty." Cousin Clarry flexed her arm and prepared to play. "Now let me get my practice," she said. "What with ghosts and actors, the place is turning into a suburb."

Chapter Nine

Cousin Clarry allowed Elinor to welcome Strone Heriot when he arrived, standing at her shoulder and waiting with ill-concealed impatience to sweep him upstairs and, under the pretext of showing him his room, find out something about him. He followed the huge figure up the stairs, sending a quizzical glance back to where Elinor and Joanna stood in the hall. Cousin Clarry reached the top stair and paused, as she always did after any form of exertion, to recover her breath. Strone watched her struggles with concern.

"You shouldn't have taken it so fast," he said.

"I don't know what you mean by fast," responded Cousin Clarry, with a touch of irritability. "I can't come up slower than one at a time, can I now? Tell me that."

"Well, perhaps"

"This way. Mind that rug there—it always slips. In here. Put your suit-cases on those little stands, will you? I always think it's a bad habit, the way people put them on a bed after they've travelled on those dirty racks in all the train-soot. I hope the mice won't disturb you—we don't seem able to get rid of them, but they don't come out.—I suppose you're glad to get back to England?"

"Yes, very."

"So's Joanna. You don't know her husband, do you?"

"No, I didn't come across—"

"Nasty sort of fellow. One couldn't say that to anyone but a relation, naturally. But"—she gave Strone a keen stare—"a husband's a husband."

"Quite," said Strone.

"You going to be out of work for long?" inquired Cousin Clarry.

Strone eased himself against the bed and prepared to enjoy himself.

"Not long, I hope," he said.

"It's a chancy sort of profession. My second cousin—I suppose she'd be some kind of connection of yours, too—Kitty Lee—she took it up for a time. Used to tell people she was on the stage, but she was more off than on. Joanna tells me you're well known, but I hadn't heard of you myself until you wrote."

"It was very kind of you to ask—"

"Well, if it had been left to me," said Cousin Clarry, "I would have kept you away; but now that you're here, I can tell you that you're a steadier fellow than I expected to find you."

"Thank you."

"And I'm here to see, relation or no relation," continued

The Greenwood Shady

Cousin Clarry, "that you don't take advantage of your position."

"What, exactly, is my position?" asked Strone.

"If you don't know, then it's time you asked Joanna to tell you. But remember—she's Mark Stirling's wife until she can arrange to get rid of him," said Cousin Clarry, making her way to the door. "Tea at four, supper at half-past seven."

Strone walked to the top of the stairs with her and watched her descent. As she disappeared into the kitchen, Joanna appeared at the door of the drawingroom, and Strone beckoned her up. Together they walked into his room: Joanna sat on the bed, and Strone began leisurely to unpack.

"I warned you, didn't I?" said Joanna. "But she's a pet."

"She's wonderful. And she's got her eye on us—or on me, I should say. And she says that a husband is a husband."

"Strone "—Joanna spoke a little abruptly—"did you mind my not telling you until you got here? About Mark coming home, I mean."

He hung two ties carefully over the back of a chair, and looked at her.

"What's the difference?" he asked. "If I knew, or if I didn't know—I'd have come all the same. If Cousin Clarry had suppressed my letter, if Elinor hadn't asked me to come—I'd have come just the same."

"But Mark's coming makes a difference, doesn't it?"

Strone stood still for a moment, considering.

"Can't say yet," he said. "In a way, I'm rather glad—it'll quicken things up in the long run. As long as you're not in this house when he comes into it, I've nothing to say."

"You mean—you mean I've got to leave before he—"

Strone, abandoning his unpacking, stared at her in astonishment.

"Good God, yes!" he exclaimed. "What else were you thinking of?"

"Well, I hadn't—"

"—given it a thought. Well, I have—all the way from the station. And now don't talk any more about it—for the moment," said Strone, coming over and sitting beside her. "Tell me what you've done since I saw you. You've put on weight."

"Do I really look fatter?"

"You look it, and you feel it," said Strone. "Especially there."

"Ow!" said Joanna, wincing. "That's Cousin Clarry's cooking. I'll walk it off now that you're here. Oh...Strone, it's so nice to have you! I've been imagining you here—in this room; I've been picturing everything we'd do together and—"

"So've I. But perhaps our pictures wouldn't agree." Strone, still sitting, pulled Joanna to her feet and held her in front of him, studying her with a slow, intent gaze.

"Well?" said Joanna, smiling.

"You're...sweet," said Strone. "Joanna, have you ever thought that the quickest way out of all this is to come away with me?"

"With you? You mean come away and—and live with you?"

"Precisely. It'll bring the thing home to Stirling far more effectively than any amount of talking's going to do."

"We're not sure yet," said Joanna slowly, "that he'll divorce me."

"He won't if he thinks there's any chance of getting you back. But if you're with me, he—"

Joanna shook her head slowly.

"You keep forgetting—no, not forgetting, but just not believing one thing," she said. "He doesn't love me. All that's finished."

"Rot!" said Strone. "He had some tricky business on hand out there, and you drifted apart. He'll come home with nothing on his mind and time on his hands, and when he sees you... but I'll take good care he doesn't see you."

"Strone, don't let's talk about it now," begged Joanna. "Let's have these next weeks without him—just getting to know each other and being able to be together all day and every day—can't we?"

He pulled her to him, and she lay unresisting in his arms.

"Anything you say," he said after a time. "For the moment, anyhow. Who shall we talk about? Me? You?"

"No," said Joanna unexpectedly. "Let's talk about Willy."

Willy came by the afternoon train on the following day

and took up his residence at Deepwood House. Cousin Clarry, after watching his friendly but detached greeting to Joanna, dismissed her suspicions and concentrated instead on trying to find out what made him look so worried. His lean frame and the furrows on his brow went straight to her sympathies, and after studying him for some time she made the suggestion that he should manage his own and Julian's breakfast in the flat and take his main meals at the Lodge. Willy, after some objections which he explained were purely perfunctory, thanked her and Elinor and warmly accepted. He superintended Julian's ablutions and brought him across, clean and fresh, to supper.

Supper over, Strone took Joanna out for a walk and Willy helped with the drying up. He then followed Elinor into the drawing-room, leaving Julian with Cousin Clarry to put away the silver and china.

"He's a nice little boy," said Elinor, placing the cigarettes beside her guest. "Does he like England?"

"He hasn't noticed England yet," said Willy. "He had his first train journey recently, and he's living for the next one. He's done a good many thousand miles by road, and by air, and by sea; but I'd forgotten he'd never been in a train—he's mad about them now."

"Is he always as quiet as this?"

"I'm afraid so. I don't know why he's never been through all the stages of small-boy hooliganism—perhaps because he led rather a lonely life out in Africa. He can sketch very well, and that's all he likes doing—that and going in trains."

The Greenwood Shady

There was silence after this; Elinor waited for her visitor to say something, but Willy was not a man who found silences awkward. Leaning back on his comfortable chair, his face in shadow, he studied Elinor silently, and found her very much to his liking. She was quiet, she put on no spurious brightness to entertain him, used make-up discreetly and made no embarrassing attempts to look less than her age.

For her part, Elinor looked at Willy, and found him unexpectedly restful. Cousin Clarry's idea of having him to meals had been a little disconcerting, suggesting, as it did, that he would have to be entertained, or at least noticed. Now she saw that he would require no attention, and she was grateful. She wondered whether he had always looked so harassed—it was already clear that the worry was only skin deep, but it made him seem older than his age. He looked, she thought, like an artist, with his long sensitive fingers and his gaze, at once absent and disturbed.

"About Strone," said Willy slowly, out of the silence. "You know, of course, that he's—that he and Joanna are—well, in love?"

"She told me," said Elinor.

"I don't know quite why I came here," said Willy, looking round the room with a puzzled air, as though the answer could be found in the furnishings. "But he and I are old friends. He's a good bit younger than I am—ten years younger, to be exact—but when he was still in linen suits he used to follow me round and refuse to be shaken off. The only time we've really been out of touch is when I went out to Africa some years back. When he knew that I was selling out and coming home for good, he flew out on a visit and we came home together. So I feel a bit responsible for what happened on the boat, and I think I came along to Deepwood to—well, to see how things were going to pan out."

"Do you know Mark Stirling?" asked Elinor.

"In a way—yes. His coming home's going to complicate things a bit," mused Willy.

There was another long silence, and Elinor finally took a turn at introducing a new topic.

"How do you like the flat?" she asked.

"The flat? Oh, it's very nice, thanks. Bit on the dolls-house scale," said Willy. "We're going to be very comfortable when we've got used to crawling in and out of the doorways on our hands and knees. I come off a lot worse than Julian.—I've met the neighbours—at least, the downstairs ones."

"You have? That was quick," commented Elinor.

"Not quicker than usual." He grinned engagingly at her. "A lone-looking man with a small boy who looks misleadingly delicate—you've no idea what a magnetic combination that is," he said. "Old ladies in trains offer us buns, and kind-hearted strangers adopt us on sight. The moment our luggage was put in the hall this afternoon out popped the old boy in the downstairs flat and said, 'Oh, isn't he a *love?*'—I think he meant Julian, though I couldn't be sure. Then he said, 'Come raht in, lad, and I'll gie thee parkin'—I hope the accent's correct?"

"It's shocking," said Elinor. "He doesn't sound anything like that.—Go on."

"Well, he certainly offered us parkin," said Willy, "and Julian's got some of it in his room now—the real thick, dark Yorkshire stuff. Then a girl came into the hall—a remarkably pretty girl."

"Francesca?"

"Yes. A nice girl, Francesca."

"Then you've met almost everybody."

"Yes." Willy dropped his voice to a whisper. "I've met even Her."

"Her?"

"Don't pretend you don't know who Her is," said Willy. "The Cheddarborough strain is famous. I'm almost too frightened to go home. Mr. Warren regards her as the Scarlet Woman and Jezebel rolled into one."

"She shocks him," admitted Elinor. "He's got that uncompromising attitude about good and bad—and of course, even by modern standards, Georgina isn't good. But you'll find her quite harmless."

"Harmless?" Willy sat upright on his chair and looked at her in surprise. "Harmless? That man-eater?"

"Well, yes. She's just got what she calls enlightened ideas."

"One of which," Willy said, "is that the male has forfeited the right of making the first advance. I haven't been so upset since I was followed in Leicester Square on Mafeking Night!"

Elinor laughed.

"Don't worry about Georgina," she reassured him. "She's busy—she's got a fascinating bearded man called Stanislaus on her hands. He plays the oboe. Will that disturb you?"

"If it does, I'll let him know," promised Willy. He rose as Cousin Clarry, with Julian, came into the room and made her a deep bow. "Madame, my chair," he offered.

"Can't stop," she said. "He's been a very helpful boy, and I'm going to give him a nice milk-shake with chocolate in it. And you look as though one wouldn't do you any harm."

"Thank you," said Willy, "but my doctor warned me about excesses. No milk-shakes, he distinctly said."

"Well, I'll make you one, Elinor—you're looking tired with all these visitors."

"I'm not tired," protested Elinor. "Mr. Hume was telling me about Georgina."

"You've met her already?" said Cousin Clarry, fixing a glance full of suspicion upon him.

"She met me. And I wonder if you'd all mind calling me Willy?—it's going to save so much time, saying one word instead of two."

"Willy. It'll come hard—I never knew a Willy before," said Cousin Clarry. "And about Georgina"—she looked at Julian and dropped her voice to a rumble. "Don't under-estimate her, you understand? Put a chair against your door."

Willy, saying good-night and walking over to the flat with the sleepy Julian beside him, pondered this last remark with something more than amusement. A modest man, he was not disposed to imagine that women loved him on sight, but there was something about Georgina which made him wish that the flats at Deepwood House were more self-contained. There was between his own and Georgina's accommodation a mere landing; an enterprising woman could cross it in three steps.

He put Julian to bed in the smaller bedroom, and then made his own preparations in the larger room.

Tired, he soon fell asleep; but it was restless slumber—the bed was too short for his length, and his feet stuck out uncomfortably at the end. He dreamed that he was running along the Deepwood drive with Georgina pressing close and ever closer behind; she had reached him and put a detaining hand on his shoulder....

Willy woke with a start. To his horror, he found that it was no dream. Georgina was beside him; her hand was on his shoulder, and she was shaking him urgently.

"Wake up! Please—oh, please, wake up!"

Willy sat up in bed and looked at her coldly. It was too much. In the morning he would write to Lord Cheddarborough and tell him that his daughter ought to be under some sort of supervision.

"Will you kindly go away?" he asked.

"No." Georgina gave a convulsive shudder, and Willy, looking up at her, saw that she was labouring under some strong emotion. It was obvious that Stanislaus had done a great deal more than play the oboe. Resolving to deal calmly with the situation, he got out of bed, walked to the door and put out a hand to open it. With surprising strength, Georgina pulled him back.

"Don't, whatever you do—don't open that door!" she said shudderingly. "There's something...someone...outside."

Willy faced her.

"It's no use my trying to do anything with him," he said. "The best thing for a foreign character like that is—"

"Oh, Stanislaus!" Georgina's voice was savage with contempt. "I'm not talking about Stanislaus. I'm talking about"—she shuddered—"about him!"

Willy began to feel anxious. If there was going to be an affair of passion and pistols on his very doorstep—

"I'm awfully sorry," he began, "but—"

"Don't talk," broke in Georgina abruptly. "Get me a drink, will you?"

"There isn't," said Willy with satisfaction, "a drink in the place."

There was a moan from Georgina; she sank on to Willy's bed, and it struck him for the first time that, for a woman caught between two lovers, she had taken remarkably few pains. Her dressing-gown was caught about her untidily and her hair was in wild disorder. Looking further, he saw that she was deathly pale and shivering.

"What's the matter with you?" he inquired. "Have you caught a chill?"

"I've just seen a ghost," said Georgina. "Don't look like that—I tell you I *have*—"

"Oh." Willy gave the matter some thought. "Well, personally," he said, "I don't believe in them. Are you sure you—"

"I don't believe in them either," said Georgina, recovering a little self-command. "I still don't believe in them, but I swear to you that I've just seen one."

"Where?"

"In my flat. Something woke me, and I couldn't get off again, so at last I got up to get myself a drink. And—and there it was, just going out of the door of the drawing-room."

"Well...what did it look like?" asked Willy, at a loss.

"I don't know—I mean I was too paralysed to take in details. I wanted to scream, but nothing came out. All I can tell you is that he—it—was holding something."

"A head?"

"A head?" repeated Georgina in bewilderment.

"Well, you know what I mean—these chaps usually carry one."

"Well, this one didn't. He—it—had its back to me, and then it turned, and I saw that it had a shirt in its hand."

"Shirt?"

"Yes, shirt." Georgina was recovering, and impatience sounded in her voice. "You've got to believe me. I was wide awake and cold sober. I'm not an imaginative woman and I'm highly intelligent. I saw that thing—whatever it was. I *saw* it, I tell you."

"Why did you come to me?" asked Willy. "You've got that—"

"Foreigners," said Georgina, "are all very well for some things, but they're not the slightest use when there's any sort of crisis. If I told Stanislaus I'd seen a ghost, I'd have him on my hands."

"Where's that servant of yours?" asked Willy.

"Curzon? In his room, I suppose. But you needn't think it was Curzon I saw, because he's over six feet, and broad; and this—this thing was shorter and slimmer and—"

"What period did he look?" asked Willy. "Tudor, Plantagenet?—Did he wear knee-breeches and a ruffle?"

"Stark," said Georgina.

Willy stared.

"Great Scott! You mean he was just carrying his shirt round?"

"Yes. Could I *imagine* such a thing? If I'd imagined I saw a ghost, wouldn't I see an orthodox one, like the ones you suggested? I tell you, he was smaller than Curzon, but well made—and he was good-looking—and he was carrying a shirt—or perhaps a nightshirt. It looked large."

"Well, let's go across the way," suggested Willy, "and see

The Greenwood Shady

whether Stanislaus or Curzon saw anything."

"Leave Stanislaus out of this," said Georgina.

She walked cautiously on to the landing and led the way into her flat. Willy knocked on the door of the room she indicated, and Curzon, half-asleep, stood before them. Willy noted that he showed no surprise at the sight of a man in night attire. Questioned as to his movements that night, he had little to tell. He had gone to bed at half-past ten and had been asleep ever since. He had seen nothing and heard nothing. After hearing this evidence, Willy decided that there was nothing further for him to do.

"Your mistress has had a fright," he said. "See that she gets a drink—a hot one, I'd advise."

He left them and went back to bed. When he woke in the morning, Georgina was in his room, fully dressed and looking her usual confident self. Willy shook the sleep from his eyes and looked at her with a scowl.

"Not another ghost?" he muttered.

"No, the same one," said Georgina calmly.

"You've seen him again?"

"No. But I've seen Curzon, and he's very worried."

"Worried? Worried what for?"

"He laid out a clean shirt on his chair last night," said Georgina, "and it's gone."

"Gone?"

"That's what I said," said Georgina. "Somebody took it."

Chapter Ten

Before ten o'clock on the following morning, everyone in Deepwood, Easton and Weston was in possession of all the facts of the ghost-story. Georgina, unlike Mrs. Warren, had desired no concealment: she had seen a ghost, and she said so. What other people felt of belief or disbelief interested her not at all. On meeting Mr. Warren in the hall on her way out, she gave him brief details of her experience, and was pleased to learn that her story had backing: his wife, admitted Mr. Warren in a gush of relief, had seen it, too. Listening to Georgina's breezy and uninhibited account, he came nearer to liking her than he could have thought possible. She was all that he most distrusted: he regarded her as an aristocrat of the wrong sort, a bad example and a thoroughly wrong 'un. In spite of a good deal of cinema-going and a dogged determination to read every book recommended by the girl in Boots, Mr. Warren still considered chastity a spinster's glory and pride, and Georgina's open flouting of all his standards angered and offended him. Now he had to admit that, by knowing a ghost when she saw one, she had done him a great service and removed a weight of doubt and worry from his mind.

The Greenwood Shady

The ghost was everywhere acknowledged to be Mrs. Warren's. She had seen it first, but it was not this fact that made the neighbourhood grant her possession; it was the fact that her words, few and infrequent though they were, carried much more weight than Georgina's. Georgina was looked up to, but not respected. If she had asserted, without Mrs. Warren's corroboration, that a ghost had walked at Deepwood House, the district would have smiled, shrugged and put the story down as another of her eccentricities.

Sightseers came in groups, but there were no crowds. Frobisher, who had been ordered by Mrs. Fleury to keep the expected masses outside the iron gates, went back to his resting-place behind the tool-shed and settled down once more.

It was a spot he cared little for, but the areas in which he could spend his leisure were narrowing in direct ratio to Mrs. Fleury's confidence in his skill. Pushing his hat still farther down over his eyes, Frobisher brushed away some troublesome buzzes, for once envying Telemachus, who, on guard a few paces away, could keep himself fly-free with a mere twitch of the tail. In a little while, reflected Frobisher, Mrs. Fleury would be out again and on the prowl; she had given him orders to transplant the dimorphotheca, and she knew, and Frobisher knew that she knew, that he and dimorphotheca were utter strangers. Matters were working up to an awkward climax, but Colonel and Mrs. Fleury had been chosen to represent Wiltshire at the forthcoming inter-county Bridge contest at Brighton: they were to leave soon, and they would not be back before Mark Stirling's arrival. It was unlikely that Mrs. Fleury would challenge the gardener before she left; when she came back, Frobisher realised with relief, he would be where dimorphotheca could trouble him no more.

He settled himself against a tree-stump, and was wondering whether it was safe to go back to his more comfortable place by the kitchen garden, when he heard a sound from Telemachus, but it was not a warning sound—it was a gasp of astonishment. Frobisher, looking round to see what had caused it, saw, peeping cautiously round the tool-shed, the head of Captain Vandeleur.

"Oh, it's you," he muttered.

"It's 'im orl right," stated Telemachus. "Wait till you see wot 'e's got on!"

"You're properly dressed, I hope?" said Frobisher coldly. "If not, you'd—"

He stopped. The Captain had stepped forward and stood before them, dressed in Curzon's shirt. It was too broad and too long, and it hung in folds to the Captain's knees. Conscious of the sorry figure he cut, and aware of Telemachus's open jeering, he began an explanation.

"You must forgive this disarray," he said. "It was the only garment upon which I could—"

"Your tail's showing," put in Telemachus.

"And so," said the Captain, goaded beyond endurance, "is yours." He drew himself up, and looked, in spite of his flap-

The Greenwood Shady

ping shirt, oddly dignified. "You don't seem to understand, my good sirs, that I left—in that house—my uniform and my sword. And now I can find no sign of either. I have looked in the nooks and in the cupboards, I have looked in the secret drawer in the panelling, and I have climbed through the trap door to the roof in order to see if by any chance the things were thrown up there."

"Weren't they down the well?" asked Frobisher.

"No. I should have felt far more comfortable if they had been. What," he asked, "do you think could have become of them?"

"Dunno," said Telemachus, indifferently. "When people don't want their uniforms no more it don't matter much what becomes of 'em, does it?"

"It matters a great deal," stated the Captain. "In my uniform I have a certain position—a certain standing. Without it, as you see, I command no respect.—Neither of you appears to be doing any special duty," he pleaded. "Could we not all make a thorough search?"

"Wot, take up all the floor-boards looking for your old regimentals?" exclaimed Telemachus. "Not likely! 'Slong as you're dressed proper, we don't mind 'ow you look—do we, Guv?"

The Captain sighed, gathered his shirt-tails round him and sat disconsolately beside Frobisher, staring towards the house with a brooding and melancholy expression. "'Ow long did you live there?" asked Telemachus.

"Live where?"

"In the 'ouse."

"That house? I didn't live there at all," said the Captain, with a touch of disdain. "The Vandeleurs come from Castle Van Faber, in Northumberland."

"Then wot," enquired Telemachus, "was your uniform doin' 'ere?"

"I was on a visit," said the Captain. "A short visit. A visit of a night."

"Go on!" Telemachus drew nearer. "An' who pinched your uniform, eh?"

"Your questions," said the Captain, "are impertinent and indiscreet."

"O.K., O.K., O.K.," acknowledged Telemachus good-humouredly. "But jest answer 'em."

"Why were you here?" supplemented Frobisher. The Captain sighed—a long and plaintive sound.

"I came to see a lady," he said. "A young and very beautiful one. Her husband—"

"Speak up," said Telemachus. "I can't 'ear you."

"She was the toast of the regiment," said the Captain, in a dreamy tone. "She could have married any one of us: myself, Lord Stag, Georgie Finck—Georgie was wild about her. But she looked above us—not in rank, but in fortune—and she chose a man who was reputed to own half the property in Wiltshire. She married him, but she found that the fortune was

The Greenwood Shady

hard-earned. He brought her, from London, to this stagnant spot, where she saw no one and met no one. But fortunately he had to be away a great deal, and—naturally—one or other of us used to come down and visit her, to keep up her spirits."

"Advertisin' it a bit, wasn't it, to come down in full dress?" commented Telemachus.

"We were not usually indiscreet. I was on special duty connected with the passing of the Prince Consort; I found myself in the neighbouring country, and I knew—"

"—the lady was on her own. So you galloped up on your charger and fell into the well," put in Telemachus, who liked his stories to flow.

"I came to see her. She was alone, but—alas!—her husband's suspicions had been aroused, or one of the servants had played the spy. He returned and burst in upon us. I placed my lady behind me and faced him, and he flourished my sword—*my* sword—in my face and shouted, 'The Devil take you!'"

"And then 'e ran you through?"

"No. I fell, but not at his hands. Before he could strike," said the Captain, "the blow came—from behind."

There was a long silence as his hearers digested this unexpected climax. Frobisher turned to him inquiringly.

"You mean that she—"

The Captain nodded.

"With a candlestick. Just on that spot."

He indicated a bump on his skull, and the others inspected it with sympathy. It was a hard end for a lover.

"But the well?" asked Telemachus.

"I can only suppose," said the Captain, "that they took me out between them and dropped me down. Then I suppose they hid or disposed of my uniform. You see, there would be no scandal; nobody knew I was here, nobody would ask any questions. When I came to myself, the well was closed. Until you came, I waited down there...waited, waited. And now that you are here, I would like to go with you looking as fine a figure as I always used to."

"Well," said Telemachus after reflection, "the on'y place you'd get what you're after is in a museum, I reckon. They"—he broke off abruptly and made a signal for silence. "Someone coming," he hissed. "You'd better 'op it, Cap'n."

The Captain rose swiftly and, with a gliding movement, vanished behind the tool-shed. Telemachus made a further reconnaissance and whispered his report.

"It's orl right, Guv—it's only the kid. An' 'e's snuffling again."

A small boy—Julian Hume—came slowly into sight. As Telemachus had said, he was crying.

Julian Hume had seldom cried—had, indeed, seldom had anything to cry about. He had been happy in Africa, happy on the boat, happy in England, and especially happy in the train. Life, until he came to Deepwood, had been very good, and he had enjoyed it. Even life at Deepwood had been pleasant until

The Greenwood Shady

he had—on an impulse which he now regretted with all his heart—asked his father to send him to the Deepwood school.

He gave a sob and reviewed his reasons for wanting to go. The school house had looked like the pictures in the old fairy-tales; the boys had looked strong and good-humoured; going to school and getting to know them all would be fun.

It had been far from fun. He understood now his father's hesitation when he had made the request; he also understood the remark made by Mrs. Sprule, that it seemed like throwing someone to the lions. He knew, now, exactly what lions were.

It was a double blow, for he had always looked forward to going to school. He had been told by his father that school was a place in which everybody was happy. He had seen photographs of his father at school at his own age, looking very happy indeed.

But Deepwood school was different—Julian was certain of it. It was peopled, not by small boys like himself, but by savages. He had done them no harm whatsoever, and they had pulled his hair, knocked him down, torn up his drawing-book and rubbed his nose in the mud. He would have liked to tell his father, but something—he hardly knew what—prevented him; some feeling that his father would be disappointed had held the words back. But this morning, on reaching the iron gates, Julian had walked into an ambush, and he had emerged with his clothes torn to shreds, his face and hair muddied and one eye blackened. He was crying not so much from pain or fear, but from an inability to see a way out of his difficulties.

If he couldn't go to his father—and he couldn't—then where was he to go?

He gave a gulp and a sob, rounded the corner and came upon the gardener lying on the grass, his hat shading his eyes. Julian side-stepped to avoid him and gave another involuntary sob.

"I hope," said Frobisher, "you're not going to cry here."

"Well—no," said Julian.

"I'm busy," said the gardener.

The glaring inaccuracy of this statement had the effect of diverting Julian's mind for a few moments from his woes. He stared down at the recumbent form, and Frobisher made a movement of impatience.

"You're late for school, aren't you?" he asked.

The tears started to Julian's eyes.

"Y-yes," he said. "I went, but the boys were all waiting for me outside the gate, and they—they tore my clothes."

"Are those the only clothes you've got?" enquired Frobisher coldly.

"Well—no. Not 'zactly."

"Then I can't see what's worrying you."

"They—they knocked me over," explained Julian.

"Oh?"

"And they bumped my head in the mud."

"Really?" There was no mistaking the contempt in Frobisher's tone, and Julian flushed. "Didn't anybody ever tell

The Greenwood Shady

you anything about boxing?" went on Frobisher.

"N-no."

"That's more than half the trouble," muttered Frobisher, to himself. "Letting a boy go out into the world without knowing how to box.—Do you mean you've never used a right hook?"

"N-no."

"You've never heard of a straight left, swing, jab, upper-cut?"

"N-never."

"Well, in that case, there's nothing to be done," said Frobisher, "but to resort to the jungle. Now if you'll kindly go and—"

"W-what jungle?" asked Julian.

"If a boy," said Frobisher, in accents of weary boredom—"if a boy can't bite the ear of the nearest aggressor; if he can't take hold of the next two and knock their heads together; if he can't land a strategic fist on unwarily exposed noses; if he can't pull some hair out here and knock some teeth out there; if he can't kick and scratch his way out of trouble, then the point I wish to make is that he deserves to be in it. Now that's all, my good young fellow. As I said, I'm busy."

Julian turned without a word and walked slowly back the way he had come. With slow steps he approached the iron gates. Pausing for a moment, he passed through them and walked towards the school house. All was quiet, but as he reached the little wooden gate the doors opened and the inmates poured out for the morning break. Julian halted; at the same moment, he was seen; five boys, with a concerted howl of joy, bore down upon him. He stood quite still, waiting. His cheeks were flushed, and in his eyes was a light which his enemies saw only when it was too late. As they reached him, he opened his mouth and released a war cry that made their blood curdle and knocked Grand-dad Robbins' pewter mug off its bracket. With the cry still on his lips, Julian Hume went into action.

Chapter Eleven

Willy found that his sojourn at Deepwood was to be a leisurely one. With Julian at school, he was left with nothing to do but go for walks by himself or spend his time at the Lodge.

He chose the latter alternative, and passed his days talking to Elinor, following her from room to room and sometimes helping her with whatever work she was engaged in.

Joanna and Strone were seldom seen; they went out soon after breakfast, and usually spent the day out. Mr. Warren, after studying Strone and deciding that he was a fine young chap, drove them out to his weekend cottage—a high-sounding title which he had given to a primitive two-roomed shack set on a hill about eleven miles away, and where he and his wife had spent many a happy week-end during the years he was in business.

Cousin Clarry cooked, played her cello and watched Willy. An idea had come to her—an idea so bright that it almost dazzled her with its possibilities. She turned it over and over, and found that it looked equally good at all angles, and at last decided to put it into effect.

The first step was to get to know something of Willy's circumstances, and with a view to doing a little preliminary investigation, she demanded his services in the kitchen and set him down at the table to chop parsley. Settling herself down opposite to him, she spread a large newspaper out in front of her and began to shell a heap of peas.

"Where's Julian's mother?" she asked, without preamble.

Willy's soul lifted in delight. A good many other women had wanted to know this fact, but none had used this enchantingly simple method of finding out. He settled himself more comfortably in his chair.

"Julian's mother? She's in America," he said.

"Did she divorce you?" inquired Cousin Clarry.

"No—I divorced her."

"Wasn't done in my day," commented Cousin Clarry. "The man used to take the onus."

"That's when there *was* an onus," Willy reminded her, in his soft tones. "But look how we've progressed—just look."

"What went wrong?" proceeded Cousin Clarry, not to be lured into a general discussion.

Willy, knife in mid-air, considered the question.

"Well, I suppose I did," he decided finally. "I turned out less interesting than I looked, I suppose."

Cousin Clarry got up and opened the oven door, peered in and banged the door again.

"How long were you married?" she asked.

The Greenwood Shady

"Before she left me? Oh, not long. It was a year or two after Julian was born."

"You mean," said Cousin Clarry, shocked, "that she just went away and left that poor mite?"

"Well, not exactly. She was rather bored with life on an African farm, with nobody to talk to but me. She used to go into Nairobi to meet her friends and stay with them for a month or two. Then she met a party of Americans who were going shooting, and she arranged to join them—it was exactly her cup of tea. In fact, I don't think she would have married me if she hadn't thought that we'd spend our time striding through the undergrowth potting away at lions; but it didn't turn out like that at all—all I did was to try to raise crops, which is much less dangerous."

"And what happened to her?"

"Oh, she married one of the Americans. They must find her very useful in New York when they want any lions got out of the way—she's a dead shot."

"Did Julian—well, no, he couldn't miss her, of course; he was too young."

"Fortunately, yes," said Willy.

"But children need a mother," stated Cousin Clarry. "Didn't you ever try to get him one?"

"Never," said Willy, separating the chopped from the unchopped. "The affair seemed to sap my confidence."

"Well, now that you're home," said Cousin Clarry, "you'd

better look round. You won't find parcels of black men waiting to do your cooking and housekeeping for you, and you won't find white women, either, unless you marry one."

"Ah—romance!" sighed Willy.

"Don't breathe on the food. A single man can usually find a housekeeper, but you've got a child—they won't come to you so readily, you'll find. Where do you plan to live?"

"In my own house in Gloucestershire," said Willy. "The tenants, fortunately, want to move, otherwise who knows when I could have got rid of them? But they're going, and I shall move in when I leave here."

"What sort of house?" asked Cousin Clarry.

"Oh, one of those nice grey stone-built houses in the Cotswolds—and thirty acres, mostly hilly."

"Large? The house, I mean."

"So-so."

Cousin Clarry was preparing to approach the question of income when there came an interruption. Elinor appeared at the door, ushering in Mrs. Fleury.

"No, don't move! I asked Mrs. Stirling to bring me in here," said the visitor, "so that I wouldn't disturb you. No, do sit down, Mr. Hume—please!"

Willy placed two hard-seated chairs for the newcomers and resumed his chopping. Mrs. Fleury sat down and addressed the company with unusual animation.

"You've heard, I suppose, about our ghost?" she asked.

The Greenwood Shady

"When I say ' our ', I mean, of course, Mrs. Warren's and Georgina's ghost."

"Why shouldn't there be two ghosts?" inquired Cousin Clarry. "There's one with a shirt and one without a shirt, isn't there?"

"It's the same one," stated Mrs. Fleury. "Speaking for myself, I don't believe in anything of that kind. If Georgina had been the only one to see it, I would have said at once that it was only to be expected—she's an odd woman and she'll end up by seeing all sorts of things—but I *am* surprised that Mrs. Warren should come forward with a story of that kind."

"Their stories agree," pointed out Elinor. "That is, from their description, the apparition—whatever it is—appears to be the same. Are you nervous about it?"

"I can't say I am," replied Mrs. Fleury. "I'm not attempting to throw any doubt on either Mrs. Warren or Georgina, but I'm not expecting to see anything myself. The best cure for that sort of thing is to keep busy, and I'm busy enough, I can tell you! The ghost story is going the rounds. If it gets beyond Easton and Weston we shall have to put guards at the gates. I'm going to speak to Georgina about getting the thing looked into by the Psychical Research people—I'm not sure that one of the members doesn't live just near Lord Cheddarborough.—But I didn't really come here to talk about ghosts," she went on. "I called to ask a favour." She turned to Elinor. "I wonder, would you be so kind as to take my place on the Parade Committee? They insist on having me year after year, but I'm usually away at this time, and I promised to find them a substitute. There's very little to do—you'll have to write out a few notices and post them."

"You write them, I'll post them," offered Willy.

"Thank you," said Elinor drily. "That'll be an enormous help.—Well, I'll do what I can," she promised Mrs. Fleury.

"Where you off?" inquired Cousin Clarry. "Oh, yes, I remember—this Bridge thing."

"Yes, the tournament. It was really rather an honour to be asked, and we felt we couldn't very well refuse. And besides, it'll be a nice change for Francesca."

"You taking her?" inquired Cousin Clarry.

"Oh, but yes!" Mrs. Fleury's smile was sweet, but edged with a little cold surprise.

"Pity. Not much there for her," commented Cousin Clarry intrepidly.

Mrs. Fleury released a little more genuine feeling.

"In Brighton? Nothing to do in Brighton? Francesca *adores* Brighton," she declared. "We were there the year before last, in September, and she enjoyed every minute of it. We went on coach tours, we went to the theatre, to cinemas—we hadn't a free moment!"

"We hoped," said Elinor, "that you'd leave her here for us to look after. We—"

"Leave her alone in the flat? With all the ghosts?"

"Well, you wouldn't leave her alone in the flat when there

weren't any ghosts, if you remember," said Cousin Clarry.

"That I admit. Yes, that I admit," said Mrs. Fleury magnanimously. "But in my young days one didn't go away and leave a young girl alone. I know it's done freely now, but Francesca isn't like other girls."

"You mean," put in Willy, with his most disarming smile and in his gentlest voice—you mean that she *is* like other girls!"

Mrs. Fleury gave him a cold, blank stare and rose.

"Well, Mrs. Stirling," she asked, "can I count on you to fill my place on the Committee?"

"Well—yes," said Elinor reluctantly. "We shall miss you."

"Nonsense, nonsense!" said Mrs. Fleury briskly. "Everybody'll look very smart, and nobody will notice whether we're there or not.—I must go—I've such a lot to do. No, don't get up, Mr. Hume."

Elinor saw her out, and came back into the kitchen, meeting Cousin Clarry's grin with a smile of her own.

"Year after year," said Cousin Clarry grimly. "That woman can't play second fiddle."

"Who's asking her to?" asked Willy.

"It's the Parade," explained Elinor. "It's rather a silly affair, really—it's held in June every year on the Weston cricket-ground. All that happens is that they charge an entrance fee, which goes to various missionary societies, and in the afternoon there's a parade of children in fancy dress, and in the evening a parade of grown-ups in fancy dress. That's all—they just parade twice round the arena, or whatever you call it, and then prizes are awarded."

"And *that*," said Cousin Clarry, "is where Mrs. Fleury comes in. Before Georgina settled here—before Mrs. Fleury came to live at Deep wood House, before I came to live with Elinor here, it used to be a simple affair, and Mrs. Fleury always walked off with the prize. But gradually it's become more and more elaborate, and now that we've got Georgina, she wipes the floor."

"Ah!" said Willy. "First prize, Georgina; second fiddle, Mrs. Fleury."

"It's rather hard," put in Elinor. "Georgina can draw on such a wonderful stock. There's a rule that no professional costumes can be hired—they must either be made locally, or be a costume belonging to a grandmother or someone of that kind. Georgina came last year as the most magnificent figure, in the dress of a Georgina Finck who used to be lady-in-waiting to Queen Charlotte. How can Weston compete with that?"

"And Mrs. Fleury walked out?"

"She doesn't walk in any more," said Cousin Clarry. "She usually finds she has to go away for the day. This year she's lucky—she's got a real excuse, for a change."

"Tell me," said Willy, in the soft voice which Elinor now knew meant that he was more serious than usual. "How long will they be away?"

The Greenwood Shady

"About a fortnight, I imagine," said Elinor. "They're not going just yet."

"But before they do," said Willy, "can't we do something to help that girl?"

"Girl? Oh, Francesca! How do you mean?" asked Elinor.

"Well "—Willy drew his hand backwards across his hair—"this business of the young doctor fellow—Beale—Heal?"

"Beale."

"Beale. He was there—at the Fleurys—last night when I dined with them. I never saw a man so swamped in love; and what chance did he get?" Willy pushed aside the parsley and, taking a small pudding-basin from the table, held it up and squinted at it earnestly. "'Now you see, don't you,'" he said in Colonel Fleury's somewhat staccato tones—"'you see that in order to rewind the weight, you must have a rotating barrel carrying the rope without disturbing the wheels position—or else, as you see, the hands would be disturbed at every winding. Now take this mechanism'"—Willy put down the basin and flourished the flour-sifter— "take this ratchet and click mechanism. The—'"

"You needn't go on," said Cousin Clarry. "We've all dined there. I wouldn't mind the ratchet and click in the clocks, but when they put it on your plate and call it rabbit and leek, then I do draw the line, I can tell you."

"Well, it isn't the way to encourage young love," said

Willy. "Ghosts, clocks, clocks, ghosts and some Bridge hands thrown in. Can't you give them some sort of hint?" he asked.

"We've done more than hint," said Elinor. "We used to invite Francesca by herself and ask her young man—not this one, but the earlier ones; but it didn't do much good. Colonel Fleury would appear just as it was time to go, and say something silly about escorting the princess back to the tower, or some idiocy of that kind.—We gave it up."

"But don't they realise that if they go on like this they'll—I mean, I realise that she's their only child, but wouldn't you say they'd like to see her happy and settled in life? Now wouldn't you?"

Elinor spoke with some reluctance.

"I hardly know," she said slowly. "I can't believe that they really think that any harm can come to Francesca if she's given a free hand. They're old-fashioned, and they detest the way young people go on nowadays—perhaps they're determined to protect her from what they feel is a too-free world. There's one other thing, although I feel it's a dreadful accusation to make—and that is, that they're quite satisfied to keep her at home. She doesn't do the housework—they have a woman in to do that—but Francesca does quite a lot of the cooking on the days the woman isn't there, and she gets all the Bridge things ready, and she helps her father with the clocks and does the family shopping and writes the family letters....It all adds up, you know, and she must be very useful. Perhaps they don't realise...and perhaps they do."

The Greenwood Shady

"Well, I tell you what," said Willy. "Suppose you and I go into partnership and see what we can do? It's rather an urgent matter, as you know; that young doctor fellow'll be off soon. Shall we see if we can fix things so's Francesca can go with him?"

Elinor rose and walked slowly into the drawingroom, and he followed her.

"Isn't that unwarrantable interference?" she asked.

"I don't think so. I like that girl—what's more, she's cut out for a doctor's wife. You can see it sticking out a mile. Let's try to get them together, shall we?"

Elinor smiled at his earnestness. He was standing at the window looking over to the House and at Francesca's window, clearly visible from where he stood.

"I'll help in any way I can," she promised. "But I advise you to stick to looking after Julian."

"Julian? Julian doesn't want any looking after," said Willy. "Julian's safe at school, and besides, he—"

He broke off abruptly, and Elinor saw that he had caught sight of something outside. At the look on his face she came across the room and, standing beside him, looked out at the oddly-assorted group approaching the Lodge.

At the head of the procession walked Julian, his arm firmly in Mrs. Sprule's grasp. His clothes were torn, his hair wild; one eye was black and his nose was bleeding. Willy's face slowly whitened, and Elinor, glancing up at him, heard his muttered words.

"I've been afraid of this," he said. "I've been afraid of it for—for years...."

Elinor put a hand impulsively on his arm. The gesture was steadying, but she spoke in a puzzled tone.

"But—but, Willy," she said. "Look at the—the others."

Willy looked. Tommy Robbins, supported by his mother, was behind Mrs. Sprule. Next to him, limping, came Fatty du Cane; behind him were the Jenner twins, both sobbing, with Mrs. Jenner between them.

Without a word, Elinor and Willy made for the front door and, opening it, faced the procession. Mrs. Sprule held Julian out at arm's length and glared at his father.

"You ought to be *ashamed*!" she brought out passionately on a middle register.

"Ashamed!" roared Mrs. Robbins on low G. "So you ought to be!"

"Ashamed!" squeaked Mrs. Jenner, on a tremulo soprano note. "To send a boy like him into a decent school, among decent boys—"

"You deceived me, Mr. Hume," said Mrs. Sprule, dignity replacing passion. "You brought me that boy, and you led me to suppose that he was as mild-mannered and gentle as—"

"Brought up with heathens," pointed out Mrs. Robbins. "Let loose among a lot of Zulus and Hottentots, and then put with decently-brought-up boys."

"Look!" piped Mrs. Jenner, exhibiting a bump on a twin.

The Greenwood Shady

"Look at his poor head! Look at that lump—and wait till his father sees it! Size of a cricket-ball!"

"Look at this," invited Mrs. Robbins. "Teeth-marks! You'll hear more of *that* from his father. And look at poor little Fatty's nose, all swollen. And show him the hair, Fatty."

Fatty advanced and held out a handful of hair plainly pulled from his bright-red poll. Waiting for the sympathetic hisses of the women to subside, he held out a shin on which a bruise was darkening.

"Kicked me," he explained, with a gulp.

There was a disturbance in the hall, and Cousin Clarry, pushing her way between Elinor and Willy, stood on the doorstep and, with a swift glance, took in the damage.

"Fighting!" she trumpeted.

"It's that boy," proclaimed Mrs. Jenner, pointing at Julian. "Look what he's done!"

"What—all that?" said Cousin Clarry in astonishment. She turned to Willy for confirmation, and met the blaze of triumph in his eyes. "You mean Julian did all that?"

"Every bit," said Willy, struggling to inject a note of modesty into the words.

"And when his father sees *this*," said Mrs. Jenner, drawing the other twin forward, "he'll—"

"Now, now, now," said Cousin Clarry. "Boys will be boys."

"They needn't be savages," pointed out Mrs. Sprule. "Mr. Hume, I'm sorry to say this, but—Julian is expelled."

"Well, I'm sorry about that," said Willy, with genuine regret, looking at the still undamaged areas of the victims. "I—"

"Zulus and Hottentots," said Mrs. Robbins again.

"Oh, nonsense!" said Cousin Clarry. "Now don't stand there: you've all got free doctors—go and use them. Now, you boys, you go back to school with Mrs. Sprule, and she'll tell you a little story about a worm that turned. Dangerous things, worms. That ought to teach you to keep your hands off them until you've found out whether they can fight back."

The victims were led away, and Willy looked down at the small form left on the drive.

"Julian!"

Julian, hitching up his short trousers, advanced and looked up expectantly.

"Julian, did they go for you first?" asked his father.

"No. Not to-day, they didn't," said Julian.

"I see. Was this attack unwarranted—that is, did you set on them for nothing?"

"Not for nothing," said Julian. "I owed them an awful lot."

"Ah."

Willy held out a hand, and Julian slipped his into it. They walked together into the hall, and Cousin Clarry, fetching a large square of clean rag, proceeded to mop up his wounds. Willy looked at Elinor thoughtfully.

"I wonder," he said, "if you could let me have a copy of the Queensberry rules?"

Chapter Twelve

Francesca's well-being was being considered by a good many people. Mr. Warren, freed from his anxiety about his wife, reverted to his habit of glowering at Colonel and Mrs. Fleury and brooding over plans for uniting their daughter to young Doctor Beale, who was considered by Mr. Warren to be far and away the finest young man who had set his cap at her. Not only had Doctor Beale a Yorkshire mother, but he had been born not six miles from Mr. Warren's own birthplace near Halifax. He watched with real distress the approach of the day which was to remove the doctor.

Joanna watched with equal distress. She remembered, with a little regret, her impulsive promise to do something to help. Sitting with Strone Heriot on a hard green bench outside Mr. Warren's country cottage, she brought the subject up ruefully.

"He'll be gone soon," she said, "and I've not done a thing."

Strone, sitting cross-legged on the grass at her feet, made no reply. Pulling a blade of grass and chewing it absently, he was thinking not of Doctor Beale, who was going, but of Mark

Stirling, who was coming. He was not in a mood to interest himself in anybody else's difficulties.

"You're not listening," complained Joanna.

"No. Well," he amended, "I'm not interested. We've got troubles of our own, haven't we?"

"Well, in a way," said Joanna slowly. She slipped off the bench and settled herself beside him, frowning. "It's a muddle, isn't it, Strone? There's Francesca down there, free as air, and the doctor even freer, and yet they can't get together. And we're always together, and yet we're—at least, I'm—not free."

"Well, she's over twenty-one, isn't she?" said Strone, with a touch of irritation. "It only needs a few minutes to pack a suit-case and tell her father and mother to go to hell—and there's her boy-friend waiting outside in the car. Where's the difficulty? If the girl had half an ounce of guts she wouldn't need you and me and Cousin Clarry and Elinor and Willy, to say nothing of Uncle Tom Warren and all, sitting up at night and eating our hearts out over her."

"All right, all right," said Joanna softly. "Don't get cross. This is a very difficult case—one of those knotted, tied-up psychological situations you read about in those books that write about them. If you were a writer instead of an actor, you could make a lovely morbid book out of it."

"What, out of Francesca?"

"Out of the Fleury trio. Look how nice they all are—the best parents and the best upbringing and a real English home atmosphere. And yet, look at the effect they have on even such a nice coom-fortable character as Mr. Warren. Nobody can say a word against Colonel and Mrs. Fleury. Then why are we all fighting to get Francesca out of their clutches?"

"Who's fighting?" inquired Strone, pulling a fresh supply of grass. "Me?"

"No, not you—you're such a selfish pig, you're too wrapped up in your own affairs. You—"

"Affair," corrected Strone. "I'm only having one."

"Well, if you weren't, you'd be like the rest of us—planning how to outwit Mother and Father. And that's where the psychological twist comes in: are they a charming, well-bred English couple, wrapped up in bridge and their charming daughter, or are they setting out to keep her single all her life?"

"Both."

"Hm?"

"I said both. By which I meant they're charming, but they're like a lot of other parents—they don't realise how time passes. They still think of Francesca as a dewy sixteen, too young to think of marrying. So they don't take suitors seriously. So they don't encourage them. So the suitors go away. So Doctor Beale too will go away. So Francesca'll have to look round for something else.—For God's sake, can't we talk about something else?"

Joanna turned and, leaning forward, put her lips softly to the lines of irritation on his brow. Strone pulled her against him, and she lay with her head on his shoulder.

"Sorry I was cross," he said. "But we haven't got much time together, and we've got to get a future mapped out. Joanna...I love you so much!"

There was no reply. Joanna, with a forefinger, was tracing the veins on the back of his hand.

"Attraction's an awfully funny thing, Strone, isn't it?" she said musingly after a time. "Can you define it?"

"Why define it? Why not just acknowledge it's there and leave it at that?"

"Well, it's so *reasonless,* and it's so *quick*! The first time I ever looked at you I felt something. Well, *why*?"

"Because I felt something, too," said Strone. "That's why."

"No wonder marriages don't always come off," mused Joanna. "You don't get a chance to go about it in the right way. Before you can say to yourself: Is he good, is he sensible, is he rich, is he likely to get on...plingggg! it's got you. You can't think soberly any more; all you can do is moon. You know, Strone, I moon about you all the time. I moon about you in bed at night, and I wake up and start mooning again. I can see other people, and I can hear them, and I can talk to them and answer their questions, but through them all I can hear and see you. All the time, like a sort of undercurrent.—Do men go moony like that?"

"Not unless they've got it really badly," said Strone. "I'm

a bit moony just now because I've got to work out what's the best thing to be done."

"But it shows you that Nature doesn't really care whether you're happy or not," pursued Joanna. "Nature knocks you over with this attraction business, and so you marry without your head, and that's why you land in such messes. You love me, but what do you really know about me?"

"Oh...one or two things," said Strone. "I know you're tender-hearted, because you were sorry for the over-worked mothers on board. I know you like children, or you wouldn't have been able to stand those screaming Harris kids. I know you're loyal, because you wouldn't take sides against Stirling. I know you're pure, because you miss half the openings I give you. And I know you're strong, and a good sailor. And I know one or two rather important things, too—the way your hair grows round the back of your ears here, and the way your eyes go up just at the end, and the way your hands curl up every time I try to smooth them out. I know you've got lovely soft lips and good lungs—I counted twelve, slowly, last time I kissed you. If you're interested, I could give you a fairly accurate list of all your measurements. Brain...well, I don't know yet. Have you decided whether the Amazon is in Africa or America?"

"It's the Z that does it. The Zambesi's got one too, and it gets me all mixed. But I'm fairly clear about the Dee and the Don and the Ouse and the Humber."

"Good. And the Hudson?"

"Oh, that's easy. Canada. Or is it in New York?"

Strone laughed. "Oh, Joanna, you're hopeless!"

Joanna, leaning back a little to look at him, spoke seriously.

"Strone."

"Well?"

"I only wanted to say that—well, perhaps you won't like the subject very much, but I'd like you to know something."

"Go on."

"Well...about being in love. It wouldn't be true to say that I wasn't in love when I married. I must have been, because everybody tried to stop me, and I wouldn't be stopped. But I just want to say that nothing I felt before was ever like...this. I promise."

Strone pressed her head back to its position against his heart and put a quiet question.

"How did it happen, Joanna—that first time?"

Joanna sighed.

"Oh, it was all rather quick, and it wasn't a happy time. Everybody argued and—"

"Who's everybody?"

"The relations—the Clarences and the rest. I had no parents, so I was everybody's child—I'd spent my holidays with almost all of them at different times, and of course they felt that that gave them the right to interfere when I got married. I met him when I came down to Deepwood to see Aunt Ellie. He was staying with her—he used to come down on business sometimes. I was pleasantly surprised when I saw him—he took after his uncle, Alexander, who was Aunt Ellie's husband, and a much more attractive man than Mark. Well, we went for walks, and then we went for some more walks, and then—well, then we discovered we were in love. I'll never forget that day I told Aunt Ellie...."

"What did she say?"

"Oh, what everybody else said, only of course she could tell me from her own experience with Alexander. She begged and begged me to go away and think about it, but there was nowhere much to go, except to the other relations, or back to my job—I had a job teaching juniors in a school in Sussex. I asked Aunt Ellie what she had against him, and she couldn't give me any facts—just as I, at this moment, couldn't give you any facts about why I've left him. There aren't any facts. If you ask anybody who was out in Africa—if you ask Willy, you'd find he couldn't tell you anything concrete. So there it was—we were married and we went straight out to Africa. Sometimes—afterwards—I used to wonder whether it was the fact that he was the first man I'd ever really known...."

"Could be," said Strone.

"But making a mistake like that ought to be a sort of guarantee against falling too hard in the future, oughtn't it?" asked Joanna.

"Depends what you trip over," said Strone, pushing back her hair and dropping a series of kisses along her forehead. "You hadn't much chance against highly-trained charm like mine. How could you hold out against love making...like... this?"

"Why don't they make you the hero in all those films you do?" asked Joanna, after a time. "You'd make a lovely one. I'd go for you every time."

"Thank you. Joanna—"

"Hm?"

"Joanna." Strone's voice was low. "Will you come away with me?"

Joanna disengaged herself slowly from his arms and sat up. She looked at him with troubled eyes, and Strone took one of her hands firmly in his.

"Look at it this way," he pleaded. "Look at the position we're in. You've no grounds for divorce, and neither has Stirling. He'll be here pretty soon, and if you try to settle the matter on a wordy basis, nobody'll get anywhere. If you separate, you'll have to wait years. But if he comes home and finds you're with me, there'll be no need for any talking—it'll be too late for talking.—-Will he divorce you?"

"Ye-es," said Joanna slowly. "Yes, he's not the kind of man who'd refuse a divorce just out of spite. But—"

"But what?"

"But only this," said Joanna. "Last time I got married, it was all done on the wrong foot. I fell in love with the wrong man; nobody was pleased, and everybody showed it. Nobody except my father-in-law and Aunt Elbe came to the wedding,

The Greenwood Shady

nobody wished us happiness. Nobody except Aunt Elbe saw us off when we sailed. Nobody on the boat would talk to Mark. Nobody greeted me when I arrived and nobody minded when I left. Do you call that a marriage?"

"No. But—"

"Well, this time," said Joanna, "I'd like to do things the old story-book way. I don't want to sound terribly old-world, but I don't want to live in sin—even with you; though when I wake up in the middle of the night and think about you and how wonderful it would be, I weaken a bit. I'd like to treat this feeling I've got for you as if it was something tough and lasting and—and deep. I love you very much, Strone darling; but I'd like to wait until I am a really free woman. I want to get married out in the open, with heaps and heaps of people at our wedding. I want to be pointed out as Mrs. Heriot Strone, wife of the actor. I want to have a nice house and lots of children— nice legitimate children. I don't want any more shadiness, Strone—I've had more than enough! I want the future to be all out in the daylight. I want to know that you love me enough to wait for me. I want Oh, Strone, waiting's going to be so hard!"

She stopped and, taking a handkerchief from his pocket, shook it open and dried her tears. He watched her with a half-smile and then, rising, put out a hand and pulled her to her feet.

"Feeling better?" he asked.

"Strone, were you listening?"

"Every word," said Strone.

"Don't you...agree with me?"

"Not in any one particular." His smile became wider. "I think you ought to come back to London with me week after next and let me save all that money I pay a couple—a *married* couple—to do for me."

"But—"

"But I love you. Whatever you say, Sister Joanna, is all right. I'll rig up a picket fence between us and look at you over the top now and again. And now sit on the bench and stop telling me what we can't do and tell me what we can do. I've got to start rehearsals for a show as soon as I leave here. And I don't leave here—as I told you before—until I've seen you out of the house. Where," he inquired, "do you intend to go?"

Joanna considered.

"Well, if you're in London," she said, "couldn't I go there, too? There are two Clarences at Bayswater and one just behind the Roosevelt statue and another just near Earl's Court Underground. Cousin Clarry knows them all—I could ask her which of them I could stay with."

"I shouldn't stay with any of them," advised Strone. "I made an exception in your case, but as a rule I never stay with people nowadays. You either have to follow your hostess to and from the kitchen offering to help with the washing-up, or you have to sit, quite alone, in the drawing-room listening to your host arguing that there isn't the slightest need to get out the best china. You can't demand morning tea, and you have to say you never take coffee at eleven. And for breakfast you have

The Greenwood Shady

to eat sawdust out of a packet because your hostess objects to cooking porridge. You have to offer to shave in the bathroom, and you have to be careful to be pleasant to the woman who's cleaning the front steps when you go out. The whole thing's the most terrible strain, and if you're wise, you'll go to a decent hotel where you don't have to apologise for giving trouble."

"Hotels cost too much," said Joanna. "Even if I got what Cousin Clarry calls *ong-pongsiong* terms.—What I might do, Strone, is get a job."

"You will not," said Strone, "get a job."

"But why? It's better than doing nothing all day in London."

"Nobody," stated Strone, "could do nothing all day in London. Unless they were mentally deficient, which I trust you're not, though I'm keeping an open mind. Have you ever been to the British Museum?"

"Good heavens, no!"

"Tate Gallery?"

"No—well, yes. Or was it—"

"Have you seen the Mint?"

"Mint?"

"Have you been over the National Gallery?"

"Certainly I have."

"When?"

"Well...I was twelve. And I've been to the Zoo. Oh—and the Tower. And Madame Tussaud's, including the Chamber."

"Petticoat Lane?"

"Well—no."

"Wallace Collection?"

"N-no."

"The Monument? The London Bridge? The Docks? The Old Bailey? Houses of Parliament? Smithfield Market? The Cheshire Cheese?"

"If you'll only buy me a guide-book and a tall, handsome guide," promised Joanna, "I'll do the lot. When do I see you?"

"Leave that to me. And now, what time is it?"

"Oh—you want tea, don't you?"

"Well, if you can hold the kettle under that trickle that runs down there, I'll get the Warren Primus going."

"You'll find some stores in that rickety cupboard inside," said Joanna. "I'll unpack the sandwiches."

"What d'you suppose they did up here?" asked Strone, going in and looking round the plainly-furnished interior.

"She said it reminded them of their moors. Does this look like a Yorkshire moor to you?"

"Well, I see their idea," acknowledged Strone. "I wouldn't mind spending a honeymoon in a place like this. There wouldn't be any disturbances."

"It makes me feel mean, the way we spend lovely days up here when poor Francesca doesn't get—"

"Not Francesca *again*?"

"Why not? How would you like to entertain your mother's

The Greenwood Shady

bridge friends and listen to those clocks going bing-bang bing-bang all day and all night?"

"Rum hobby," commented Strone. "Old Fleury must have been like that fellow in the song—you know:

'And in watching the pendulum swing to and fro
Many years did he spend as a boy!'"

Joanna laughed.

"It's not really funny," she said. "What with his conversation and Mrs. Fleury's gardening terms—"

"Which reminds me," said Strone, lifting the Primus on to a deal table and examining it. "That gardener of theirs could do with a bit of watching."

"Watching? You mean he's—well, dishonest or something?"

"No—bats."

"Oh, you mean talking to himself? But that's quite harmless. Cousin Clarry often talks to herself."

"He doesn't talk to himself. He talks to someone he thinks he's got with him."

Joanna stared.

"How do you know?"

"I heard him. I was hanging about waiting for you, and I took a turn among Mrs. Fleury's ranunculus. No, never mind what it is—just picture me among it. I stopped to light a cigarette, and I heard the gardener discoursing away to himself somewhere in the region of the tool-shed. I couldn't hear what he was saying, and I didn't care to do any private investigating, but I did notice that he stopped, waited for a few moments and then spoke again. I'm not mistaken—he was carrying on a full-sized conversation. I know he was alone, because I could see his reflection in the tool-house window."

"Well, is there much difference between—"

"Between talking to yourself and doing a duologue with someone who isn't there? I'd say so. One's a pretty general and usually harmless habit, and the other, to my mind, edges over towards hallucinations."

"Well, he doesn't drink, and he never leaves the grounds, and he sticks to his gardening," pointed out Joanna.

"He wasn't sticking very close to it when I saw him. And as far as I could see most of the plants were looking pretty tired."

"How could they look anything else in this weather? We've had boiling hot days ever since I came home. How can the poor flowers thrive in this scorch?"

"Everybody else's seem to be doing all right. But—damn this stove!—as I said, it isn't my show."

"His references were a bit thin, I think Mrs. Fleury said. Do you think he's got a criminal record or something?"

"Couldn't say. But when you engage our gardener, don't take on anybody who hides behind the tool-shed talking to himself in a voice that would get him a good job on any stage."

"Well, perhaps that's what he is!" exclaimed Joanna.

"What?"

"What you'll be one day," said Joanna. "A broken-down actor."

Chapter Thirteen

Mrs. Fleury was not at all surprised to hear that Julian had failed to settle at Mrs. Sprule's. In a long and private talk with his father she confided that, on hearing he was to attend the village school, she had had qualms. She had nothing, she explained, against either Mrs. Sprule or the school, but Fatty du Cane was Fatty du Cane, and Julian Hume was...well, Julian Hume. The gulf, though not as wide as it had been in her day, was not yet entirely bridged, and until it was, it was no use putting up temporary structures.

At this point Mrs. Fleury paused, pleased with the term. Willy, waiting patiently for her to come to the point, filled in time by admiring her really fine complexion and the silky whiteness of her hair. Age, as personified by Mrs. Fleury, was a gracious and still pleasing spectacle. He took in her figure, her carriage and clothes and accorded them the sincerest admiration, and, at the same time, wished very much that she would release him and let him go and talk to Cousin Clarry, for whom he was beginning to entertain feelings which gave him almost as much uneasiness as those which the sight of Elinor Stirling had roused in him.

Coming to himself with a start, he found that Mrs. Fleury had moved from Deepwood to Weston. Here, she told him, was the school to which Julian should have been sent in the first place. It was in every way suitable; it was just the right size for boys of Julian's age—twenty juniors and eighteen seniors. It was run on sound lines, and it only admitted—in these days when one never knew who was what—the children of parents personally recommended to the Principal, Miss Condiment. It was on the bus route, and children were seen across the road by one of the mistresses. Lunch was provided for those children who attended both morning and afternoon school. The fees were moderate—negligible, said Mrs. Fleury, with a remembrance of the exorbitant rent Willy was paying for the flat. Finally, she was prepared to speak to Miss Condiment herself, though the term had already begun, and say a word for Julian.

Willy thanked her and passed some of the information on to Julian, who said it might be all right. Satisfied, Willy strolled across to the Lodge, where breakfast had just come to an end, and told Elinor the news.

"I'm glad," she said. "Perhaps he'll be better there—I mean, perhaps Miss—who did you say she was?"

"Condiment."

"Good heavens! Well, perhaps she can keep the boys from fighting."

Willy looked disappointed.

"I never went to a dame school myself," he said, following her into the kitchen. "I always had a lot of men to look after

The Greenwood Shady

me."

"Some women would give a lot to be able to say that," commented Cousin Clarry, unloading the morning's purchases from the string bags. "Now go out of this kitchen, Willy Hume—you can see it's crowded already."

Willy took a chair and looked in admiration at Strone's expert drying-up. Joanna, at the sink, wrung out her cloth and addressed Willy.

"I'm glad you've come," she said. "Strone was going across to fetch you."

"He doesn't want fetching," commented Clarry. "He's never out of the place. What did you want him for?"

"To get him up to date," said Strone. "Joanna and I have been making plans."

"Well, let's hear them," demanded Cousin Clarry. "And remember what I said to you the day you came here."

"I remember perfectly. You said a husband's a husband."

"I did."

"Well, that's just what Joanna said, too. So we've decided," said Strone, giving a final polish to the spoons, "or rather, I've decided, that she's to go up to London and stay there. I'll be there, too, and—"

"Ho?" said Cousin Clarry.

"I don't know what 'ho' means," said Strone, "but I've got a bit of rehearsing to do for what's called a forthcoming play. What we want to decide is, where Joanna's to stay. Which

Clarence connection, in other words, is the best bet? Joanna won't agree that a hotel would be the best place, so we've got to work through the relations."

Cousin Clarry unwrapped a particularly large shoulder of mutton and transferred it to a plate.

"Put that out in the larder," she directed Willy. "Not near the window, now—I've known that Mrs. Fleury to stop and have more than a peep as she's passing. Now, Clarences. Let me see. What about Florrie?"

"Who's she?" asked Joanna.

"Florrie? She's Edwin's widow, but she's buried two since Edwin," said Cousin Clarry. "She lives in Park Terrace or Gardens or Crescent or Square, whichever it is—a large house, and she takes in boarders, though you must never mention it. That is to say, when you've been there a week she'll bring you a little list and say, 'Here are a few of the things I've had to get for you, dear,' and you pay up. She doesn't like you to behave as though she's charging you anything. You'd be all right there if you could put up with her sister-in-law—not Edwin's sister, but the sister of her next husband. She's a nice woman, but she's on the peculiar side—she thinks she's Madame de Sévigne, nobody knows why, and she talks French to you all the time. Rushes across the room as agile as you please, though she must be eighty, and kisses you on both cheeks and says *chérie,* as though she were offering you a drink."

"Thank you," said Joanna. "I think not. Who else is there?"

The Greenwood Shady

"Let me see." Cousin Clarry, considering, got out the large white cloth she tied over her hair when she cooked and, assisted with the utmost politeness by Strone and Willy, swathed it round her head. "Thank you. Thank you. Now let me see. How about Anna Heriot, Strone's third or fourth cousin?"

"I've never heard of her," said Strone. "Who does she imagine she is?"

"Nobody," said Cousin Clarry. "She's a very nice woman, and accomplished. Really accomplished. She lives near Regent's Park—you can hear the roars every feeding time—and she plays the harp and mandolin. Beautifully. It was she who made me take up the cello. 'I'm too old,' I said, and she said, 'Nonsense, Clarry, nonsense—you're only in your thirties, and by the time you're fifty you'll have been playing for fifteen years.' She gives little concerts now and again—you'll enjoy them, Joanna."

"I shan't," said Joanna, "because I shan't be there. Where else is there?"

"I've got an aunt in Sloane Square," offered Willy, "who keeps marmosets."

"What about those cousins in that lovely little house in Chelsea?" asked Elinor. "Won't they do?"

"Those? *Those?*" said Cousin Clarry in her deepest and most disdainful tones. "Do you know what those two are doing?"

"No. What?" asked Joanna. "Taking up the zither?"

"They go out, both of them—Emily and James—to evening parties—not, mark you, as guests, but as cook and butler. They hire themselves out at so much an evening; she prepares a dinner, and he gets into his tails and serves it."

"Well, what am I waiting for?" Joanna asked the company. "I join them as washer-upper. They sound the very thing, Cousin Clarry. What are you looking so disdainful about?"

"To think," said Cousin Clarry ponderously—"to think of people paying good money to eat one of Emily Clarence's dinners! Why—"

"I know," said Joanna. "Horse, whale and old boot. But what does that matter? They sound sensible and up to date. How old are they?"

Cousin Clarry counted up.

"Let me see—Emily's mother was born the year your Uncle Christopher died, and she married in—No, that wasn't Emily's mother, that was Agatha's. I suppose if we reckon—"

"Well, how old *roughly?*" asked Joanna.

"Well, she took up cooking in nineteen hundred," said Willy, screwing up his eyes in an effort to concentrate, "and she made her first *crème à la bombom* the year poor King Edward VII passed away. In fact, some malicious people said that it was the *crème à la—*"

"Will you all get out of this room," demanded Cousin Clarry, "and let me get on with my work, instead of—"

"But their *address,* Cousin Clarry," said Joanna. "Their

address. Emily's address. I've got to write to her."

"Don't you know the address, Elinor?" asked Cousin Clarry.

"I'm afraid not," said Elinor. "I know how to get to it, but I've forgotten the name of the street."

"Oh dear, oh dear," moaned Cousin Clarry. "I wish you'd all find your own addresses, instead of worrying me. It might be in here." She pulled out a large dresser drawer and handed Elinor a roll of greaseproof paper, two packets of envelopes, a bottle of ink, three skeins of green wool, a tea-strainer, two checked dusters, an old-fashioned family album, a bottle of cleaning-fluid and some sheets of cello music. Elinor, becoming overloaded, passed some of the articles to Willy, who passed them to Strone, who passed them to Joanna, who put them on the kitchen table.

"Gloves, nut-crackers, two packs of patience cards—here, take them, take them," muttered Cousin Clarry, now thoroughly on the scent. "Pen-knives, a—What's this? Oh yes. Look, Elinor, you don't often see anything like this nowadays. A cutting device for your quills when people wrote with quill pens. There, you see—you put the quill in there and press. Belonged to dear old Uncle Arthur. You—"

"Cousin Emily's address," said Joanna.

"Very well, very well. One can't do more than *look*," grumbled Cousin Clarry. "Table napkins, knitting-needles, that old brown teapot—what's *that* in here for? Inkwell—I must clean that up, Elinor; it's got such a pretty silver top.

Spinning-top. Now what in Heaven's name? Oh, I know. I won it at the bazaar, Elinor; don't you remember? Pass that to Willy—it'll come in nicely for Julian. It works very well—I tried it. You wind the string round and round—not *that* way, Willy—that's right. Round and round and round. Now Oh, bravo, bravo!"

The top swirled bravely on the kitchen table, mounted the greaseproof paper, cleared the tea-strainer and bounded on to the floor. Strone picked it up and held out his hand for the string.

"Oh, no, you don't," said Joanna. "You give me that top. Cousin...Emily's...*address*!"

"I wish you wouldn't drive me," said Cousin Clarry.

"It must be upstairs with my—No, wait a minute." She dived deep and came up with a leather writing-folder swollen to an abnormal size with letters and fastened by two rubber bands. "It may be in here. You can't mistake her handwriting—niggley-piggley stuff. Here! No—yes!" Triumphantly, Cousin Clarry unfolded a letter. "Yes, we've got it! Now write it down, somebody. Mrs. J. M. Clarence-Cook, 19 something or other—can you make this out, Elinor? Poke? Peake—that's it. 19 Peake Crescent, Chelsea, S.W. 3."

There was a loud knocking at the back door, and Cousin Clarry broke off, frowning.

"Now, who's that out there?"

Strone looked outside.

The Greenwood Shady

"It's a man with a pram," he announced. "But no baby."

"Oh, well now. Go away, all of you," ordered Cousin Clarry. "I've got to go and see to him."

Joanna directed the two men to replace the articles in the drawer, and took Elinor upstairs.

"I'm going to put some cream on my hands," she said. "They always feel dry after I've had them in the washing-up water. Then you can dictate me a nice fishing sort of letter to Cousin Emily."

She sat down at her dressing-table and picked up a jar of hand-cream.

"Do you use Dagmar's?" she asked. "It's expensive, but it lasts."

"I don't use any," said Elinor.

"I didn't mean hand-cream, specially. I meant face stuff."

"Oh. Well," said Elinor, "I use a sort of pinky-yellow shade of powder because they say it makes the older woman look—"

"But *whose*?"

"Well, mine, of course."

"Oh, Aunt Ellie darling, you're hopeless! I mean, what *make*!"

"Oh, what *make*? I see what you mean. Well, it depends where I am. If I'm in Easton, I—"

"But you can't just buy *anything*," pointed out Joanna. "You've got your own special kind, and you can't use any other. If I use anything that isn't Dagmar I come out in awful spots."

"You do?"

A terrible suspicion seized Joanna and, turning slowly on her seat, she faced Elinor.

"You don't mean," she said incredulously, "that you just put on anything, regardless?"

"Well, not regardless, no," said Elinor. "If it's too expensive, I give it back at once, and I wouldn't buy bright purple lipstick or pea-green powder."

"Now we're on the subject," said Joanna curiously, "what *do* you use in the way of cosmetics? Mascara?"

"No. Not mascara."

"Foundation?"

"I use a sort of creamy stuff that—"

"Eye-shadow?"

"Good gracious, no!"

"Well, I tell you what'll be the quickest," decided Joanna. "Tell me what you *do* use."

"Oh, quite a lot. I spread on my creamy stuff and then I put on powder."

"The pinky-yellow?"

"Well, yes. Then I put on my lipstick and—"

"And then here comes glamorous you." Joanna drew a deep breath. "Don't you use any skin food?" she asked. "Haven't you got any cleansing cream or astringent lotion or com-

The Greenwood Shady

plexion milk or wrinkle oil or velvetta or creama or alouette or—"

"It all sounds heavenly," said Elinor. "But, you see, I've got to get up and have a bath and dress and go downstairs and lay the breakfast table and make the coffee and clean the drawing-room and the diningroom before anybody gets down and help Cousin Clarry with the fires and—"

"I know, and I'm not being unpractical," said Joanna; "but when I run my home I shall still find time to look after my skin."

Elinor wondered how many times she had heard that vow made by earnest young women at their dressing-tables.

"I hope you will," she said. "But—"

"Do you think that when I'm Cousin Clarry's age I shall have a scaly skin like hers? No, never. I shall take trouble and I—"

"But you're young and pretty," pointed out Elinor.

"If I'm pretty, then so must you be, because we're alike. I know you can't help what age you are—I mean, nobody can—but you needn't let yourself go. You've got a nice skin, and you've got to keep it nice."

Elinor was on the point of asking what had kept it nice throughout all the years of neglect, when Strone, coming up the stairs as rapidly as their limited width would allow, hammered impatiently on the door.

"Come on, come on, come on," he shouted. "What's going on in there?" He opened the door a little way and peered cautiously through the crack. "Well, what *is* this?"

"Coming," said Joanna. She turned to Elinor. "To-night," she said, "I'm going to come in and make you up properly, and then I shall take you out and choose your proper make-up and I shall see that you buy it."

She went downstairs with Strone, and Elinor, left by herself, walked slowly to the dressing-table and fingered the pretty bottles and jars. Sitting on the little stool, she stared for a time into the mirror, her expression serious and searching.

Forty-one...nearly forty-two. Less than four years a wife, more than eleven a widow. Eleven years. Elinor glanced back at them; they were quiet years, but they had been happy ones. It was difficult to see quite how they had been passed—housework, gardening, sewing, mending. Spring cleaning. Distempering some of the rooms, changing the furniture round, making two new flower-beds near the drive and having the small coal-shed built on to the back of the Lodge. Society? There had not been a great deal; indeed, until Cousin Clarry came there had been almost none. It was easier to live quietly, making no effort to overcome shyness or the dislike of going about alone. It was easier to go out and give some time to hospitals or the Children's Home or the Orphanage at Weston.

Men? Elinor gave a wry little smile. She had met heroines, both in fact and fiction, who had declared that it was as abnormal and as unhealthy for women to live without men as for men to be expected to live without women. Literature and—if women's conversation was to be believed—life pointed to a code of behaviour which, if not quite so free as Georgina's, was tending that way. And yet...for eleven years she had never thought of men. Men were Colonel Fleury, slim, trim, boring; Mr. Warren, bluff, honest and an occasional visitor with Ada love; one or two husbands in Weston or Easton. She had been married, she had known a brief but satisfying time of passion, and it was over. She had read her novels, listened to the conversation and congratulated herself on being free from the tormenting desires of which Georgina had so much to say.

And now Elinor realised that she had congratulated herself too soon. Her outlook, though it may not have been exciting or eventful, had at least been clear; her life might have been called dull, but she had been happy. She had never before felt this odd disinclination to settle to anything, this desire to do nothing but sit on her bed staring out of the window and dreaming of what, in her few rational moments, she could only think of as absurdities. She dreamed of clothes—not the neat coat-and-skirt variety she had worn for years, but gowns: long, clinging, made of soft, gleaming fabrics. She thought of suites in luxury liners, and herself travelling in them. She conjured up colourful scenes in distant lands and in them wore a becoming variety of sombrero, mantilla, starched headdress, shimmering gauze covering or plain white topee. She owned a long, low, pearl-grey saloon, and drove it with superb skill; she belonged to several exclusive women's clubs in London and Paris, and addressed her fellow-members in rippling idiomatic French. She owned a villa at Cannes and a charming little chalet at Château d'Oex. She went, beautifully dressed, to Longchamps, Hurlingham, Lords, Ascot, Aintree, Braemar, Cowes, Wimbledon, Twickenham and Glyndebourne.

And wherever she went, Willy went with her.

Elinor drew a long, shuddering breath and closed her eyes, shutting out the picture of middle-aged serenity which still, to her infinite relief, masked the metamorphosis which was taking place behind it. Fragments from Cousin Clarry's stories, to which she had listened with amusement, never dreaming that they could have any closer application, came back to her now with appallingly sinister meaning: Cousin Belle, who had lived an exemplary life with her husband for twenty years and had, quite without warning, vanished with an artist, and was next seen in Portofino cleaning his brushes; Aunt Sybil, who, after a life of herb-culture and good music, had, at the age of forty, put on a hat—Cousin Clarry remembered the very one—and had gone forth to hunt down a man; Cousin Elvira, who had brought in her mother's medicine tray, and—forty-three years of age and known for her delicacy and reticence—had leaned out of the window and called Cooee to the curate who was passing. Elinor shivered. The fires had been banked, but they were still alight. It was, she thanked Heaven, a problem for herself alone. Full though her mind might be of Willy Hume, madly though she might recall, every night, his soft voice, long, thin hands and amused eyes, there remained paramount a desire for concealment. If she could meet him

The Greenwood Shady

with coolness for the next two or three weeks, if she could fight this unlooked-for enemy, then he would go away with Julian and she would be safe. Time and absence would do what they had so often done before—erase memory and restore her to her accustomed calm.

She opened her eyes as footsteps—slow, deliberate footsteps—sounded on the stairs. Willy's voice, a little plaintive, sounded on the landing.

"Hey!" he called.

"I'm in here." Elinor's voice was quiet and friendly. She opened the door and went outside to join him. "I've been counting Joanna's jars of cream," she said. "Dozens and dozens, all one brand. She says I'm out of touch."

"Out of touch?" Willy repeated the words softly, looking at her with an expression she strove in vain to interpret. "Yes... *that's* it. I was wondering what it was, and that just expresses it. You *are* out of touch, d'you know that? Out of touch with the great, big, bad wicked world outside. Yes, you are, Heaven be praised.—Did you ever hear of an ivory tower? Well...you must stay in yours."

Elinor went quietly past him and down the stairs.

"Yes, I will," she said, smiling. "I'll stay in it."

Chapter Fourteen

Elinor, going back to her bedroom after her bath on the following morning, was surprised to see Cousin Clarry waiting for her, the look on her face grim and purposeful.

"Oh, there you are," she said. "You've been a fine long time. It isn't healthy to lie in that hot water and boil yourself for hours on end."

"That's not what you came to tell me, is it?" asked Elinor. "You look the way you always look when you're up to something. What is it this time?"

Cousin Clarry plunged a hand into the Russian tunic and brought out a tape-measure.

"I've been watching you lately," she said. "Do you realise that you're beginning to put on weight?"

Elinor's eyes widened.

"But I've been telling you and *telling* you!" she said. "Haven't I stood on those bathroom scales and watched the hand go round and round? But you said you were pleased! You said—"

"There's weight *and* weight," said Cousin Clarry. "It all

The Greenwood Shady

depends where you put it. Now stand still while I run this tape-measure round you."

Elinor, wondering, stood still. Cousin Clarry measured her lengthwise and breadthwise and let out her breath in a gust of despair.

"Tck, tck, tck! A woman of your age, Elinor, ought to watch herself."

"But you said I wanted building up, and you—"

"When women round forty begin to spread," went on Cousin Clarry, "there's nothing to stop it but willpower. You've got to say to yourself, I *will* keep my figure—and then you do." She poked a large finger into Elinor. "Look at that—just *look* at that! What sort of corset do you use?"

"I don't really—"

"*That* thing? That tiddly-twiddly little elastic affair? What kind of pulling-in do you think that's going to do? Tell me that. When women had to have figures, how do you think they got them? Whalebone. Not fancy lacy bits, and not half a yard of elastic. Whalebone. When I'm in Easton to-morrow I'll bring back two or three pairs of proper corsets for you to try on."

"But you said that whalebone was—"

"And now I'm going to show you some exercises to take all those rolls of fat off. Come and stand in front of the glass here with me and watch while I show you. No—don't look at me; look into the glass, and then do exactly as I do. Now pull in your stomach—go on—pull! And don't look at my stomach—look at your own. I didn't have this figure when I was forty, I can promise you. Now in, in—you don't call that in, do you? You've got to hold your breath—watch now." Cousin Clarry drank in an enormous quantity of air, pulled in her chin and beat time slowly with one hand. On the tenth beat she expelled the air. "Now! Pull, pull, pull—now keep it pulled in while I count. One, two, three, four—that's only four, and I did ten. This is dreadful, dreadful—you should never have allowed yourself to go so far. I shall come up every morning and see that you do this drill. It's a case of not letting the muscles go; once the muscles go, the figure goes. Once the figure goes, the attraction goes; once the attraction goes, there's nothing to choose between a woman of forty and a woman of fifty or sixty or seventy."

"But isn't it glands and things?" pleaded Elinor. "I mean—"

"I know nothing about glands," said Cousin Clarry. "In my day we got on very well without glands. You're getting fat, and we must stop it."

"But it's that lovely *food*! If you feed me on cream soufflées and—"

"No more," said Cousin Clarry firmly.

"No *more*? You mean...no more? But you told me I needed—"

"Nothing milky, nothing creamy. And no puddings. Biscuits and cheese—I'll get some nice plain water-biscuits. And no cream soups; a little Julienne, perhaps. It's a pity you enjoy

The Greenwood Shady

your breakfast, for at your age the best thing is no breakfast, the lightest of lunches, no tea and then a fairly satisfying supper. Your Aunt Effie was the slimmest woman I ever saw, although all that family tended to fat; she used to do just what I've said: fruit-juice in the morning, a lamb-chop for lunch—you could get lamb-chops in her day, but she took nothing with it—no potatoes and no vegetables. She had no tea, and so when dinner came she felt she could let herself go without harm. She had a formula: no breakfast, no tea, no waist—that was a joke, spelt w-a-i-s-t. Nobody could look at you and say ' No waist,' could they now? Stand up straight and start breathing again."

"Do you mean to say," asked Elinor anxiously, "that from now on you're going to starve me slowly?"

"Starve? Starve?" said Cousin Clarry irritably. "Who said anything about starve? All I'm going to do is to reduce one or two of the richer things you eat, that's all. I am not—I am certainly not going to stand on one side and watch a good-looking woman like you letting yourself go. You're a very fine-looking woman. You're—"

"Talking about me?" asked Joanna from the door.

"No, I am not. I'm telling your Aunt Elinor that if she wants to keep her looks, she's got to take care of them."

"There you are, Aunt Ellie," said Joanna triumphantly, making two bounds across the room and landing on the bed. "That's just what I told you.—I told her she's got to buy some decent skin-food, Cousin Clarry, and—"

"Skin-food?"

"Yes—and cream and a decent foundation and—"

"Do you really suppose," asked Cousin Clarry with contempt—"do you really suppose your Aunt Elinor's going to waste her money getting all those rubbishy complexion aids, and waste her time smearing them on and rubbing them off, as you do?"

"Of course. Why not?"

"Because all that sort of thing is for nincompoop creatures like you, too young to know any better. If I had any capital," declared Cousin Clarry, "then I'd put it straight into complexion aids, because all you have to do is to sell them to poor, deluded women and tell them they'll look like the Queen of Sheba after the first application, and you'll get rid of the stuff as fast as you can dye it pale pink and scent it. You didn't see me going in for all that clap-trap when I was a girl, and can you look me in the face to-day and tell me that I needed it? Let me tell you something "—Cousin Clarry came a step nearer and put up a fat forefinger—"Let me tell you this: not at any time in my life have I wasted my money in your so-called beauty aids. Have you anything to say?"

"No," said Elinor.

"Not out loud," qualified Joanna. "What are you doing with that inch-tape?"

"She's been measuring me," said Elinor, "and I'm to be put on water-biscuits."

"Nothing of the sort," said Cousin Clarry, preparing to de-

The Greenwood Shady

part. "Nothing too rich, was what I said. Starved—poh!" With a grunt, she went out and marched heavily down the stairs.

Elinor's diet from that morning, if not quite at starvation level, was miserable compared with the rich and satisfying meals which she had grown used to. Her plate was passed to her by Cousin Clarry with none of the delicious additions which the others were enjoying. Joanna, passing her the cream, was severely snubbed by the watchful cook. Willy, whose enjoyment of his food was much lessened by the sight of Elinor's open envy, attempted to augment her helping and was caught red-handed. Only at supper was Elinor permitted to eat enough to make her feel really satisfied.

"What," inquired Willy, as they sat alone in the drawing-room after the meal, "is Cousin Clarry up to?"

"She thinks I've put on too much weight," said Elinor. "A month or two ago she thought I wanted feeding up. Now she's decided I want running down. I'll be glad when she changes her mind again."

"Shall I tell you something?" asked Willy.

Elinor looked at him. His face was in shadow; he was leaning back in a deep chair, his long legs crossed, his arms hanging over the chair's sides. She could not see his permanently anxious frown, and the pose—negligent and easy—was in keeping with his character.

"Well, what?" she asked.

"Characteristics can be catching, I find," said Willy. "I'm

catching one of Cousin Clarry's."

"Oh, which one?" asked Elinor.

"Her Where, Who, What approach. Whenever I look at you, I find myself Who-ing and What-ing like anything. Now—his voice dropped to its softest—"that's not polite, is it? When Cousin Clarry does it...but that's different. It wouldn't be Cousin Clarry if she passed over a single detail. But for a stranger to probe..." Willy, horrified at the idea, shook his head slowly from side to side.

"What," asked Elinor, "do you want to know?"

Willy settled himself more firmly in his chair.

"Everything," he said simply. "Piece by fascinating piece. Beginning at the very beginning. Now let me see.—You were an only child, Cousin Clarry said."

"Quite right."

"And you had an unhappy childhood."

Elinor shook her head.

"No. She's wrong there. The childhood part was quite happy. It was later—when I was growing up—things were so difficult."

"Define difficult," requested Willy.

"Oh...just difficult. You see, my parents were one of the most happily married couples there can ever have been. As a pair, they were perfect. He adored her—and she adored him—as much twenty years after they were married, as on their wedding day. It isn't a record, of course, but there can't be so many of them about. Or perhaps there are, but they're too happy to be heard about. What people air mostly is grievances—the happy people just say nothing and go on being happy. Don't you agree?"

"I'm asking the questions," Willy reminded her. "They sound a nice easy couple—what was difficult?"

"Being their daughter. As husband and wife, they were perfect. As parents, they were"—Elinor stopped and gave a little laugh, half helpless, half exasperated. "As parents, they didn't really exist. They remembered to send me to school, and sometimes they remembered to have me home for holidays, but that—and paying the fees regularly—was as far as it went. When I was seventeen the school thought it was time I left, so I left and went home. I hadn't any special talent, and I had no training of any kind, and nobody suggested my getting any. We lived in the most charming house on Exmoor—miles and miles from anywhere. My parents didn't want any society but their own, so we had none. It didn't occur to them to entertain for me, or to see that I got entertained. They got up in the morning, walked, read, looked after the garden, played two-handed patience and went to bed. And I settled down into the same routine—except that I played patience by myself." She smiled across at him. "I sound a wonderfully enterprising girl by modern standards, don't I?"

"Go on."

"Well, the point is that I didn't know how to go on. I was quite intelligent, and I was beginning to see things more clearly. I'd been brought up in the tradition that I was the luckiest girl in the world to have such charming and romantic parents; but I was beginning to see that their—I don't quite know the word—their self-engrossment wasn't going to get me very far."

"How far," inquired Willy, "did you want to go?"

"I can't remember," said Elinor. "I said something just now about modern standards, but I'm not sure that the girls themselves have changed much—I think the parents nowadays automatically steer their girls, as well as their boys, into a channel leading to some kind of job. You never hear of a girl to-day who, at eighteen, doesn't know what she's aiming at, but when I was young there were still two sorts of parents: the kind that thought a career was worth it for its own sake, and the kind that said 'It doesn't matter—she's sure to marry.' But when they said she was sure to marry, they usually took steps to see that she at least got a chance to marry. Schools, nowadays, interest themselves in a girl's future; from the time she's fifteen she hears the word job or career. When she leaves school, her parents find out what she's keen on, or what she's fit for. The Fleurys didn't, but even they, according to their lights, do something to see that Francesca meets people. It would interest me very much to place a modern girl in the position I was in, and see what she does. Even a factory girl's mother sees about the girl's first job, and takes her to interview her employer—if she didn't, I suppose the Labour Exchange would see about it. But a job on a slightly higher level presup-

The Greenwood Shady

poses some sort of training—and how can a girl get it if her parents don't lift a finger?" She broke off. "Am I boring you?"

"No. What did you do?"

"Nothing much. I got more and more restless; I felt more and more useless. Then I decided I'd go and be a nurse. I still think I'd have made a very good one. But neither my father nor my mother did the slightest thing. They said I'd look nice in a nurse's uniform but they thought I'd better wait a bit. You can't possibly understand, unless you'd known them, how impossible it was to hold their attention at all. They thought there were only two people in the world; if you'd asked either of them if they had a daughter, they'd have had to think for a moment or two before saying Yes."

"And so?" asked Willy.

"And so I remembered the relations. You know—you've heard the names dropping out of Cousin Clarry at the rate of a dozen an hour. Cousin This, Uncle That, Aunt the Other. The Clarences. I suddenly wondered, one day, if any of them could help me to get myself something to do. I'd got to the point of reading advertisements for companions—I thought the Clarence horde might know someone who knew someone....And so I went on a round of visits, and after a time a dear old uncle called Gervaise—nobody ever mentions him because he tried to push his wife off the top of a bus and he had to be shut up; Cousin Clarry's convinced that Uncle Gervaise was responsible for the present closed-in buses—well, Uncle Gervaise got me a job."

"Helping to push his wife—"

"No. They were quite friendly at that time—he was over seventy when he tried to—"

"To do her."

"Yes. But he knew a man who'd been left a large house and library and wanted somebody to look after the books—"

"And that was your first job?"

Elinor laughed.

"And my last. I was there until I was twenty-five—then I met my husband, in a train, and—well, then I got married."

"How long were you married?"

"Four years. I often think," said Elinor dreamily, "what a good thing it was I didn't have any children. Can you imagine how the poor things would have been studied and cared for and loved and trained and weighed down with all the things I thought I'd missed?"

Willy made no answer and asked, instead, another question.

"Why didn't you marry again?"

Elinor's eyebrows went up and he made a quick movement and, leaning forward, looked at her quizzically.

"Remember—I warned you," he said. "Who, how, what, when and where. When I go too far, just raise your eyebrows as you did then. It's more effective than a whole lecture on good manners."

"I—didn't know I'd done anything. You surprised me,

The Greenwood Shady

that's all."

Willy, forgetting his apologies, frowned at her intently.

"Four years," he said. "At the end of which you were about thirty. Thirty—tall, graceful, lovely hair, lovely eyes, all Joanna's looks with something that Joanna hasn't got: elegance. Thirty, with all that, and a whole heart—oh, I know that, because I saw Joanna with the other Stirling, and I know what it must have been like."

He leaned back again in the shadow, and there was a silence. When Elinor spoke again, it was not about herself.

"I always feel," she said, "that I ought to have been able to prevent that—Joanna, I mean, and Mark. But I did what I could."

"Don't worry about Joanna," advised Willy. "She's going to be happy. She'll marry Strone, when she's free, and they'll make a good couple. He's a nice fellow, Strone—do you like him?"

"Of course."

"I'm glad. He's just what he looks—strong and dependable. And he makes a lot of money in his rather unspectacular way. The girls don't tear him apart for his autograph, but he makes a good backing whenever he plays in anything—they put him into a thin bit of the production, and he makes it look as if it meant something."

"I like him," said Elinor slowly, "and I'm only afraid of one thing."

"And what's that?"

"Well "—Elinor hesitated—"they've got a long waiting time ahead, and men get impatient and—"

"Ah!" said Willy. "Well, Joanna'll have to handle that. I think you can leave that girl to handle quite a lot.—There's one more question," he added.

"Well?"

Willy rose to his feet and stood looking down at her. "Elinor"—he seemed to choose his words carefully—"how long would you have to know a man before you knew whether you liked him or not?"

Elinor's reply was unhesitating and calm.

"Are you speaking generally?"

"No. I'm being very, very particular. You've known me a matter of—-well, weeks, and what I'm trying to find out is—if you like me."

"Of course I do."

"Thank you. Well, what I've been trying to lead up to," said Willy, "is this. The first week, I liked you. The second week, I got into a peculiar kind of state and couldn't sort any of my impressions out properly: all I knew was that you'd got into my system and I couldn't get you out. And then it all cleared itself up, and I knew what was the matter with me. Elinor, I'm not much of a fellow, but I—well, I love you very much."

Elinor sat where she was, her chief thought being that, if

The Greenwood Shady

she had asked him to sum up her own feelings since his arrival, the words he had just used of himself would have done again. She clung to this thought, while there penetrated to her consciousness the knowledge that he loved her and had told her so. She felt two women; the calm one considering his words, and the trembling, happy one glorying in their significance. He watched her, seeing only the one, and his heart sank.

"If I've annoyed you—" he said hesitatingly at last.

Elinor looked up at him, and he saw that her expression was thoughtful.

"I'm sorry. I was dreaming," she said. "I—I'd like to say something; but I don't know how to—how to put it exactly."

Willy drew his chair close to hers, sat on it and took both her hands.

"Talk away," he said. "But say something kind, if you can."

"Willy," she said, "I like you—very much, and what you've told me is wonderful, but—"

"Oh, there's a but. A very small but, I hope?"

"Could we leave this for a little while? You see "—Elinor hesitated—"you see, you and I have been thrown together a good deal."

He wondered whether she realised how much of the throwing Cousin Clarry had done, but he merely nodded.

"What I'm trying to say is this," pursued Elinor. "We're more or less of an age, and we've been together day after day, and we get on well and like each other, and we've got a lot in common—Strone and Joanna, for one thing. So I'm afraid that what we feel might be the result of all this: the—"

"Propinquity," said Willy, "is the word you're looking for."

"Yes, that's it—propinquity. You know what happens to people on ships when they're thrown together. At the journey's end they wonder what made them—"

"Have you ever been on a sea trip?" inquired Willy.

"No. But I've—"

"You've heard. Well, sometimes it all dies down," acknowledged Willy; "but then, again, sometimes it doesn't. Look at Strone and Joanna. Do you see any signs of any dying down?"

"No, but—"

"You mean that you're prepared to believe I love you—for the moment—and even like me a little yourself; but you think it's because we've been too much together?"

"Yes. I don't—"

"You don't trust Johnnie-on-the-spot, is that it?"

"In a way..."

"Then what," inquired Willy gently, "would you like me to do? Shall I go away and report the state of my affections to you at regular intervals? Am I allowed to see you for short periods every so often? And at what point do you make up your mind that your absence has made my heart grow fonder?"

The Greenwood Shady

She stared at him.

"Are you laughing at me?"

"Of course," said Willy. "Who wouldn't? Darling Elinor, I'm not twenty-six—I'm forty-six. I'm not impulsive—I'm quite slow as regards the thinking processes. Ponderous, in fact. I love you and, having thought the matter over from a lot of angles, I can see only one reason why we shouldn't be married—the one reason being, of course, that you don't love me. You're a very attractive woman, and so it didn't take me long to fall in love with you; I'm not—though I wouldn't say this to everybody—anything out of the ordinary, and therefore it might be some time before you came to a realisation of my charms. I'm willing to wait; but only while you make up your mind about the state of your affections, not the state of mine."

"When you put it that way," said Elinor slowly, "you make it all sound very straightforward. But I can't—I don't seem able to make up my mind as easily as you do. I do like you very much, and perhaps I get things a little muddled. I always envy Joanna because she makes up her mind quickly and definitely and knows exactly what she wants. If you asked Joanna to marry you, she'd think for a moment and then she'd just say 'Yes' without any fuss, and you'd be married in no time."

"Never mind about Joanna," said Willy. "How long will it take you to turn 'I might' into 'I will'?"

"I—I don't know," said Elinor.

"Ah!" said Willy. "Then I must ask Cousin Clarry to find out."

Chapter Fifteen

With the date of the Parade drawing nearer, Deepwood's attention began to be focused on costumes. The question of what was to be worn was not a difficult one, for the same costumes were stored in the village, and worn year after year; the only problem was who was to wear what. This was always the cause of a great deal of acrimony, and this year there promised to be even more, for both Mrs. Robbins and her daughter-in-law, Mrs. Tate, were determined to be Boadicea. The matter was put to the vote by secret ballot, and Mrs. Tate awarded the chariot.

Mrs. Sprule closed the school for a day in order to give herself up to the task of allotting and altering costumes and finishing last year's repairs. Seventeen-year-old Griselda Robbins tried on Nell Gwynne's dress and lowered the decolletage by three inches. Everywhere was the sound of machining, and the thoughts of everyone centred upon dress.

But nobody was thinking of it more seriously than Captain Vandeleur, for he was searching desperately for a pair of trousers. A chivalrous man, the Captain was anxious to avoid causing more alarm to the ladies than he had already done; he was not prepared, however, to walk about much longer in attire that laid him open to the sneers of Frobisher and the jeers of Telemachus. His goal was clear: to find his uniform, to buckle on, once more, his sword, to appear in all his former dignity and grandeur. But in his present unseemly garb he did not care to venture far in his search.

He had spent a trying evening; he had hoped that the Warrens would go out, so that he could enter the flat and inspect Mr. Warren's wardrobe, but when evening came they were still at home, and he had been reduced to the expedient of peering through the window and estimating the size of the garments he hoped to borrow. His inspection of the short, stout Mr. Warren drove him to the conclusion that he had better seek elsewhere.

He decided to try Colonel Fleury, and here he was more fortunate, for on preparing to enter the house, he saw the Colonel and his wife going upstairs to play evening bridge with Georgina. Waiting until they were out of the way, he crept cautiously into their narrow hall. There was no sound in the drawingroom; peeping in, he saw that Francesca was in the kitchen preparing a tray-supper for herself.

Captain Vandeleur went through into the Colonel's bedroom and, sighing for the well-fitting and elegant cut of his own day, chose a pair of brown trousers with a pin stripe. With these in his hands, he went through the drawing-room and was almost at the door when Francesca came out of the kitchen and saw him.

The Captain, appalled at being caught in so unbecoming

an outfit, clutched the trousers to him and attempted a bow. The grace of his bow had moved many a maiden to admiration, but Francesca did not see it. Slowly and without a sound, she slid to the hearthrug in a swoon, and it was here that Doctor Beale, who had made a routine call on Mrs. Warren and received a friendly tip that Colonel and Mrs. Fleury were out, found her.

"Francesca!"

He was beside her in an instant, kneeling and applying unprofessional restoratives. Finally, he lifted her and placed her gently on the sofa.

"Francesca! Francesca...darling!"

Francesca opened her eyes and saw the doctor's face at closer range than she had ever before observed it. She studied it with dreamy intentness.

"Francesca darling—what happened? Do you feel all right?"

Francesca sat up slowly, still supported on the doctor's arm.

"What happened, Francesca? Can you remember?"

"Yes," said Francesca dreamily, "I saw the ghost."

The doctor's gaze became slightly more professional, and Francesca, in a calm and steady voice, repeated her statement.

"I saw the ghost," she said. "Just there, by the door."

"But darling..."

"He was wearing a long kind of nightshirt," went on Fran-

The Greenwood Shady

cesca, "and he was carrying a pair of trousers."

"Francesca, just lie back a little and—"

"Father's trousers," said Francesca.

Doctor Beale rose slowly to his feet and stared down at her.

"Don't you believe me?" she asked.

"I believe anything you say," said the doctor. "But seeing a man pinching your father's suit is one thing—I suppose you disturbed him and he tried to get away. Seeing a ghost—"

"He was standing in front of that door," said Francesca, "and I saw the door-knob through him. You're between me and the door now, but I can't see any door-knob—I can only see you."

The last words were spoken in such a soft tone that the doctor, forgetting the ghost, sat down on the sofa and gave another unprofessional demonstration. In a little while, Francesca drew herself away gently and reluctantly, and returned to the subject.

"I really did see him," she said.

The doctor looked at her with a worried frown.

"Can you remember what time this was?" he asked.

"It doesn't matter about the time," said Francesca calmly. "I was going to have supper by myself, and I went into the kitchen to get it ready. I don't know what I came out for, but I shall never laugh at Mrs. Warren or Georgina any more. I saw him."

The doctor took both her hands in his.

"If old ladies see ghosts, Francesca darling," he said, "nobody really worries. I'm giving Mrs. Warren a mild tonic, and she won't see any more ghosts. When Miss Finck sees a ghost...well, I'm afraid she'll see a good many more before she's much older. But you're quite another proposition. When *you* see a ghost, then we have to look into it."

"I'm quite well," said Francesca. "And it isn't nerves or anything, because—I know this is going to sound silly, but it's true—when I saw him...it...I wasn't really frightened. I mean, in one sense I was terrified—I suppose everyone is at other-worldliness. But the ghost himself—itself—no, himself, because he was a man—well, he wasn't frightening. He gave me, just for a second, the idea that he was sorry I'd seen him. He was sorry, and embarrassed.—David, do please believe me!"

"I've told you—I do believe you," repeated the doctor. "But you must try to see my point, darling. I don't *want* you to see ghosts. There may be quite a lot of them about—I wouldn't know—but I want you to be in the state of rude health in which you don't notice them. Do you see? The fellow may be standing in front of me now; but I can't see him, and I'd rather you didn't."

"I'd rather I didn't, too," said Francesca.

"All right, then—we'll arrange that you don't. I'll bring you round something in a bottle—something with an especially nasty taste—and then you can—"

The Greenwood Shady

"No," said Francesca. "Don't bring it."

"Don't—"

"No. Leave it across the way with the Warrens," begged Francesca. "I don't want Mother or Father to know anything about this, if you don't mind."

"Why?"

Francesca, frowning, tried to think why, and could find no definite reason, but her desire to keep the knowledge from them grew stronger each moment.

"I don't know quite why," she said.

"But I ought to—"

"I consulted you professionally," pointed out Francesca, "and you can't—I don't know how to put it—"

"Reveal the secrets of the sickroom. All right, I won't—to your parents," said the doctor; "but if you don't mind, I'd like to talk to Mrs. Stirling about it—or Miss Clarence. They're both very fond of you, and they've both got good heads—between us we might hit on something helpful."

"You can tell them, then," said Francesca, "but ask them not to say anything to anybody else."

"I promise. Francesca—"

"Yes?"

The doctor hesitated.

"You mentioned something about supper....I know," he added hastily, "that your mother doesn't like my coming when she's—when they're out, but—"

Francesca rose.

"It's only cheese on toast. Can you eat cheese on toast?"

The doctor tried to look enchanted, and almost succeeded. He also succeeded in getting down the toast, which was leathery, and the cheese, which was rubbery. Francesca, her eyes bright, her cheeks pinker than usual, made coffee and allowed him to help with the washing-up. Not until there were unmistakable sounds of the party breaking up upstairs did the doctor recall himself to the present and realise that he must hurry away in order to escape being seen.

Francesca walked with him through the hall and out into the drive.

"I'll go as far as the Lodge with you," she said. "That is, if you're going to see them now."

They went slowly; the doctor took her hand, and she let it lie quietly in his, saying nothing. Reaching the Lodge, she stopped.

"Why don't you come in too?" asked the doctor.

Francesca shook her head. The warm beauty of the night had added the last touch to her mood of quiet happiness. The moon was full, and shone brilliantly above the darkness of the wood. She lifted her head and looked up at the bright heavens.

"Look," she whispered. "It's so lovely."

The doctor looked at something which he considered even lovelier, and put his lips gently upon it. With a last light pressure of his hand, Francesca turned and walked back to-

The Greenwood Shady

wards the house, and the doctor, after watching her for some moments, opened the door of the Lodge, and, rapping on it lightly, went inside.

Francesca heard the door close, and stood still.

There was no sound, and the silence and beauty of the night stole sweetly into her senses.

Presently there was a stir in the garden, and Francesca, looking round, saw the gardener crossing a patch of moonlight. Seeing her, he touched his hat and said good night, and was passing on when Francesca, on an impulse, spoke.

"It's a lovely night," she said.

Frobisher made no reply. Telemachus and Captain Vandeleur, who were close behind him, had been rhapsodising about the moon for some time, and he was tired of the subject. The Captain, seeing Francesca's uplifted face, murmured an appreciative word to Telemachus.

"A charming girl," he said. "Charming. But not to be compared with Miss Georgina."

"An' w'y not?" demanded Telemachus.

"A matter of proportion," said the Captain. "Miss Francesca is pretty, but she lacks presence. And so does young Mrs. Stirling. Lissome, but without—"

"Presence."

"Yes. Where," inquired the Captain sadly, "are women's figures nowadays?"

"Just where they always was," said Telemachus.

"For my part," said the Captain, "I lean to a Juno. I always had an eye for a fine woman."

"With muscle," supplemented Telemachus. "Wallop on the cranium with a candlestick."

"Yes...that was a treacherous blow, indeed," mused the Captain. "I suppose," he added reflectively, "that when we leave here, I'll find that there are a good many women...."

"Nearly all women," Telemachus informed him. "Ssh!—I want to hear when the Colonel and his Missis are goin' away."

"Next week," said Francesca, in answer to Frobisher's respectful question. "To Brighton."

"Brighton?"

"Yes. Do you know it?"

"I went there once, miss, but I didn't care for it. It can be nice in the spring, but in the summer I'd rather avoid it. I can only bear it without the crowds. I like a quiet place like this."

"Do you?"

"Scarborough in the summer, yes; Torquay, perhaps; Brighton...no, miss. Good night, miss."

"Good night," said Francesca.

She walked slowly into the house and opened the door of the flat. Her mother, she saw, was a little irritable, as was usual after a session with Georgina. The Colonel was pensive—a sign that he had lost.

"Hello, Mother," said Francesca. "Did you enjoy it?"

"Well, no," said Mrs. Fleury. "I can't say the Bridge was

interesting."

"Who was the fourth?"

"Foreign chap," grunted the Colonel.

"Oh. What nationality?"

"Didn't ask," said the Colonel. "Name sounded like Kichenoffski or something of that kind. He knew as much about calling as the man in the moon."

"I didn't see him leave," observed Francesca.

The Colonel, following his policy of keeping sordid details from her ears, forbore to tell her that Mr. Kichenoffski was not leaving. Instead, he grunted.

"You weren't calling very well yourself," pointed out his wife. "Putting me up to game on three trumps to the knave was a little misleading, to say the least."

"If you could go to three on your own," said the Colonel, "then a push of one was perfectly justified."

"But don't let's argue—the game's over.—Where were you, Francesca?"

"Outside, looking at the moon," said Francesca. "It's nearly full."

"Thought I heard you talking to someone," said her father.

"The gardener. He passed me, and we said a few words."

"I see. Well, you'd better get off to bed—it's late." He walked into the dining-room and returned with a drink. "I'm tired of this hot weather," he complained. "I'll be glad of a bit of sea air."

"So will Francesca," observed her mother. "She looks pale. You must do some swimming when we get there, Francesca."

Francesca, at the door of her room, turned.

"If you don't mind, Mother, I won't go to Brighton," she said slowly.

It was a simple statement, but both Colonel and Mrs. Fleury stared at her as though she had taken leave of her senses. After a moment, Mrs. Fleury gave a little incredulous laugh.

"Not going! Francesca, my dear, what a silly remark! Of course you're going! What on earth are you talking about?"

"I'm sorry, Mother, but I'm really not going."

There was something in the tone that neither of her parents had ever heard before. Colonel Fleury spoke sharply.

"This is nonsense," he said. "Why, your room's booked!"

"Yes. It'll mean wiring," said Francesca. "I'll do it first thing to-morrow morning."

There was a stunned silence. Mrs. Fleury was the first to break it.

"Have you—can you," she asked coldly, "give any reason for this extraordinary behaviour?"

"That Beale fellow," said the Colonel suddenly, "has got something to do with this."

"I've never once mentioned Brighton to Doctor Beale," said Francesca, with an unmoved calm that convinced her hearers that she spoke the truth.

The Greenwood Shady

"Well, then, what *is* the reason?" demanded Colonel Fleury.

"Nothing much," said Francesca. "I don't care for Brighton."

"You don't care—you d-don't—" began the Colonel.

"No. It can be nice in the spring," said Francesca, "but in the summer I'd rather avoid it. I can only bear it without the crowds."

There was no reply from either of her parents, who merely stared at her. Francesca opened the door of her bedroom. Her father opened his mouth to speak, but Mrs. Fleury put up a hand.

"No arguments to-night," she said coldly. "We can discuss the thing in the morning. We shall talk about something else." She glanced at a tiny grease-spot on the Colonel's coat. "That won't come off without leaving a mark," she said. "You'll have to send it to the cleaner's."

"But dash it," said the Colonel irritably, "I was going to wear it to Brighton. Now I'll have to wear the other." He turned back to Francesca, who was waiting to say good night. "I must say I don't understand your attitude," he said.

"I'm sorry," said Francesca again. "Scarborough in the summer, yes; Torquay, perhaps; Brighton...no. Good night, Mother—good night, Father."

"Good night," said Mrs. Fleury, with determined cheerfulness. "We shall talk in the morning.—What other suit," she asked her husband, dismissing the matter, "were you referring to?"

Francesca held her door open for a moment to hear the reply.

"Suit?" said the Colonel. "Oh, I'll go in my brown."

Francesca shut the door, threw herself on her bed, and—for the first time in her life—went into a fit of helpless giggles.

Doctor Beale entered the drawing-room of the Lodge and found the family sitting down in various attitudes of after-supper comfort. In addition, there was present Mr. Warren, who had walked over for a drink and a chat.

Cousin Clarry greeted the doctor cheerfully.

"Sit down, sit down," she said. "You're looking very worried; only that might be nothing—Mr. Hume here always looks as though he's adding up the pence column and can't remember what he had to carry from the farthings and half-pennies. It's very misleading. No, don't sit in that chair—come near the window."

Doctor Beale sat down and plunged straight into his subject.

"It's Francesca. I went in to see her and she was—she'd fainted. I brought her round, and she said she'd—well, she'd seen the ghost."

The others stared at him. Elinor looked puzzled; Willy had his usual frown, and Cousin Clarry's mouth hung open while she pursued a train of thought. The doctor told his story

The Greenwood Shady

briefly, and at the end of it Cousin Clarry made a pronouncement.

"This ghost," she said, "will have to go."

"I quite agree," said Doctor Beale. "But—"

"How do you propose to make him go?" asked Willy. "I thought nobody'd established that he was really here yet—didn't Mrs. Fleury mention the Psychical—"

"Psychical fiddlesticks!" declared Cousin Clarry. "I've been thinking about this ghost, and I've got my own ideas."

"Well, what are they?" enquired Elinor.

Cousin Clarry shifted herself forward on her chair, planted her feet apart, placed her hands firmly on her knees and addressed the company.

"Now pay attention," she said. "None of us in this room has seen this phenomewhatyoumay call it. And we all think that the people who did see it were imagining it. Mrs. Warren starts off with a ghost with nothing on, and Georgina sees it with a shirt on, and Francesca says it's got a shirt and trousers on. The next person to see it will put on a collar and tie and—"

"But Mrs. Warren," pointed out Elinor, "didn't tell Georgina what she'd seen. Georgina's account was in every way the same, except that—"

"Well, don't let's worry about any detective business," said Cousin Clarry. "Your Uncle Sidney always fancied himself as an amateur one—Sidney the Sleuth, we always called him—and spent his time taking up floorboards looking for nobody knew what, and while he was doing his private investigations, his trustees made off with his money and his solicitor made off with his wife. It doesn't do at all. You're not going to tell me, I hope, that because Mrs. Warren and Georgina told similar stories, we've all got to sit here and believe that there really *is* a transparent creature gliding about among us?"

"No," said Elinor. "I was only saying that—"

"Whenever there's a scare of this kind," proceeded Cousin Clarry, "you always find it spreading."

"That's true," said the doctor. "But, as I told Francesca, I didn't feel worried when Miss Finck or Mrs. Warren saw the ghost. It's when Francesca herself—"

"I absolutely agree with you," said Cousin Clarry. "You can't have that girl laid out on the hearthrug with ghosts running in and out."

"No. But how—"

"We're going to get rid of it. We're going to find out—or tell everybody we've found out—where the fellow came from, and we're going to see he goes back there. We're going to stop up the mouse-hole."

"Please," begged Willy, "could you go more slowly, so's we can follow you?"

"Very well," said Cousin Clarry. "I'll put it another way. In my experience, when people say they've seen a ghost, then it's no use telling them they haven't. It's no use Doctor Beale, there, giving Mrs. Warren a pink pill and Georgina a blue pill

The Greenwood Shady

and Francesca a green pill and telling them it's their stomach. As fast as you give them pills, they see more ghosts. The first time is never the last time. And, what's more, these things grow like snowballs. See for yourself—first the ghost comes in with nothing on, and then he equips himself with a shirt and a pair of trousers. The next time he'll have a plumed hat. But try to tell people that they didn't see a ghost and a plumed hat, and you're in trouble. When Bertie Clarence said he saw a mermaid in the English Channel, did his wife contradict him? No. She told them to stop the yacht, and they went round and round in circles with their faces straight, looking for it. Then she told him that the mermaid had probably decided to go away and come back when his wife wasn't aboard. You humour them, and it pays. People don't like to be told they've seen what isn't there.—So what we'll do is, we'll deal with the ghost on his own level."

"And what," inquired Willy, "is his own level?"

"I'll tell you. You may think it sounds silly, but if it sounds more silly than a ghost in Curzon's shirt, I'll be surprised. Now. You know the well?"

Her three listeners stared at her in bewilderment.

"What well? The one in the village?" inquired Doctor Beale at last.

"No. The well in the garden. Let me tell you about it," said Cousin Clarry. "There's an old well out there—between the lilac bush and the asparagus bed—that's been boarded up as long as people can remember. A week or two ago it got un-

Elizabeth Cadell

boarded, and nobody could find out why. Mrs. Fleury thinks the gardener did it; but why should a gardener—and especially a gardener as lazy as that one—go to a lot of trouble pulling the boarding off a well? In my opinion, Fatty du Cane and those other boys had something to do with it, but we needn't worry about that. What we're going to do is this: we're going to say to everybody: 'Yes, there is a ghost', and 'Yes, he's walking.' But why hasn't he walked before? Because he's suddenly been let out of some place in which he was perfectly happy. Where would that be? The well! So what do we do? We all go out there one night, and we have the well boarded up again."

"What for?" asked Doctor Beale.

Cousin Clarry looked at him with her mouth open. "What for? You ask me what for? I've just told you what for. I've talked for three-quarters of an hour and you haven't grasped a word of what I've been saying."

"But why *do* we board up the well?" asked Elinor.

"Because," explained Willy, "to shut in the ghost. It's quite a sound idea. The doctor here must do his bit; he's got to cancel all the pills and go in for the psychological approach. He's got to lay his patients down on the sofa and walk three times round them"—Willy rose and, with eyes half closed and an arm outstretched, walked round and round his chair—"'The ghost is down the well. The ghost is down the well. The ghost is—'"

"All right—sit down, sit down," said Cousin Clarry testily. "If the doctor hasn't seen it yet, then he never will. Now, is

The Greenwood Shady

it a good idea, or isn't it?"

After a great deal of explanation and argument, it was pronounced a good idea and given general approval. The question of who was to do the boarding up was then raised, and Mr. Warren, Willy and Strone agreed to share the work between them.

"I don't see," observed Mr. Warren, "why that good-for-nothing gardener chap shouldn't give us a hand. I've never seen him do any work yet."

"No, not him," said Cousin Clarry in so decided a tone that Elinor looked at her curiously.

"Why not?" she asked.

"I don't like him," said Cousin Clarry. "The more I see of him, the less I think of him. He looks like your Uncle Felix, and we all know what a low-down rascal *he* turned out. He's big and loose-looking, and he spends all his time out of sight. People say he talks to himself, and Strone says he talks to somebody he thinks he's got with him. That's either drink or delusions, and a man like that oughtn't to be allowed about the place. What's more, he isn't a gardener. Mrs. Fleury said so once to me, and I didn't pay any attention, but for once in her life she was right. He doesn't know a pea from a potato. I know we've had weeks of hot, dry weather, but Elinor and I have managed to keep our bit of garden going. But look over at the House gardens—" Cousin Clarry waved a hand. "You can't see them now, but look at them tomorrow, and you'll see what I mean. I look out of my kitchen window—day after day, browner and browner. Scorched. The grass all burnt up, the flowers all dying and the bushes all drooping. I'd like to give him a piece of my mind, but he's too shifty a customer for me. And why doesn't he look you in the eye, eh? Answer me that. He touches his hat when he sees you, but does he look at you? No. Too shifty."

Mr. Warren spoke in a thoughtful tone.

"Ah'll tell you a funny thing about him," he said slowly. "Rum."

"Well?" asked Willy.

"Have you ever seen a dog inside those gates lately?" asked Mr. Warren. "We used to have quite a lot of trouble chasing 'em out, if you remember. That pup of Mrs. Jenner's and the old bulldog—Ah remember that old bulldog used to come and visit us every morning and get his bit of this or that. And now try and get him past those gates. He won't come through 'em. Ah've put a juicy bit of bone just inside for him, and he's crept in, caught sight of the gardener and given a yelp and made off hard's he could go. Now what would you make of that?"

"He's been ill-treating them," declared Cousin Clarry.

"If you ill-treat dogs," observed Strone, "they make quite a lot of noise, as a rule. But I had an idea about this gardener fellow—I gave it quite a bit of thought after I'd heard him talking to an imaginary companion. I wondered if he's a ventriloquist out of a job."

The Greenwood Shady

"Ven-tril-o-quist?" said Cousin Clarry. "Now why? Tell me that."

"I've always thought there was something theatrical about him—his voice, for instance," said Strone. "He talks like a man who's addressed crowds or audiences. And another thing. I said he talked to someone he thought was there. Well, I think now that he just sits there and practises his ventriloquial effects—I've never liked to get near enough to listen in, but I'm pretty sure I've heard a second voice. I bet you'll find that I'm right—he's either a ventriloquist, or he's speaking the words of a bit of duologue and supplying the other part."

"That wouldn't account for the dogs," said Mr. Warren. "But I tell you what would."

His voice dropped and his listeners waited. Mr. Warren gave a glance round and then spoke slowly.

"If the fellow," he said, "was a bit of a loony—if he'd escaped from an institution somewhere—then that'd explain everything. It would explain the dogs—they always sense that sort of thing. It would explain why he pretended to be a gardener and took a job that kept him inside these grounds—he never leaves them. It would explain all that back-chat he does to himself...."

A slight chill fell on the company. Nobody spoke for some time, and there was general relief when the bold, confident voice of Georgina was heard at the door.

"Hey there!" she called.

"Come in," said Elinor.

"Don't get up," said Georgina, from the doorway. "I saw the doctor's car outside and I need him."

"Somebody ill?" asked Doctor Beale.

"My current lover," said Georgina, "is chasing me round the flat brandishing a bottle of vodka. Come and do something; Curzon's out."

"We'll all come," said Willy. "All the men, that is."

"All? What for?" demanded Georgina.

"Well, you entice him, I'll hold him, Strone'll hit him, Mr. Warren will relieve him of the vodka and the doctor'll bring him round."

"Forward march," said Georgina.

Chapter Sixteen

Late on the following morning, Willy, on his way across to the Lodge, heard his name called, and turned to find Mrs. Fleury beckoning to him.

He went back with a little trepidation. The task of subduing Georgina's friend the night before had been a noisy one, and the party had ended on a far less belligerent note than that on which it had begun. Willy considered swiftly the possibility of convincing Mrs. Fleury that he had been in bed, trying in vain to sleep through the noise, but he dismissed it; he distinctly remembered leading the male voice quartette in a dirge over the recumbent body of the foreigner and—much later—giving Georgina a solo rendering of 'Ich Liebe Dich'. He had been too often assured by friends who had heard his performances that if they could mistake the sounds for singing they could never mistake them for anybody else's singing.

He gave Mrs. Fleury his best bow and prepared his best apology, but, to his surprise, her greeting was cordial.

"Good morning," she said. "I've been looking for you upstairs, but you'd just gone. Do come inside, won't you?—Miss Condiment is anxious to see you."

Willy followed her into the drawing-room feeling a little, but not much, relieved. His apologies might soon be needed for Julian's lack of attention or disinclination to apply himself. An apple for the teacher, thought Willy hazily, going through his best bow again, this time for Miss Condiment. "How do you do," she said. "It's such a pleasure to meet you again."

Willy murmured a suitable phrase and, waiting until the ladies had seated themselves, disposed himself on an uncomfortable period piece. Miss Condiment looked at him with a grave smile.

"You can guess," she said, "that I am here to talk about Julian."

"Well, yes," said Willy.

Miss Condiment looked as sad as her rigid figure and stern features would allow. She raised both hands in a gesture of helplessness and let them fall again before she spoke.

"Mr. Hume," she said, "I want to make a confession."

"Er—yes?" said Willy.

"I want to confess that, in all my years with children, this is the first time I have had to say to a parent: 'I cannot'. This is the first case in which my experience has proved useless. This is the first time I have had to come to the conclusion—how reluctantly, I cannot tell you"—she looked at Mrs. Fleury and Mrs. Fleury shook her head gently, to indicate that she couldn't tell him either—"the conclusion that the presence of one child—your child, Mr. Hume—is a danger to the others."

The Greenwood Shady

"Danger?" repeated Willy.

Miss Condiment bowed her head.

"What sort of danger?" he inquired.

"Miss Condiment means physical danger," explained Mrs. Fleury. "Julian has been fighting again."

"I am having"—Miss Condiment opened her bag and took a paper from it—"I am having a most difficult time with parents. I have nine mothers, all complaining."

Having made this unusual claim, Miss Condiment leaned forward, handed the list to Willy and sat bolt upright once more. Willy studied the names with a show of concern and handed it back.

"Miss Condiment hasn't done this without a struggle," put in Mrs. Fleury.

"No. Indeed, indeed I have not. But Mr. Hume, I'm afraid—I'm very much afraid—that you must remove Julian. He is to stay to-day and come home at the usual time, but I shall be grateful if you would not send him again."

"I'm so sorry about this," said Willy. "What exactly has he done? Fighting, you said. Do you mean he's been attacking the other boys without cause?"

"Without cause and without provocation," said Miss Condiment. "Julian interprets the most simple acts as a challenge. A boy only has to put out a foot for Julian to imagine he's tripping him up. A child only has to mention the word 'Zulu' to make Julian think an insult is intended. If three boys make a playful rush at him, he mistakes it for an attack. In fact, Mr. Hume, Julian loves fighting and is glad of an excuse."

"Oh. Well—I'm very sorry," said Willy again.

Miss Condiment rose and held out a hand.

"Before I go," she said, "there's just one other thing. It's about Julian's talent for sketching."

"Oh"—Willy brushed this aside modestly—"he's always been pretty good."

"Yes." There was a certain amount of reserve in Miss Condiment's voice. "Yes, he has talent—but he misapplies it." She opened her bag once more and took from it several small sketches and handed them to Willy. "Those," she said primly, "are no doubt clever, for a child of that age, but they are also, in my opinion...precocious."

Willy gazed unbelievingly at the sketches in his hand. The outlines were those which he recognised—crude, but showing great promise, with the lines of bird or beast caught and put down remarkably well. There was the owl, but Willy saw, with his soul filling with delight, that its face was the face of Miss Condiment. The little donkey—unfinished but unmistakable—had exactly the Condiment turn of feature. The three little pigs were recognisably Sprule, and the pair of skunks pure Jenner twin.

Willy folded up the sketches without comment and slipped them into his pocket.

"Yes," he murmured. "You must forgive him—he's too

The Greenwood Shady

young to realise...I'm sorry..."

"I'm sorry too," said Miss Condiment. "You must be careful when you choose his prep school—he needs rather special handling."

She went out with Mrs. Fleury, and Willy followed them. As he stood in the hall, hesitating, he heard a curious scratching sound near by. Turning, he saw that Mr. Warren had opened his front door slightly and was beckoning urgently through the crack.

"Here...hsst...here," he whispered.

Willy walked towards the door, and it opened to admit him. Mr. Warren shut it cautiously and, finger on lips, drew Willy into the drawing-room. Pressing him into a chair, he spoke in a low voice, gesticulating with a fat thumb over his shoulder.

"That vinegary piece out there—that's Miss Condiment, isn't it?"

Willy nodded.

"Ah thought so. Yes, Ah thought so," said Mr. Warren, nodding his head. "Trouble with t'lad?"

"Yes," said Willy. "Fighting. Expelled."

"Expelled, eh?" Mr. Warren rubbed his hands together with every appearance of glee. "Expelled I Ah knew it. Ah knew how it'd be. Ah said to Ada, Ah said, ' Ada love,' Ah said, you watch—that lad won't last long in that female atmosphere,' Ah said. And Ah was right—he didn't last long."

"No," admitted Willy. "He—"

"He's a fighter, and good luck to him," said Mr. Warren. "He's a go-er, is that lad, and if Ah'd known you a bit better, Ah'd have said a word to you about sending a high-spirited lad like yours to—"

"The point is," said Willy, "that he isn't particularly high-spirited. He's always been rather a quiet chap. Until we came here, he—"

"Ah, but he's de-vel-oping, don't you see?" cried Mr. Warren, throwing a glance out of the window to make sure that Miss Condiment had gone. "He's de-vel-oping. English air, English food—it's what the lad was missing. Why, you don't want him to behave like a softy all his life, do you?"

"No," said Willy, "but—"

"When you were a lad, did you do any fighting?" inquired Mr. Warren.

Willy drew himself up.

"I was known and feared—"

"—within a radius of ten mile. Ah know, ah know," said Mr. Warren. "And quite right too. Fighting's good training for boys, and Ah believe in it. That's why Ah was proper upset when Ah heard you'd sent him to Clare Condiment. She knows as much about boys, does Clare, as that Mrs. Fleury does, and that's less than half nothing. You shouldn't have listened to them. What that boy wants "—Mr. Warren took a short turn about the room and returned to tap Willy impressively on the

The Greenwood Shady

knee—"what that boy wants is...men!"

"Men? Oh, you mean a—"

"A man's hand. A boy," said Mr. Warren, "ought to be brought up as a boy. Let his sister go to the sissy school; let his sister go to the Clare Condiments; but keep a boy with men, and then he'll be one himself in time. When Ah was a lad—just about six or seven Ah'd be—my father said, 'Now, no more females'; and from that time there was no more. Nowadays, a lad's no better than his sister; he gets sent to a kindergarten with a lot of girls and then he gets sent to a school with a lot of females to teach him. It isn't what Ah believe in, and that's why Ah fetched you in here—to tell you about an idea Ah've got." Willy leaned back.

"Well?" he asked.

Mr. Warren pulled a chair forward and sat on it.

"Well, it's like this," he said. "Ah was in business in Easton for a fair time, as you know."

"Yes."

"Well, Ah know most of the people there, and they know me. Ah don't know the chap who's in charge of the boys' school there, but Ah know his dad, old Joshua Barwell. If Ah get hold of old Josh and give him the word, he'll—"

"But I only came to Deepwood for about a month," said Willy, "and Julian's been in two schools already. Do you really think it's worth—"

"What?" Mr. Warren shot the word out with horror.

221

"What? You tell me you're going to let those females throw your little lad out and let the poor little fellow think he's at fault? What's he *done*?" asked Mr. Warren passionately. "Just tell me what he's *done*! He's seen through those nasty deep Weston lads and done a bit of fighting in the open. They're not used to that—they're used to taking it out of each other in quiet ways when teacher's not looking. Now, your lad wouldn't stand for that, and he was right, and you've got to show him he was right. You've got to tell him he was at the wrong school, and you've got to see he gets to the right one—a lad among lads. You leave it to me, Mr. Hume; Ah'll see this chap Ah know first thing to-morrow morning, and we'll have the thing fixed up."

"But—"

"You leave this to me now," urged Mr. Warren.

"It's very kind of you," said Willy, "but it hardly seems worth bothering about, does it? We shall be leaving here in about—"

"It's the principle," said Mr. Warren slowly and emphatically. "It's the prin-ci-ple. It's not right to put the boy in the wrong and take him away from here feeling he's done something he ought to be ashamed of. Put him in wi' t'lads and let him find his feet, and then when you go away he'll be ready to take his place in any school and hold up his head."

Willy, seeing that there was nothing to be gained by opposing this kind scheme, rose.

"Well, you're very good," he said. "I—"

The Greenwood Shady

Mr. Warren, following him to the door, put a hand on his shoulder and spoke confidentially into his ear.

"The trouble was," he said, "that you went to the wrong place. You went to Weston instead of Easton. Ah've nothing to say against those in Weston, mind you; but they're not the good, sturdy kind you get in Easton. They look down on us, and call us oom-droom, and they go on with their arts and their crafts and their tea-parties—but it's at Easton that you'll get the good hard heads and the straight thinking. You send that lad in among the Easton lads, Mr. Hume, and you'll never regret it."

Willy thanked him and walked thoughtfully back to the Lodge. Cousin Clarry, seeing him approach, met him at the front door and led him into the kitchen.

"Now," she said, pushing a chair towards him, "I won't ask you what Mrs. Fleury's been saying to you, because I know."

"You do?" said Willy, surprised.

"It's all over the town. I had it first from the grocer—she'd rung up to say he needn't send back her ration-book as she wouldn't need it."

"Wouldn't need...What," inquired Willy, "are you talking about?"

Cousin Clarry stared.

"Weren't we talking about Mrs. Fleury? I saw her telling you all about it. They say she's as sour as a stick, and I believe them. Thank goodness that girl has shown some spirit at last."

223

"See here," said Willy, his soft voice at odds with the tone of command. "Begin at the beginning—we're at cross purposes."

"Well, if she wasn't talking to you about that, then what was she going on about?"

"You first."

"Well, it's Francesca. She told her parents last night that she wasn't going to trail down to Brighton with them. So they've cancelled their trip."

Willy whistled.

"You mean that just because she won't go, they've given up the Bridge tournament? I thought they were very keen on Bridge."

"So they are; but they're keener still on keeping that girl hanging about them all their lives. They wired this morning—the milkman was at the back door and heard Mrs. Fleury telephoning the message through, so there's no mistake."

"Poor Francesca!" said Willy softly.

"Strone and Joanna went across, as soon as I told them the news, and took her out—they've all gone up to Mr. Warren's cottage for the day. That'll save her from a lot of unpleasantness for one day, at any rate. The whole place is on Francesca's side, I can tell you.—Now, what was Mrs. Fleury saying to you? If it wasn't about Francesca, then it was about those disgraceful goings-on last night."

"No," said Willy. "She didn't even mention last night."

The Greenwood Shady

"Then she's saving it for Georgina. There's nothing she enjoys more than a good skirmish of that kind.—Well, then, I suppose she wanted you to do something for her."

Willy turned the chair round, seated himself a-straddle and gazed at her over the back.

"You're wronging that good, kind creature," he said in soft and reproachful tones. "*She* was doing something for me—standing by while Miss Condiment said—"

"Condiment?" Cousin Clarry put her huge hands on the table and leaned on them, staring at Willy in dismay. "You mean Julian—"

"He's been thrown out," said Willy, not without pride.

"Fighting again?"

"Yes. Miss Condiment has nine mothers, and they all complained. I've heard of nine lives, but—"

"Sniffity-piffity little misses, that's all her boys are," declared Cousin Clarry. "If you'd asked me before sending that poor little creature to Clare Condiment, I could have told you that you were wasting your money and Julian's time. And now what are you going to do? Tell me that?"

"I don't have to do anything," said Willy. "As fast as Julian gets thrown out of one school, he gets thrown into another. He's going to the Easton school for boys who want to be boys."

"Good! Splendid!" Cousin Clarry thumped her hands on the table. "That's where he should have gone in the first place. Clare Condiment. Ha! Mrs. Sprule. Ha!"

"It was his own idea," Willy reminded her.

"And it was your idea," said Cousin Clarry, "that he was a—"

"Sniffity-piffity? No, I never went as far as that," said Willy. "But I didn't think he'd ever beat my record of juvenile exploits, and now I'm not so sure. I began earlier; I was only five, I believe, when I threw a large brick at the postman for not bringing me a parcel on my birthday. And six when I attacked the doctor for making my baby sister cry when he vaccinated her. And seven when I—"

"Am I here," demanded Cousin Clarry, "to listen to your life history beginning at five? Write it down, write it down and read it out to me of an evening. I've got something to say to you.—Wait a minute, though—there's someone at the door. See who it is."

Willy went to investigate, and came back bearing two large parcels wrapped in newspaper.

"Policeman outside," he announced. "Not making any arrests—he says these are for you."

"Oh yes," said Cousin Clarry. "How much?"

"Two and three this one, three and sevenpence that," said Willy, using his chin as a pointer.

Cousin Clarry counted out the money and gave it to him. Willy paid the bearer, and came back to find Cousin Clarry putting the packages into the larder.

"A little bit on the side, I doubt not," he said meaningly.

The Greenwood Shady

"My godfather always used to say," remarked Cousin Clarry, "that people ought to use their ears and save their tongues."

"I was using my nose," explained Willy. "Those parcels weren't scent-proof, you know. I know what's in them—but what I can't understand is why a policeman should bring them."

"Do you think he'd bring anything he oughtn't to? Tell me that?"

"If he did, I suppose he'd ask more than three and sevenpence for it," said Willy. "It's all very tantalising."

"Well, when you get it, it'll be very, very tasty. Now what were we talking about."

Willy crossed his arms on the back of the chair and rested his chin on them.

"You had something to say to me," he said. "Off we go."

"This is it," said Cousin Clarry. "But if Elinor comes in, I'll start talking about something else, because this is my own idea, you understand?"

"Perfectly," said Willy.

"Now," said Cousin Clarry, "you know that Joanna's husband is coming next week?"

"Yes."

"Very well, then. He's coming, and Joanna's going off to London with Strone."

"Not very accurately put," said Willy. "She's going to stay

with relations in London."

"Well, whatever she's going to do, she's going, and she's asked Elinor to explain the situation to Mark Stirling and to write and tell her what the position is."

"I didn't know that," said Willy. "I think it's a—"

"It's an unpleasant sort of job to have to do, and that's putting it mildly," said Cousin Clarry. "In my opinion, it's asking just a little bit too much—but Elinor's agreed to do it. She's going to talk to Mark and ask him to arrange some kind of divorce."

"There's only," pointed out Willy, "one kind of divorce."

"Well, then," said Cousin Clarry, unmoved, "we'll have that one. But it isn't going to be pleasant for Elinor, especially if he turns nasty. For one thing, he'll want to get Joanna's address out of her, and she isn't going to let him have it. Now, when you stand between a man and his wife, there's always trouble, even when there's as little between them as there was between those two. And what I'm asking you is this: don't go away yet. When your month comes to an end, stay on for a bit. Nobody else wants to get into the flat."

"How do you know?"

"How does anyone know? By asking," said Cousin Clarry irritably. "I asked the house agent, and he told me. There's nothing of that kind to prevent you from staying; you've only to say the word, and you can stay on. Well, now, are you going to say it?"

To her surprise, Willy made no reply. His eyes were fixed thoughtfully on the glow from the boiler fire; his brow was more corrugated than ever.

"Well, come on, come on," urged Cousin Clarry at last. "It doesn't want all that thinking out, does it? Julian at the boys' school and you with only yourself to think of.—Well?"

"It all depends," said Willy slowly.

"On what?"

Willy rose from his seat and walked over to the small cracked mirror which Cousin Clarry kept on a nail inside a cupboard door. He examined his lean, lined face, stroked his thinning hair and gave a deep sigh.

"None of *that* kind of appeal," he said regretfully. "At my age, a woman has to love a man for his mind—or for his money." He turned and faced the puzzled Cousin Clarry. "You know," he went on thoughtfully, "there has been a tremendous change in the status of the unattached man in England. Cast your mind back: some years ago, to be an unattached man was to be sought, to be courted—for lunches, dinners, theatres... even in marriage. Especially in marriage. A man of any age between twenty-two and seventy-two could be certain that somewhere there was some woman who would be glad to have him.—And now?"

"Well, look at the work they make," said Cousin Clarry. "Look at the feeding they want. Look at their washing—heavy shirts, thick socks. Speaking for myself, I wouldn't have a man if you gave him to me with a bag of gold—but, mark you, I would have said the same thing twenty or thirty years ago."

"And now," murmured Willy, "they all say it. A man is no longer the provider and the protector. The woman who used to dread loneliness now congratulates herself on having only one plate to wash up. The wife and mother, who could once say patronisingly, 'Poor Lydia! with no man to look after her,' now says, 'Lucky Lydia, with no man to look after.' The single woman says to the married woman, with pity in her tone, 'Oh, but poor you, with a man on your hands.' The—"

"When do we get to the point?" demanded Cousin Clarry. "And what has this got to do with your staying on here?"

"Just this," said Willy. "Elinor has been infected with this desire to keep herself free from heavy shirts and thick socks. She doesn't want to be burdened with a man to feed."

There was silence. Then, as usual, Cousin Clarry dispensed with finesse.

"What did you say, and what did she say?" she enquired.

"I said 'Elinor, I love you,' and she said that I only felt like that because we'd been seeing too much of one another.—So if I tell her that we're planning—you and I—that she shall see still more, how shall my suit advance?"

Cousin Clarry drew a deep breath.

"*What* did she say," she asked, puzzled. "I don't understand."

"Propinquity was the word. She said that it made people imagine they liked each other."

The Greenwood Shady

"And did you ever," demanded Cousin Clarry passionately, "did you ever hear such miffling-piffling balderdash?"

"Never," declared Willy. "That's why I feel that there must be some other reason for her treating me so harshly. Shirts and thick socks. If you could assure her that I wear the—"

"Now don't *talk*" said Cousin Clarry. "Are you serious?"

"Serious?"

"That's what I said. Serious."

"If you mean do I want to marry Elinor," said Willy slowly, "then let me assure you that I've never been more serious in my life."

"You love her?"

"Who wouldn't?" asked Willy.

Cousin Clarry drummed for some time on the table. "It's funny," she mused. "She hasn't been herself lately. I've noticed it several times."

"Is that a good sign," asked Willy, "or a bad?"

"I can't say. You'll have to leave this to me. I don't mind telling you—now that you've come out into the open—that this idea came into my head some time ago."

"It did?" said Willy, with as much surprise as he could assume.

"It did. You've got to thank me for a good many opportunities you wouldn't otherwise have had."

"Well, I do thank you," said Willy. "But now I want more than opportunities. I'm willing to stay here indefinitely if you think you can do anything to make Elinor believe I'm young and handsome. But my main idea is to get her to marry me and come and live in Gloucestershire."

A shadow passed swiftly over Cousin Clarry's face. It was there and gone in an instant, but Willy saw it and understood it.

"You leave it to me," she said firmly.

"I will. And there's one thing. I—"

"And as I was saying," said Cousin Clarry suddenly, "chops are one thing and cutlets another."

For a moment Willy gaped at her in astonishment, but the sound of the kitchen door opening brought enlightenment.

"You mean," he said, "that a chop is a chop and a cutlet is a...Oh, hel-*lo,* Elinor. Come in, come in."

Chapter Seventeen

Julian accepted his change of school philosophically. He watched Elinor remove the Condiment badge from his cap and sew on the Barwell arms. Thanking her, he gave her the smile which was so like his father's, and went quietly away.

"You wouldn't think," observed Elinor to Cousin Clarry, as they watched him go—"you wouldn't think that that self-contained little morsel could have been the terror of two schools, would you?"

"Schools? You don't call those schools, do you?" said Cousin Clarry contemptuously. "Mrs. Sprule and Clare Condiment—pooh!"

Elinor laughed and rose to carry her work-basket upstairs.

"No, don't go," said Cousin Clarry. "I don't see much of you by yourself nowadays. Sit down. No, wait a minute: there's somebody at the back door. Go and see, Elinor."

Elinor investigated, and came back with her report. "It's a man in a van—three parcels for you."

"Oh. How much?"

"Eight and fourpence the three, he said."

"Well, give it to him," instructed Cousin Clarry. Elinor paid the man, put the three parcels in the larder and returned. She looked at Cousin Clarry with a touch of anxiety.

"You're looking a bit tired," she said. "Cooking for six is a good deal more strenuous than cooking for two. Why don't you let Joanna do some of it for you?"

"Joanna? No. All she wants to do is come into the kitchen and learn how to make Strone's favourite dishes. Let Cousin Emily teach her in London when she goes."

"Oh, is it finally fixed up?" asked Elinor.

"Yes, Joanna got a letter from her this morning, and gave it to me to read. I had a job, I can tell you, with that handwriting—niggley-piggley stuff, as I told you. She says she and James will be delighted, so I only hope Joanna'll be delighted, too, when she gets there. She won't find Cousin Emily throwing her money away on stuff to smear on her face every night, either. I helped her to dress the night she made her dayboo—a dusting of cornflour just round the nose, and no more. But she got James Clarence-Cook before the season was out, and without a penny wasted on jars and bottles. Cosmetics and hair-dos and all this clapperty-trappery that women go in for—it always makes me laugh. They really think that men see it, when all that men look at is their figures. Now, a man *does* like a good figure on a woman, and that's why I cut down your diet. Men like to see a waist, and now you've got one to show them. Do you think Willy would have given you a second look if you'd weighed what you did when he came, no matter how much Joanna smeared on your face? Do you? Tell me that. And now tell me something else: having got a fine man like Willy in your pocket, what's all this shillying-shallying about? Here's a man of suitable age, gentle, kind, with a head on his shoulders, a good income and a house all ready to go into. He tells you he wants to marry you, and what do you say? Not a plain sensible 'Yes' or 'No', but a lot of Advice to Women that you've been reading in the magazines.—Now, don't say anything. It's high time that somebody allowed *me* to say something. Don't think," lied Cousin Clarry—"don't think that I haven't brooded for years about this question of your marrying again. Don't think that I haven't looked round to see what there is. Don't think that I haven't overlooked a good many men I could mention in Easton or Weston. And who was there suitable? Nobody. Not one. Rather than see you encouraging a single one of them, I would have put you into a tumbril with my own hands. And now, what happens? Tell me that. A man comes along, falls in love with you, asks you to marry him, and you give him no encouragement whatsoever."

Cousin Clarry paused, panting. It had been a long and vigorously delivered speech. Half-way through, Elinor had taken out the littered contents of her work-basket and replaced them in neat rows. She said nothing when Cousin Clarry ended, but sat admiring her handiwork.

"Well," demanded Cousin Clarry, tired of waiting, "what have you to say?"

Elinor looked up and spoke a little absently.

"Nothing much," she said. "At least, nothing that makes much sense."

"Then why *think* it? Why *think* it?—Don't you *like* Willy?"

"Yes."

"Could you—are you in love with him?"

"Yes."

Cousin Clarry drew up her shoulders and held out her hands helplessly.

"Then why—why—why? Why won't you marry him?"

"I might," said Elinor slowly. "All I wanted was time to think, that's all."

"Well, all right. You wanted time to think, and you got time to think. What did you think of?"

"Oh...a lot of things," said Elinor. "Whether it would be nice to live with someone again, or not. Whether I want to leave the Lodge and go away to Gloucestershire. Whether I feel competent to take on another woman's child. Whether I could be—day in and day out, and every night—a help and companion to a man. And...chiefly...whether I'm really in love with Willy at all. You see, Cousin Clarry, all I know is that I lie awake at night thinking about him, and then wake up and dream about him. I know everything about the way he talks and moves and laughs and looks at me. I know that I'm feeling younger and more vital than I've ever felt in my life. But...then I remember that I'm at the age which people say is a dangerous one for a woman—the age at which they suffer from the delusion that they're still attractive and can still attract men. I'm in love—but what woman wouldn't be if a man paid her some attention after an interval of eleven years? Did Willy make me feel like this, or would any man who happened to be near me and who said a few kind things to me have produced the same feeling? Countless other women at my age—the dangerous age—have behaved like fools. How do I know that I'm any different? How," she asked in gentle mimicry of Cousin Clarry's urgent question, "how, how, how?"

Cousin Clarry looked at her with grim displeasure.

"The trouble with you," she diagnosed, "is that you've been reading too much."

"I'm not talking about fiction. Glands are fact."

"Glands? glands? There you go again," said Cousin Clarry in disgust. "All that rubbish! What makes you think you've got glands?"

"Glands," said Elinor, without too much certainty, "are the things that cause all the trouble. They're the things that make you fat and the things that make you thin—it depends which ones they are, or which way they work."

"Glands! glands!" shouted Cousin Clarry. "Good God! is Willy a man, or is he a gland? Tell me that.—And tell me who has been filling you up with these old wives' tales."

"You have."

"Me? Why, I never had a gland in my whole—"

"You've told me, over and over again, how ridiculous women can make themselves when they get into their forties. Don't you remember telling me about poor Cousin Belle, who went off—when she was my age—with that artist and cleaned his brushes? You told me that—"

"Cousin Belle," said Cousin Clarry with dignity, "was without exception the silliest woman who ever lived. She used to call her husband *Caro mio* and wear daisy-chains. Is it on account of that poor creature that you—"

"And Aunt Sybil. You said yourself—you remembered the very hat, you said, and—"

"Your poor Aunt Sybil was Connie Strange's daughter, and you know that Connie was a poor wander-wit and ended by being shut up for chasing policemen. Do you seriously mean to compare Aunt Sybil—"

"Well, then, Cousin Elvira."

"Ah, there you *have* a case. Cousin Elvira *did*, I grant you, go right off her head at the age of forty-three. But you didn't know her mother, who pretended to be an invalid for over twenty years and threatened to put an end to herself if ever Elvira left her. Well, Elvira banked down her fires too long, and one day they flared up and she went up with them, and I for one wished her luck—not that she ever got any. But I can see now the kind of thing that even a woman of your intelligence will swallow."

"There's nothing to swallow," said Elinor. "It's something that does happen, and I just want to make certain that I'm real-

The Greenwood Shady

ly in love, and not just suffering from what they call sex-hunger."

"Is that what they call it nowadays?" asked Cousin Clarry, with genuine interest. "Well! I must say they've come out into the open. They're overdoing it, but when people have got over the novelty of saying all those shocking words out loud, they'll realise that reticence wasn't such a bad thing. I like listening to Joanna—she's always coming out with medical terms and looking at me to see whether I'm shocked. But I don't expect sense from a girl of her age. I do from a woman of yours. Tell me, did this sex-hunger come over you before you saw Willy?"

"Well, no."

"Then you ought to give him credit for having roused it. Do you feel peculiar when Mr. Warren comes near you?"

"Peculiar?"

"I can see you don't, but if you had the disease you're so sure you've got, I can promise you that Mr. Warren would have quite an electric effect. And Colonel Fleury—does he loower you?"

"Colonel *Fleury*?"

"Yes; you see, you don't like him. You may be hungry, but it's obvious that you only want to eat one man. So my advice to you is this: stop reading for a bit; try to forget the year you were born. And take more exercise. When you feel hungry, take Willy into your confidence and see if he can do anything for you. And if I were you, I'd stop thinking about glands or whatever you call them'. You'll be far better off without them. Go on your knees and give thanks for the chance of getting a good husband for a change. Get married and enjoy yourself. And forget yourself, and think of Willy instead. Women like you give a great deal of unnecessary trouble. They think too much, and they brood over matters which are perfectly straightforward, and make a dreadful sniggle-snarl out of them.—And now," she ended, "I've got work to do. Now will you promise me you won't mention the word 'gland' to me ever again?"

"I promise," said Elinor.

Left by herself, she sat still, staring unseeingly at the work-basket and wishing, for the first time, that there was a woman of her own age in whom she could confide. Joanna was too young; beside her freshness and youth, Elinor felt that her own affairs were sadly middle-aged. Joanna considered that love in the late twenties was a pale affair, in the thirties regrettable and in the forties indecent. She looked upon Elinor as an ageing aunt. Cousin Clarry was...Cousin Clarry. There was Georgina, but Elinor had heard all her sentiments, and disagreed with most of them. It would have been helpful—or perhaps not helpful, but comfortable—to sit down with a sensible middle-aged woman who had lived a rather less nun-like existence over the past eleven or twelve years.

Elinor sighed. Joanna, Cousin Clarry, Georgina. It was a poor choice.

The door burst open, and Joanna came in in a frock which Elinor considered more suitable to a seaside than a woodland

The Greenwood Shady

setting.

"Oh, you're here, Aunt Ellie."

"Yes. Where's Strone?"

"Gone up to Willy's flat to tell him about my letter from Cousin Emily. Did Cousin Clarry tell you?"

"Yes. When do you go?"

"The day Mark arrives."

"Oh. Don't you think that's leaving it a little late?" asked Elinor.

"A bit, perhaps. But it's the day of the Parade—we shan't stay to see the actual thing, but we'd like to see the children all dressed up. And we might have a glimpse of Georgina in her finery, too. Strone's decided that so long as we're on our way before Mark's due to arrive, we'll be all right, and so we want to stay as long as we can."

"Well, make sure you *are* out of the way."

"Don't worry—Strone's much too anxious to make any mistake. Oh...Aunt Elinor."

"Well?"

Joanna curled herself up on a big chair, her feet tucked under her.

"Aunt Elinor," she said, "the place is full of rumours."

"Rumours?" In spite of herself, Elinor's colour rose.

"Yes, rumours. There's a pretty strong one blowing about Willy staying on here after we've gone. Is it true?"

"Cousin Clarry asked him to stay, and so he's staying,"

said Elinor.

"That's not what the rumour said. The rumour said that he's hanging on in the hope of getting you to marry him. Is that right?"

"When you say rumour," enquired Elinor, "who exactly do you mean?"

"Strone and me. Is that good grammar? Strone and I. Us. We've been watching, but we haven't quite agreed on it. He says you're both in love; I said Willy might be, but you're not. So I told him I'd do some private investigating, like Cousin Clarry. Come on, Aunt Ellie," she coaxed. "Put the king and queen on the table, face up."

Elinor gave a little sigh.

"I wonder," she mused, "if I could have a nice private affair some time, without the benefit of friends and relations. When I married Alexander Stirling, advice poured in from every Clarence source. The advice was all like Punch's: Don't— and I grew to understand, in time, that they were all quite right in trying to hold me back; but what I'm trying to say is that there was nothing quiet or private about the matter. Everybody had a say in it. And now it seems that—"

"That we're all shoving our noses. Well, *I'm* not, for one," declared Joanna. "All I told Strone was that I knew you fairly well, and you weren't the kind of person who'd fall in love—I mean, at your—I mean"—she grew a little confused, but Elinor declined to help her out. "I mean, I don't want to imply that you're at the bath-chair stage. I think you're very nice to look at, and when you let me make up your face, you look quite young. I know that lots of older women marry; but what I meant was that they weren't your type. You're the shy sort, and if Willy came at you, you'd scream the place down."

"Really?"

"Yes. Don't get huffy, Aunt Ellie—I always put things the wrong way. I'm sorry—but when I came in here just now and bounced off a phrase or two about you and Willy, I honestly thought you'd laugh your head off. But you...you didn't. I hope I haven't opened my big mouth again."

"If there's anything to laugh at," offered Elinor, "I'll laugh as much as you like."

A great deal of Joanna's self-confidence had left her. She rose from her chair and, pushing the work-basket to one side, perched herself on the table and looked down at Elinor.

"Are you and Willy going to get married?" she asked simply.

"I don't know," said Elinor. "Cousin Clarry has just been in here haranguing me, so I was a little irritated at having to go through it all again. If you're interested, Willy has asked me to marry him and I don't know whether I will or whether I won't."

"Oh. But it seems to me a very simple matter, Aunt Ellie. If you love him, you marry him; if you don't, you don't."

"It isn't as simple as all that."

"What isn't? You're both free, and he's quite well off. Is it

Julian that's worrying you?"

"No."

"Well, then, there isn't a hitch anywhere. He's got a nice house, and it isn't like marrying a Stirling that nobody knows anything about—Strone knows his history from the word go. I suppose"—she hesitated—"I suppose what's really worrying you is that you feel you're a bit too—I don't mean old really, but I mean too old for...for this sort of thing."

"I don't," said Elinor, reaching round her for the work-basket and getting to her feet—"I don't feel too old for anything. I'm forty-one, and I feel younger than I did at your age—but it isn't any use telling anybody of your age that. You can tell Strone that I'm grateful for his interest in my affairs—or my affair—and I'm grateful for your interest, too, and for Cousin Clarry's; but if you don't mind, I'd like to think matters out in my own way and make my own decision. And when I've done that, I shall tell you what it is, and you can put an end to all these interesting rumours." The door closed behind her.

"Well!" said Joanna, to nobody in particular.

She was still sitting on the table when Willy came in twenty minutes later. She greeted him moodily and, after a glance at her face, he took a chair facing her and waited for her to speak.

"Where's Strone?" enquired Joanna.

"He's with the doctor trying to stop him from going in and mangling the Colonel and his missus."

The Greenwood Shady

"Well, he's an idiot, then," said Joanna shortly. "A good mangling is just what those two need. And while we're on the subject, I'll tell you that there's only one love affair round here that's being conducted on sane lines—and that's mine. Yours seems to me to be proceeding—if it's proceeding at all—by a process of patience and meditation. And Francesca Fleury is going to sit there and let her parents ruin her life for her. Mangling? I'd mangle them! If she had the spirit of a louse, she'd mangle them too."

"The trouble with you," said Willy in his usual soft tones, "is that you're short on imagination. You're a nice girl, but you don't know how to put yourself into other people's places. You're asking Francesca, for instance, to do something she's incapable of doing—throwing off the training of a lifetime and rounding on the hand that's been feeding it to her. And it's been good training, too. I can't speak for the girls' schools of the future now that they're mixing up the social levels, but I can tell you from personal experience that the girls' public school of my day aimed at turning out a fine product. My mother's sister—you won't mention this to anybody, will you?—was the headmistress of a girls' school, and what I used to learn on my frequent visits to her, during working hours, opened my eyes. You had one of those sketchy educations—a sort of hit-and-miss affair—but Francesca spent her life in places where they taught her all the finest lessons—among them, to love, honour and obey her parents."

"And now," said Joanna in a loud, exasperated tone, "it's

ruining her life. Where's the moral?"

"Ssh, ssh!" said Willy soothingly. "There isn't any moral. She's got a strong sense of duty, and that's why the doctor's leaning on Strone's shoulder borrowing his handkerchief."

"I promised to do something to help him," mourned Joanna, "but how could I? How could anyone? All her parents are doing now is seeing she doesn't catch sight of the doctor before he leaves. You can get her out of their sight, but only when she's promised that she won't meet the doctor clan—clandes—"

"Without their knowledge," helped Willy.

"Yes. My God, it's—it's unbelievable! It's—it's medieval! The next thing, they'll have her chained up in one of those chastity contraptions the Crusaders used to wear. That—"

"The Crusaders' wives, dear," put in Willy.

"Well, it ought to have been the other way round, and then there'd been have some sense in it."

"Dear me," said Willy; "you're awfully edgy this morning."

"And so would you be. I said two words to Aunt Ellie, and she went upstairs in a huff."

"Ah!" said Willy. "Which two words were they?"

"Oh..." Joanna made a sound, half disgust, half penitence. "I opened my mouth and, as usual, it said what it liked. I gave her the idea—I didn't mean to, naturally—that she was a bit past the passionate stage."

The Greenwood Shady

Willy sighed.

"Oh dear, oh dear. The work of weeks overthrown."

"Well, I'm sorry," said Joanna. "I *like* Aunt Ellie. I think she's wonderful. But—oh, Willy, let's face it—she *is* over forty!"

Willy grunted. In a few moments he began to speak in a slow, dreamy voice.

"When I was twenty," he said, "my mother died. I was fond of my mother, and as I sat in the dreadful little carriage with the black horses at the head of the other dreadful little carriages with the other black horses, following the hearse, I felt very low. But two facts sustained me: one was that my mother had lived to see me grow to full manhood, and the other was that she had lived a long and happy life and could only have expected about a year or two more of activity. That was when I was twenty. Well, when I was clearing up things in Africa just before leaving, I cleared out a lot of old papers and letters, and while I was doing that, a dreadful realisation came to me—something that, strangely enough, had never struck me before, I don't know why."

"Well?"

"My mother," said Willy, "died at the age of forty-four—just two years younger than I am to-day. But as I sit here and talk to you, feeling a fine, upstanding young man, I can't bring myself to think of my mother as anything but an old, old woman.—You see? You're nearly twenty years younger than Elinor, and it's quite impossible for you, having seen her all through your childhood, to place her as anything but a tottering old lady. But look at history, and see how many women past what you consider their best have ruled men's hearts. Look at Madame de Maintenon."

"Yes, I see what you mean," admitted Joanna. "And that l'Enclos."

"Well, I—"

"And the Pompadour and the Montespan," said Joanna, her mind broadening every moment.

"Well, we—"

The door opened and Cousin Clarry stood before them.

"Lay the table for lunch, you two," she directed. "What are you sitting here for?"

"We're discussing the great women of history," said Willy.

"Oh. Well, don't forget the greatest," said Cousin Clarry.

"Come on—"

"Who's that?" asked Joanna.

"Mrs. Beeton," said Cousin Clarry. "Come on, now—to work, to work."

Chapter Eighteen

Two events were now imminent: the doctor's departure and the day of the Parade. By a change in the sailing date, it was learned that both would take place on the same day. When Deepwood remembered that Mark Stirling was also due on that day, it was felt that twenty-four hours was scarcely enough to contain so much excitement.

If Colonel and Mrs. Fleury regretted their rather hasty decision to cancel their trip, they gave little sign of it, though they could not have been unaware of the disapproving glances that rested on them wherever they went. Francesca remained her quiet, pleasant self, a shade paler and perhaps a little quieter. The doctor paid his visits to Mrs. Warren and drove away with his face set in lines of misery. Mr. Warren drove Strone, Joanna and Francesca up to the cottage and left them there for the day, while Willy spent his time with Cousin Clarry and Elinor and made no further reference to the state of his affections. He was to stay on at Deepwood, and he was content to wait for Elinor to make up her mind in her own slow way.

Details regarding the costumes for the Parade became clearer as the day grew near. Mrs. Fleury, determined to hold up her head, decided to do so under a striking medieval headdress—a horn-like creation, jewel-studded, with high peaks and a fall of muslin at the back. Her dress, in a corresponding fifteenth-century design, was said to be correct in every detail and wonderful to behold. The Colonel had borrowed one of Cousin Clarry's Russian tunics and was adapting it to the requirements of a fifteenth-century man.

Of Georgina's dress, nobody knew anything except that it was to come from the Castle and that she was having her hair dressed in a special period fashion on the morning of the Parade.

Captain Vandeleur made cautious appearances to look at the costumes, and decided that there was nothing suitable enough for him to wear. He was going through a difficult time, for Curzon's shirt was too large and the Colonel's trousers were too tight and were also in jeopardy, for Frobisher wanted them—not for himself, but to demonstrate to Mrs. Fleury his innocence in the matter of their disappearance. There had been no mention of trousers, but on the morning they had been missed, she had come out into the garden and, in her most curt manner, given him notice. He had touched his hat and said nothing, but he would have liked to leave the Colonel's trousers as a little puzzle for her to solve.

On the day before the Parade, Willy and Mr. Warren walked across to the Lodge to arrange the details of the boarding up of the well. The time was fixed and the working party chosen, and they were on their way back when Francesca

The Greenwood Shady

came to meet them.

"Somebody wants to see you," she said.

"Me, love?"

"Yes, you—and Mr. Hume too, he said."

"Me and Mr. Hume?" Mr. Warren's voice sang with astonishment. "Now, whoever could want to...ooohh!" There was realisation in the sound.

"Well?" asked Willy.

Mr. Warren looked at him soberly and put a steadying hand on his shoulder.

"Ah can't say for sure, lad," he said, "but Ah think it'll be that chap from the school—Mr. Barwell."

"That's the name—Barwell," said Francesca. "He's waiting for you in Mr. Hume's drawing-room."

The two men walked slowly up to the flat, Mr. Warren making small sounds of distress. As they went up the stairs, he began to say something, but thought better of it. In silence they opened the door and went in. Mr. Barwell rose from a chair and addressed Mr. Warren.

"Good afternoon," he said. "I think you know me?"

"Ah don't know you—Ah know your father, though. Sit down, sit down. I suppose you've come about young Julian, eh?"

"Yes. I'm afraid"

"Oh well," sighed Mr. Warren, "and Ah'm afraid too. And Ah was the one that persuaded Mr. Hume here to send him to you. Well "—he leaned back and blew out his cheeks, as though blowing up his courage—"well, what's he done?"

Mr. Barwell cleared his throat.

"He is," he said, "a most—a most extraordinary child."

There was nothing complimentary about the tone. Willy waited, and Mr. Warren fidgeted impatiently.

"Well, go on, go on," he urged at last. "What's he done? Let's have it and get to know."

Mr. Barwell, who had prepared a very fine introductory passage on juvenile psychology, abandoned it and came to the point.

"He's a fighter," he said.

"A fighter? Well"—Mr. Warren was plainly waiting for more—"and what's wrong with being a fighter? At that age Ah was a fighter. At that age Mr. Hume was a fighter—weren't you, Willy, m'lad?"

Mr. Barwell looked at him indulgently.

"There are forty boys in my school, Mr. Warren," he said. "All healthy. They can all use their fists, and most of them do. There's nothing out of the way in one boy punching another boy on the nose. It does them both good. But Julian, as I said, is a fighter. He waits for the smallest—the slightest shadow of provocation, and then attacks. He doesn't go in for a small punch in a small way—he takes on two, three, four or five boys, preferably big ones, and—"

"OoooOps!" The extraordinary sound popped out of Mr.

The Greenwood Shady

Warren like a cork flying from a bottle.

Mr. Barwell, staring at him, saw that his cheeks were red, his mouth open and his eyes shining in what was unmistakably admiration. When he spoke his accent had broadened.

"That's the boy!" he ejaculated. "Three foower, five...did tha hear that, Willy lad? Ah can see him"—Mr. Warren doubled his fists and, bouncing up and down on his chair, rained punches on an imaginary opponent. "Ah...would you? There's *that* for you...and *that*...."

He swivelled round to plant a cunning left and, meeting Mr. Barwell's astonished glance, made a lame sound of apology and sat back in his chair.

"I don't think you understand," said Mr. Barwell. "I'm not questioning the boy's courage; I'm here to explain that one can't run a school with a storm-centre threatening to—"

"But you admitted," interrupted Willy, "that Julian was provoked, even if only slightly."

Mr. Barwell hesitated.

"The fact is," he said at last,"that Julian's appearance is very misleading. I confess that it misled me—I didn't really place much reliance on the stories you told me of his previous history. His fair skin and blue eyes, his hair and his gentle expression make the more aggressive of his companions think— not unnaturally, perhaps—that they're on to a good thing. I was nervous, to tell you the truth, about three of them: the Richie brothers, who—"

"Ah know them!" exclaimed Mr. Warren. "Ah know those three. Now, if you want fighters, then—"

"Exactly. When I saw the three Richies eyeing Julian on the second or third day of school," said Mr. Barwell, "I wondered whether it would be necessary to interfere. It was—but not on account of Julian." His words faltered and a reminiscent look came into his eyes. "I was called out," he said slowly, "and I went, expecting to see bad trouble...for Julian. And I got to the scene and I stood there and—"

He broke off, puzzled. "He had an odd look on his face," he went on. "A half smile, as though—"

"He *did*?" Willy was leaning forward, his eyes gleaming. "He did? Do you know"—he spoke eagerly—"do you know, I always looked like that when I went into a fight. Oh yes...I was a great fighter. I was known, I heard afterwards, as Golden Punch—my hair and my fists. I can remember my father telling me that I could fight, but that there was no need to look pleased about it."

"Well, that's where he gets it, then," said Mr. Barwell. "And I suppose that's where he gets that left, too."

"He uses his left?" said Willy in ecstasy. "He does?"

"Goo on, goo on," urged Mr. Warren, giving Mr. Barwell a prod. "Goo on and tell us how he downed the Richie brothers."

Mr. Barwell pulled his chair closer and began his tale. "There was a crowd of boys standing round, all yelling. I

The Greenwood Shady

couldn't get near, just at first, and when I did, I saw Julian..."

"Well?" asked Willy.

"Goo on, goo on," said Mr. Warren.

"It was amazing," said Mr. Barwell. "Listen...."

At the end of the commentary the three men were within a ring of chairs which had been placed, backs facing inward, round the centre of the room. All three had their coats off. On the floor lay Mr. Barwell in the attitude of a felled pugilist; over him stood Willy, panting realistically. Mr. Warren, one fist beating time, was shouting at the top of his voice.

"—seven, eight, nine—ten! That's the lot, Bar-well, lad. Oop tha' get."

Mr. Barwell got to his feet, and the three men turned the chairs round and sat on them.

"Ah enjoyed that," said Mr. Warren, wiping his brow.

Mr. Barwell rose and got into his coat.

"This is all very well," he said. "But there's something else."

He took from his coat pocket some sheets of paper, and Willy gave a cry.

"Not more sketches?"

"Ah—he's done some of these before, has he?" said Mr. Barwell. "You didn't tell me."

"Well, he drew Miss Condiment."

"Well, he's paid me the compliment of leaving me out," said Mr. Barwell. "But he's got some of your neighbours nicely caricatured."

"Let me see," said Mr. Warren, leaning over his shoulder. "Oh, oh—look, that's me! Ho, ho, ho, ho, ho!" he roared. "Come on, lad, let's look at them. Hand 'em over."

Mr. Barwell handed them over.

Elinor went upstairs, and found Cousin Clarry looking through some clean linen.

"Look what that laundry's done," she said. "How do they do it? Do they bite the things? Do they shred them for fun? Tell me that.—Where's Willy?"

"Someone called to see him—a man called Barwell. Mr. Warren said he was from the school."

"School? Julian, I suppose."

"Yes. Do you think there's more trouble?" asked Elinor.

"Trouble? No, I don't," said Cousin Clarry. "Dying's trouble; being buried's trouble."

She put the linen back on the shelf and followed Elinor into her room.

"He can't get thrown out of every school in the country, can he?" pointed out Elinor. "At least, if he's only going to stay a week in each, then he'll have to. Do I make myself clear?"

"No, you don't," said Cousin Clarry. "Elinor, I want to talk to you."

"I thought you did," murmured Elinor.

"Very well, then. Are you," inquired Cousin Clarry—"are you going to say Yes to Willy?"

The Greenwood Shady

Elinor sat down at her dressing-table and looked at the array of jars that now graced it. She unscrewed a pale pink cream-jar and sniffed at it, closing her eyes in appreciation of the delicate scent.

"Yes," she said at last, "I am."

Looking in the mirror, she saw Cousin Clarry's mouth drop open and counted the two familiar snaps of the jaw.

"Oh..." Cousin Clarry, for once, had nothing to add.

She plunged a hand into the voluminous tunic and groped without result. A tear appeared on one puffy cheek and rolled slowly down it. Elinor got out a handkerchief and held it out silently. Cousin Clarry looked down at it, gave a great sniff and pushed it indignantly aside.

"What's the use of a wisp like that to anybody?" she asked angrily. "Tell me that? When I want to blow my nose, I want a handkerchief, not one of those pale-pink-and-lace affairs that your Great-aunt Maudie always used to carry to drop every time she passed a good-looking man.—I never thought you'd have the sense, Elinor, upon my word I didn't. I thought those glands had got into you for good. And if you'd ordered a man and had him cut out to pattern, you couldn't have found one to suit you better. Now give me a kiss"—she offered the dry cheek—"and mind you look after Willy. A good man, that, and I'll tell you something. If you hadn't had him, then I would have had a try for him myself. Have you anything to say?"

"Nothing," said Elinor.

They walked downstairs. Cousin Clarry stumped into the kitchen, and Elinor, hearing sounds in the drive, opened the front door and stepped outside.

At the door of Deepwood House stood Mr. Barwell's car. The owner, helpless with laughter, was being helped into it by Mr. Warren and Willy, who themselves appeared to be on the verge of apoplexy. Elinor listened to their uproarious mirth; if she had not known that Willy kept his drinks at the Lodge, she would have felt certain that he had been pouring them into the company. She walked down the drive towards them, and Willy, seeing her, put out a hand and drew her into the party.

"This is a noisy gathering," she observed.

"It's disgraceful," said Mr. Warren, between the roars. "It's this chap Barwell here who's the cause of it all."

He pushed Mr. Barwell in with a final thump on his back, and Mr. Barwell, with obvious reluctance, prepared to drive away.

"Good-bye, Barwell, lad—good-bye, good-bye."

"Good-bye—good-bye, Hume."

"Good-bye. Come round any time! Glad to see you!" called Willy.

The car drove out of sight, and Mr. Warren and Willy, apparently remembering the same joke at the same time, burst into fresh roars of laughter.

"Oh—ah!" gasped Mr. Warren, recovering.

"What did Mr. Barwell come for?" asked Elinor.

The Greenwood Shady

She regretted the question, for it brought on the worst paroxysm Mr. Warren had yet had. He leaned against Willy, and Elinor waited for them both to recover.

"Well?" she asked.

"Oh, nothing much," said Willy. "Julian's expelled."

"That's right. Choocked out," corroborated Mr. Warren. "Ho, ho, ho, ho, ho, hee hee hee..."

Chapter Nineteen

The night before the Parade was still and moonlit. Nature was in her quietest mood and Deepwood in its most agitated. The village seethed with the irritation of women overtired with stitching and machining. Mr. Warren had made a last-minute decision to appear as Sancho Panza to Willy's Don Quixote. Only the fact that Mark Stirling was arriving saved Elinor from being dressed as a damsel in distress, and Cousin Clarry from being disguised as a windmill. Francesca had steadily refused to dress up, but had spent a good deal of time on Julian's costume, a pretty affair which, with his fair hair and angelic expression, was to turn him into a perfect copy of the Bubbles of the well-known picture and—his father hoped—arouse grave doubts in the minds of the spectators as to whether he was really the terror he was reputed to be.

The working party which was to board up the well assembled at the Lodge after supper. In high spirits they marched out into the quiet moonlit garden and began to fit the new boards into position.

Cousin Clarry followed a little later. For some reason which she could not define, she felt tired and depressed. Everything was turning out all right—Strone would look after Joanna, Willy would marry Elinor and take her away to be happy ever afterwards. Mark Stirling—there was no reason to suppose he would refuse a divorce. There was nothing to be depressed about.

She stood watching the work going on and listening to the instructions of Mr. Warren, the self-appointed foreman. When the last board was in position, Willy stood upon it and made a short announcement.

"From now on," he said, "no ghost."

"No ghost," said Mr. Warren. "Let's all go and have a drink on it."

"That's an idea," said Strone. "My party, at the King's Men."

There was a general movement towards the iron gates, but Cousin Clarry stayed where she was.

"I'm tired," she said, "and I'm going indoors."

She watched the merry party out of sight and prepared to go towards the Lodge. She gave a last glance at the well, and smiled a little at the absurdity of the ceremony which had just taken place there. Switching on her torch, she flashed it over the newly-placed boards and the ground surrounding the well. Switching it off again, she turned away, and had taken a step or two when the significance of something she had just seen reached her brain. Her mouth opened and her chin quivered; she steeled herself to go back, to put on the torch again and to look...if she dared. She felt waves of heat and cold flowing through her body, and longed to hurry as fast as her trembling legs could carry her in the direction of home. But she had to see. She had to make sure....

She turned and made two slow and deliberate steps back to the spot on which she had been standing. Switching on her torch, she directed it downward, and then stood frozen. She had not been mistaken, and her imagination had not played tricks. What she was looking at was clear and plain—an imprint, and an imprint made recently.

The print of a cloven hoof.

There was a movement behind her, and Cousin Clarry, with a gasp, dropped the torch and wheeled round to find the gardener at her elbow. Without speaking, he stooped and picked up the torch and handed it to her. Making a tremendous effort, Cousin Clarry took it from him. As she did so, his hand touched hers for an instant.

She turned and stumbled towards the Lodge, her breath coming in loud, uneven gasps. She closed the front door after her, and sinking on to a chair in the hall, waited for her limbs to cease their trembling. The thudding of her heart gradually grew less, and she sat breathing in long, shuddering sighs. After some time she stood up, steadied herself and walked into the drawing-room. Switching on the most powerful of the lights, she lifted the hand which had touched the gardener's and stared for a long time at the mark on it....

The Greenwood Shady

Willy did not stay long at the King's Men. He drank two beers, and led Elinor out into the moonlit night.

"Home?" he asked.

Elinor nodded.

"Yes. It's getting late."

They walked slowly towards the Lodge, and Willy spoke in a thoughtful tone.

"This time to-morrow," he said, "Strone and Joanna'll be gone. And Stirling will be here."

"Yes."

"I've been thinking," said Willy. "He won't be too pleased to see me—I know too much about his reputation out in Africa. But if he's going to make himself troublesome in the matter of the divorce, I can't see that I'm going to be much help unless I have a sort of official position." He stopped in the shadow of a tree and turned to Elinor. "As a friend of the family, I won't carry much weight. As a man of the family, I'd be quite a factor. Wouldn't I?"

He waited. There was no reply.

"Elinor," he said, "have you thought over the question of marrying me?"

"Yes," said Elinor.

"I see. And did you come to any conclusion."

Elinor smiled faintly.

"Not any conclusion, exactly," she said. "I like you very much."

"Is that all?"

"No."

"Do you love me, Elinor?"

"Yes. But—"

"One moment," said Willy, "before we tackle the buts."

The moment was a long one. Elinor, in his arms, was shaken by a gust of feeling which left her slightly dazed. Willy looked down into her eyes and gave a little laugh.

"What does that mean?" asked Elinor, somewhat breathlessly.

"It means that it's going to be fun teaching you how to demonstrate your passion for me. Have you forgotten how to kiss back?"

"Well—yes."

"Making love," said Willy, "is a game for two. I'll teach you all the moves."

Elinor rubbed her cheek gently against his.

"I know the moves, Willy," she said, "but I—"

"You'll get used to me."

"It isn't that. It's getting used to myself. It's getting used to the fact that at—at my age I can feel like this. It's rather frightening."

"Why? Did you think that all your senses went to sleep before you got to this advanced age?"

"Not to sleep, no. But—will this hurt you?"

The Greenwood Shady

"Tell me, and I'll see," invited Willy.

"Well, I think of love—of passion—as something that looks most fitting on the young. Young love, fresh love—that's how I always pictured it. Later marriages always struck me as being odd, in some way—a matter of coolness and companionship. I never thought that love could take hold of someone older and shake them to—to this extent."

"You've got a lot to learn," said Willy, "and it'll be—if you put yourself in my hands—a very pleasant lesson. When you're young, you fall in love—the phrase is a good one and an exact one. You feel, but you hardly know what you're feeling. It's what the songs call it—delicious, delightful, delirious—all that, but it's unaware. What makes me tremble now, with you in my arms, is the awareness of what I'm feeling for you. I've never loved before with my head, my heart and my body. I wouldn't exchange what I feel for you for anything in the world. I've loved before—when I was young—but no young man could feel what I'm feeling now."

There was silence. Presently the two walked slowly towards the house and stopped at the door.

"There's one thing more," said Willy. His voice dropped to a low note, and he took Elinor's hands in his. "It's a confession I feel bound to make."

"Well?"

"Just this: there's another woman in my life. I want you to do your best not to be jealous. You see, I can't do without her. She's necessary to my wellbeing, and I want to bring her—

permanently—into our home."

"Oh...Willy!" Elinor's arms went round his neck, and she laid her cheek against his. "Oh Willy, you've taken such a weight off my heart. I thought it would be asking so much, but I couldn't bear the thought of leaving her. She's not everybody's idea of a companion, but you've no idea what she's done for me, and she hasn't any other home! I really do love her."

"Well, so do I. Haven't I been telling you? She's the only woman I've ever known who regards food reverently, who knows what's due to it, who knows its potentialities, who can bring out the best in it. After eating Cousin Clarry's food, do you think I could ever bear anybody else's?—But will she agree to come and live with us?"

"Why not? I suppose she could always stay on here while I was alive, and live by herself; but I think she loves me, and somehow I think she'd like to be where we are."

"So do I. Well, you can ask her when you feel it's a propitious moment. Just when she's finishing her cello practice is a good time—she's always got a soft, far-away look in her eyes. And now let me see whether you've forgotten how to say good night."

When Elinor went into the house, she heard, with surprise, sounds from the kitchen indicating that Cousin Clarry was not only still up, but apparently still working. Going to the door of the kitchen, she opened it, looked in and stared in amazement.

The Greenwood Shady

The door leading to the back entrance was open. In the small space outside, Cousin Clarry had put a table, and on this was piled an assortment of tins, jars and unopened parcels which Elinor remembered having taken in at intervals during the past weeks. Clambering up to high shelves, groping in low ones, Cousin Clarry filled her arms and staggered out to deposit fresh loads on the table. As soon as astonishment allowed her to move, Elinor went forward.

"Cousin Clarry—what on *earth*—"

Cousin Clarry turned to her a face looking curiously grey. Elinor saw that one of her hands was bandaged.

"What on earth are you doing?"

"Getting these things out. Here, take these and put them on that table out there. Careful with them. Here."

Elinor walked out with a load and came back for another.

"But I don't understand—"

"It's plain enough, isn't it?" said Cousin Clarry in her usual downright fashion. "I'm just clearing out a few things. In the morning I shall label them and send them back where they came from."

"But...but *why*?"

"Been collecting too much stuff, that's all. Just having a turn-out."

The tone told Elinor that she would learn nothing more. She helped with the remaining loads, saying nothing, and then looked at Cousin Clarry, noting that her face was less ashy and the colour returning to her cheeks.

"Aren't you going to bed?" she asked gently.

"This minute. But I felt I wanted to do that before I went up."

They walked upstairs slowly, and stood for a moment on the landing.

"I want you to do something for me first thing in the morning," said Cousin Clarry.

"Well?"

"Ring up that garage man—Armstrong—and tell him I want a taxi after lunch. And I'll want him to go round with me delivering some parcels."

"Parcels? You mean all that lot downstairs?"

"Yes. And now, good night to you."

"Oh—your hand," said Elinor, remembering. "What happened—is it a cut?"

"No," said Cousin Clarry. "It's a scorch."

Chapter Twenty

The last Friday in June of that year was to be remembered in Deepwood for many reasons unconnected with the Parade. The first of these was the news that the elder Mrs. Stirling was going to be married to the man whose only designation in the locality was That Boy's Father. Deepwood, while regretting the connection in one way, liked it in another; a woman, in the general opinion, ought to have a man to look after her, and everybody hoped that Elinor had got a good one.

The second item of news came like a bombshell, and spread a general feeling of bereavement: Miss Clarence was to leave Deepwood and go away with Elinor. The circus was leaving.

It is difficult to say exactly how Deepwood regarded Cousin Clarry, but she had become part—and a large part—of life, and nobody knew what it was going to be like without her. The big form had lumbered, year after year, past the cottages and clambered on to the bus; the cloak and the Trilby in winter, the Russian tunic and the straw boater in summer, were sights as familiar as the inn sign or the big iron gates. The deep roar of greeting, the shrewd questions and caustic comment would be heard no more. There would be nothing for the girls to giggle at or the boys to imitate.

The news threw a shadow over the preparations for the Parade. Mrs. Jenner, dressing the twins in their Tweedledum and Tweedledee outfits, pushed the padding into the wrong places and felt unaccountably irritable. Mrs. Sprule, getting the Peter Pan group ready, with none of her usual enthusiasm, mislaid Captain Hook's hook and fell over it in her search, badly bruising her shin. Grand-dad Robbins displayed more than his usual truculence over getting into his Father Time suit, giving as his reason his conviction that, in his absence, something was going to happen to his pewter mug. The hired buses, which usually carried away loads of merry passengers, had an unusually dispirited cargo to drive into Weston.

Georgina was to drive over to Cheddarborough during the morning to fetch her costume from the Castle. She was also to bring back the stirrups which had been lent—together with the white horse and splendid embroidered trappings—by Lord Cheddarborough to Joan of Arc. The horse and trappings had arrived, but the stirrups had been forgotten. She left Deepwood early, taking with her the handsome Spaniard, Señor Cortes, who had been her companion during the past few days. He had been more popular at the King's Men than most of her visitors, for he had sat with Georgina at the little bar, regaling the company with Spanish stories that, translated by Georgina, took so much salt with the swallowing that the business of the inn had reached a new ceiling. Landlord Robbins saw him go

The Greenwood Shady

by in the car and rubbed his hands: the drive would make him thirsty, and he would be on his stool at the bar by noon.

Nobody saw Georgina return, but Cousin Clarry, glancing out hopefully before lunch, saw the elegant little car in front of the House, and was just in time to see Curzon disappearing inside with two large parcels and also a long package that might have been a walking stick. Cousin Clarry, inventing an excuse to go in and see Mrs. Warren, came back and informed Elinor that Georgina was going as Britannia, and the long parcel was possibly a trident.

"She'll make a good Britannia," said Elinor. "She's got that fine, imposing figure that Britannia has."

"That Britannia used to have," corrected Cousin Clarry. "But what would Lord Cheddarborough be doing with a Britannia outfit? No. Must be something else. Can you think of any period costume that would have a long pole?"

"Well a—a friar would carry a staff," suggested Elinor.

"Friar? Friar? Now," demanded Cousin Clarry, "would Georgina come as a friar? Did the friars show their figures off, as she's anxious to do? No, it won't be a friar. Well, it doesn't matter—we'll soon see."

Georgina ate her lunch and, chancing to look out of the window, saw Francesca in the garden, walking disconsolately along one of the paths. She leaned out and called her.

"Oh, you're back," said Francesca.

"Yes. Stay there—I'm coming down," called Georgina.

She stopped to light a cigarette, and then went downstairs and joined Francesca. She looked at her pale face speculatively.

"You look a bit under the weather," she commented. "It's this heat, I suppose. I've never known six weeks unbroken heat in this country before—it's unnatural."

"Yes. Look at the garden," said Francesca, indicating the brown grass and the drooping flowers. "Everything looks scorched."

"Everything *is* scorched. I wish your mother would say something to that gardener. Or, better still, I wish she'd sacked him earlier. The place has never been in this state before."

She swept round the path leading to the shrubbery, and Captain Vandeleur and Telemachus, who had been peering out of the bushes, had to move quickly to avoid her. The Captain looked with admiration at her tall, handsome form.

"If you say presence again," said Telemachus, "I'll unboard that well that they took all the trouble to board up and shove you down again. I've 'eard of a woman bein' conspicuous by 'er absence lots o' times, but never by her presence."

"You'll allow she's handsome?"

"She's a good looker, yes—but so's the little 'un."

"The little Francesca?" The Captain sighed. "She reminds me of a dainty form I once held in—"

"Now, go easy," said Telemachus.

"The little Francesca," said the Captain, "is charming.

The Greenwood Shady

Charming. She moves with grace, and she holds her head proudly. But the other—Miss Finck—she is magnificent."

"She's talking secrets," commented Telemachus. "Look—bending down to say somethin'. Somethin' about that ole rip, her father, I wouldn't mind betting. If you come nearer, we'll be able to 'ear."

The Captain, unable to bring himself to eavesdrop, stayed where he was. Telemachus went forward and stationed himself close enough to hear what was being said.

"If you like—and if you promise not to say a word about it to anybody—you can come up and see it," said Georgina. "It's on my bed."

"It sounds wonderful," said Francesca. "But did it actually belong to somebody—I mean, to an ancestor?"

"Of course it did—why do you think I want to wear it?" said Georgina. "It's the actual uniform worn by Georgie Finck, and it fits me like my own skin. I wondered whether people would guess something when I came back with my hair done in this Prince Albert style, but I had to risk it."

"I'd love to see it," said Francesca.

"Well, come on up. But I don't want that bloodhound Clarry on my track. Come on."

Telemachus watched them go and gave a long, low whistle. The Captain came to his side, and looked at him with a touch of disdain.

"Orl right—I listened," admitted Telemachus. "And wot

wouldn't you give to know what she said?"

"I do not care to know."

"Ah-ha!" Telemachus gave his tail a derisive swish. "Well, don't ask, then. I'll keep it to myself. But didn't you tell me you fought with a Georgie Finck?"

"Fought? We fought together, we lived and loved and wined and wenched together. We—"

"That's what I thought. Well, you know they're having a fancy-dress parade this evening?"

"Yes. But we shall be gone by then. We leave at five."

"We leave a bit before. But they'll all put on fancy dress, and Miss Finck is going to wear something that'll knock 'em all off their perches."

"Well?"

"She brought it back today, all nicely parcelled up, from her father's house. Old Lord Cheddarborough keeps a lot of these old family outfits in glass cases and such. She goes down and picks 'er choice. 'Gimme that one, dad,' she says—'that red one with the facings. It'll fit me a treat, and I'll look like Georgie Finck 'imself. I'll put on—'"

"Stop!" commanded Captain Vandeleur, and Telemachus stopped. "You say that she proposes to wear the uniform—that she has brought to this house the uniform of—of—"

"'Sright," said Telemachus, through his teeth. "And the sword."

The Captain drew himself up, and Telemachus saw for

The Greenwood Shady

the first time his height and breadth. He turned and, without a word, walked forward until he stood beneath Georgina's window, looking up at it.

"I'll keep a look-out," said Telemachus, behind him, "and give you the tip when to nip up and get it."

"I thank you," said the Captain, without turning. "I thank you, my friend."

After lunch at the Lodge, Joan of Arc knocked at the back door to see if Georgina had brought over the stirrups. She had called previously at the flat, but had found Georgina out.

Cousin Clarry sent her away, promising to look into the matter. She returned thoughtfully to the dining-room.

"Georgina's out," she said.

"Ah," said Willy. "So if you just go across for the stirrups, you might get a glimpse of her costume—is that it?"

"Yes," admitted Cousin Clarry, without shame. "But what about that Spanish bit of nonsense they say she's got with her? If he's there, I shall have to ask him for the stirrups. And he won't know what I'm talking about."

"Try *estribos*," suggested Willy.

"*Estribos?* Why should I try *estribos*? Now tell me that."

"Spanish stirrups," said Willy. "And if you can't manage the *estribos*, you can always fall back on *caballo*."

"*Ca* who?"

"*Caballo*. Spanish horse. Now run along," said Willy.

"What'll I do if he comes at me with some Spanish?" asked Cousin Clarry uneasily.

"Oh, he won't, Cousin Clarry, he won't," Elinor assured her.

Cousin Clarry went across to the House and walked upstairs to Georgina's flat. Breathing heavily after the climb, she knocked on the door and, finding it open, went inside. A young man standing at the window turned and looked expectantly at her, and Cousin Clarry was interested to find that he did not look in the least Spanish.

This was not surprising. Señor Cortes had been driven by Georgina to Weston station, and was now sitting in a train, London-bound. The young man standing before Cousin Clarry was an American named Curtis Lyle. He had been staying with Lord Cheddarborough, and Georgina had brought him to Deepwood that morning to show him something of English village life. He was an ingenuous young man and had, as yet, no idea of the amount of life he was going to see. His eyes, taking in Cousin Clarry, widened, and then narrowed as she advanced a step or two, smiled winningly and uttered one word.

"*Estribos!*"

Mr. Lyle stared, speechless, and Cousin Clarry felt sorry for him. People ought not to go to countries without knowing something of the language—one might as well leave one's tongue at home.

"*Estribos?*" she tried once more, waving her hand in the air in a stirrup pattern. "*Es-tri-bos.*"

The Greenwood Shady

Mr. Lyle moved cautiously behind a chair and eyed her. Cousin Clarry flexed her knees, assumed the position of one sitting on a horse, and urged an imaginary steed forward.

"Chkk, chkk, chkk, chkk, chkk," she said. "*Estribos!*"

Mr. Lyle made a quick movement and covered the space intervening between himself and a larger chair, and gave his visitor a placating smile.

"*Caballo!*" shouted Cousin Clarry triumphantly. "*Caballo—estribos.*"

"Sure, sure," muttered Mr. Lyle, measuring the distance to Georgina's bedroom door.

He saw Cousin Clarry looking desperately round the room for what he presumed was a weapon. With a bound, he reached the bedroom, raced inside and locked himself in. Cousin Clarry, at the same moment, saw the stirrups on the floor near the window, picked them up and bore them home in triumph.

Georgina came home twenty minutes later, but Mr. Lyle was still in her bedroom. Hearing her voice, he emerged cautiously.

"You're pale," remarked Georgina. "Come and have a drink."

Mr. Lyle took one thankfully and looked at Georgina over his glass.

"Look—don't leave me alone again, will you?" he said.

Georgina put her drink down and advanced.

"Why...*Curtis!*" she promised. "But of *course* not...."

Chapter Twenty-One

Doctor Beale's last visit of farewell was to Mrs. Warren. He went to see her after lunch on the day of the Parade, congratulated her on her recovery and told her, with a confidence that communicated itself to her, that no ghost would ever again disturb her slumbers. Bidding her good-bye, he walked to the door with her husband.

They stood in the hall, and Mr. Warren held out a hand.

"Well, Ah'm grateful to you, lad," he said. "You've put her on her feet again."

The doctor's response was scarcely lively: Mr. Warren, looking more closely at him, saw that since leaving Mrs. Warren's presence he had dropped his calm, professional manner and was looking the picture of misery. He held out his hand and shook Mr. Warren's.

"I'll say good-bye to you," he said. "I shan't be seeing you again."

"Ah suppose not." Mr. Warren strove to find words of comfort, and could not utter one. "Ah suppose not. You'll be going...you'll be going across the way to say good-bye?" he asked hesitatingly.

"If they let me," said the doctor bitterly.

"Let you?" Mr. Warren's voice rose to an indignant falsetto. "Let you? How can they stop you from saying good-bye? What possible reason could they—"

"Oh, they've got a reason," said Doctor Beale wearily. "They've found out that Francesca saw—or thought she saw—the ghost, and that we kept them in ignorance." He looked round the little hall in vague misery and continued, "Ever since Francesca said she wouldn't go to Brighton, they've suspected something—God knows what—but they've been on at her, questioning her and suggesting all sorts of reasons for her refusal. And Francesca's not very good at hiding anything—and last night it all came out. Francesca rang me up from Georgina's flat and told me early this morning."

He came to an end, and Mr. Warren gazed at him with feelings of impotent pity.

"Lad," he said slowly, "if Ah could help you—if any of us could have done anything for you, then we'd—"

"I know ''—the doctor laid a grateful hand on his arm for a moment. "I know. But it was no use. I ought to have seen, but somehow I always went on expecting something—I didn't know quite what—to turn up. I even"—he gave a wry smile—"I even arranged a passage for her. Something kept nagging at me and saying that even if things looked sunk, they'd come right in the end.—Well, this is the end. I'm going to say good-bye to her...if they let me."

Mr. Warren stood at his door and watched the doctor ring the bell opposite. Unable to bear the sight of his being turned away, he went impulsively out of the house and walked up and down the drive. After two or three turns, he relaxed a little; it was obvious that the doctor had been at any rate admitted.

Hands sunk deep in his pockets, his eyes fixed on the ground, Mr. Warren paced up and down, brooding. They had all promised to do something, and what had it added up to? There was the young chap in there, he reflected, looking his last at that pretty lass and going away to eat his heart out. It was all over—and all because of two smug, stuck-up, hypocritical, selfish—Mr. Warren paused for breath—people. If he'd had a lass, by gum, he wouldn't have let any shadow get into her eyes, no, he wouldn't. He would have lived to see her happy, whatever it cost him, and so would Ada. Ada wouldn't have—

Mr. Warren's soliloquy came to a stop. He had reached a flower-bed which he knew was to have been sown with anemone seed. He thought the ground looked exactly as it had done when he had glanced at it that morning, and he wondered with sudden suspicion why the gardener was coming away from the spot with the air of one who had done a good job well. He waited until the man was beside him.

"Seeds all in?" he inquired.

"Yes, sir."

"Doesn't look touched to me," said Mr. Warren stolidly. "You're sure you've finished it?"

The Greenwood Shady

"Yes, sir."

Mr. Warren hunched his shoulders.

"Well, Ah'm not a gardener myself," he said bluntly, "but Ah think you'll find Mrs. Fleury more than dissatisfied with that job."

Frobisher hesitated, and then decided that nothing could be lost by boldness. This was the last day; in a few hours his mission would have been accomplished and he would be on his way with Telemachus and the Captain. Mrs. Fleury's opinion was no longer of any account.

"She will be dissatisfied, sir," he said confidently.

"Eh?" Mr. Warren gazed with open amazement, but it was impossible to see the gardener's eyes. "Eh?"

"I shall tell Mrs. Fleury, sir, that the seeds are in the ground. The seeds, sir "—Frobisher's tone was respectful—"are not in the ground; but I shall assert, with confidence, that they are. Mrs. Fleury will find it very hard, sir, to prove the contrary. When people are presented with a *fait accompli*, or with a statement made with—may I put it, sir?—a certain force, they need a little time to act, in order to prove that statement inaccurate. Mrs. Fleury will not have the necessary—"

Mr. Warren was no longer listening. His mouth had dropped open, and he was staring with bulging eyes into space. After a few moments he muttered a word or two and, swinging round on his heel, gazed back at Deepwood House. Yes! The doctor's car was still there. The doctor was still there. The—

Mr. Warren took his hands out of his pockets and ran, as he had not run for years, in the direction of the Lodge. He burst in at the front door and gave a hoarse shout.

"Hi. Hi there!"

There were three simultaneous responses. Strone and Joanna, ready for their journey, appeared on the landing above. Willy and Elinor opened the door of the drawing-room, and Cousin Clarry, dressed in her cloak and best black Homburg, strode forth from the kitchen. They all looked with dumb amazement at the panting, quivering frame of Mr. Warren.

"C-come with me," he gasped breathlessly. "Come on—quick."

"Oh, Mr. Warren—what's happened?" cried Elinor.

He glanced at her pale, frightened face, and the sight steadied him. With an effort, he forced himself to speak more calmly, but he caught her hand as he spoke and dragged her out of the door, throwing the words over his shoulder.

"Francesca," he said. "The doctor chap. Engaged. Fixed up. A—a *fait accompli*."

There was an instant chorus of delight.

"Horray!" shouted Joanna, coming downstairs in a rush.

"Oh—wonderful!" said Elinor jerkily, pulled by Mr. Warren in the direction of the House.

"Good show," said Willy, taking her other arm and supporting her.

"Bravo, bravo!" trumpeted Cousin Clarry, bringing up the

The Greenwood Shady

rear between Strone and Joanna.

"We'll only just have time for congratulations, Joanna," Strone reminded her as they hurried along.

"I know—but we must see them! Come on!"

Mr. Warren, in the lead, bounded into the hall and made for the Fleurys' door. Standing there, white-faced, was the doctor, obviously on the point of leaving. Mr. Warren gave a loud shout of joy, pushed him backwards into the drawing-room, seized his hands and wrung them up and down heartily.

"Oh, congratulations, congratulations, con-gratu-la-tions!" he shouted. "Lad, Ah'm as pleased as if 'twere my own son."

The Colonel had just opened his mouth to speak, when Cousin Clarry gave him a thump on the back that effectively stopped him.

"Splendid, splendid, bravo, bravo, bravo!" she cried, one hand beating the air. "I never thought you'd have the sense. Shake hands. I've been doing you an injustice. I thought you were a ratterty-tatterty old curmudgeon, doing your daughter out of her life's happiness. Shake hands, Colonel, shake hands."

Mr. Warren had detached Francesca from Mrs. Fleury, and placed her in a corner with the doctor.

"Kiss her, lad. Kiss her!" he cried. "There you are, Miss Francesca—there you are, there's your young man with his arms round you. Don't be shy now, don't be shy."

Elizabeth Cadell

He had to raise his voice, for the din in the room had mounted. Elinor and Joanna, having kissed Francesca, were both talking at once in an endeavour to make up to Mrs. Fleury for all the hard things they had thought about her. Strone was joining the hands of the young couple and giving them his blessing. Willy congratulated the Colonel and, catching one or two words of the staccato, spluttering reply, stood aside for a moment to size up the situation. He gave a swift glance round: Mrs. Fleury was pale and speechless; Francesca and the doctor were wisely making the most of the moment and allowing explanations to wait, but the Colonel would soon become coherent. Willy got to Mr. Warren's shoulder and the eyes of the two men met. In Mr. Warren's was a desperate appeal.

"Stick by me, Willy," he breathed.

Willy became busy. He led the overjoyed Cousin Clarry to the Colonel, and saw with relief that the second thump had knocked the breath out of his lungs. He joined Mrs. Fleury's group and, embarking on a long and congratulatory speech, gave Strone a look that put him in touch with the less obvious aspects of the situation. Strone raised his voice in happy chatter, and for once the sound of ticking was stilled.

A bad moment occurred a little later; the Colonel, at last in possession of his breath and determined to be heard, pulled forward a stool and stood upon it. Prepared for a speech, the party fell silent. Mr. Warren threw a glance of agony at Willy, and Willy gave an imperceptible nod of reassurance.

"Ahem," said the Colonel fiercely.

The Greenwood Shady

"Bravo, bravo!" shouted Cousin Clarry. "Speech, speeeech!"

"I wish to tell you all," said the Colonel, "that there has been a terrible—"

"Hurrah!" shouted Willy, Strone and Mr. Warren in unison.

"Bravo!" yelled Cousin Clarry.

"Silence!" thundered the Colonel. "I wish to say that—"

"For he's a jolly good fellow," sang Willy.

"For he's a jolly good fellow," shouted Strone and Mr. Warren.

"For he's a jolly good fe-hell-lo," boomed Cousin Clarry in dreadful bass.

"And so say all of us," sang the visitors in unison.

"And so say all of us."

"Sus, sus," rollicked Cousin Clarry, with a thump that dislodged the Colonel from his perch.

"And so say all of us."

"Sus, sus," hissed Willy into the doctor's ear. "Up to you from now on, Beale."

"For he's a jolly good fellow," carolled the doctor, realisation flooding over him.

"For he's a jolly good fellow," he yelled, wringing Mr. Warren's hand.

"For he's a jolly good fell-hel-lo!" screamed the chorus, crowding round Colonel and Mrs. Fleury.

"And so say All of Us!"

"Horray! hooray!" yelled Cousin Clarry, seizing a rose-bowl and holding it up. "The Colonel and his missus."

The company lifted the nearest container to hand and drank an imaginary toast. With renewed congratulations, shepherded by Willy, they then took their leave and went outside into the hall. Georgina, roused by the noise, appeared on the landing in a revealing negligee.

"What moves?" she called.

"Francesca—she's engaged!"

"Good God!"

Georgina trailed downstairs, kissed Francesca, enfolded the doctor in a verbena-scented embrace, offered a cheek to Mrs. Fleury and allowed the bathrobe to slip off one shoulder as she passed the Colonel. She went upstairs again and the company dispersed. Strone seized Joanna and raced with her back to the Lodge.

"Come on—we'll never make it!" he said. "But hats off to old Uncle Warren for his bright little plot."

"Plot?"

"I thought you said," said Strone, hurrying her upstairs, "that women had intuition.—Where's that suit-case of yours?—Is it properly shut?"

"Yes. What intuition?"

"When I say shut, I mean shut," said Strone, testing the lock. "I don't want the contents strewn all over the station.

And when I say intuition, I mean intuition. Those two were no more engaged than you and I are. Less, in fact."

Joanna stared.

"You mean that it was all a—"

"It was a fine bit of intuition on old Uncle Warren's part, that's what it was."

"But—but I saw you joining their hands and—"

"I was merely being theatrical—giving it a good touch here and there. Willy put me wise. Now get a move on."

"Well, I'm ready," said Joanna.

"All right, then. But first—"

Strone stopped her as she reached the door, swung her into his arms and put his lips on hers. He raised his head after some time and looked at her.

"Joanna—oh Joanna, my sweet....Say something!"

"....eleven, twelve, thirteen, fourteen...." counted Joanna with her eyes closed.

The two taxis—Strone, Joanna and Elinor in one, Willy, Cousin Clarry and the Homburg in the other—went through the iron gates and in the direction of Weston. Soon there followed Mr. and Mrs. Warren in their grey saloon. Upstairs, Georgina could be seen through the open window of her bathroom applying make-up and preparing to affix the trim side-whiskers.

It was the moment for which Captain Vandeleur had long

watched and waited. He hurried round to the front door of the House and slipped into the hall. Pausing for a moment, he listened: voices were coming from the flat occupied by the Fleurys. The Captain, who had in his day become familiar with the sound of parents' voices raised in anger, sighed for the little Francesca. For a moment he contemplated opening the door and putting an end to the dispute, but time pressed—in a few moments Georgina would emerge and don the uniform which meant so much to him....A pity. But there might be a moment—afterwards—to let Francesca see him in his full glory, proud, gallant. No woman had ever been able to resist the sight. He went swiftly up the stairs, thinking of how her cheeks would flush with surprise and her eyes flash into incredulous admiration....

He was on the landing...in Georgina's hall...across the drawing-room, and then at last, standing in her bedroom. And there before him, outspread on the bed, lay a sight that made him utter a cry of triumph.

At last! At last, at last! There, before him, was the only uniform in the world—other than his own—that he could have worn—which he would have worn. How well he remembered advising Georgie about the slight alterations! What a difference the half-inch here and there had made! He had slipped the scarlet tunic on to show Georgie the effect, and how he had stared! What a pair they had made; what a peerless pair in their brilliant uniforms, which only their reputations for gallantry could outshine. Women had looked, smiled and been

The Greenwood Shady

kind—ah! how kind. And now it only remained for him to step into the well-fitting garments, to buckle Georgie's sword about him and once more he could hold up his head and be the debonair, the dashing Anthony Vandeleur.

With swift delight he dressed, the hated Curzon shirt, the abhorred Fleury trousers kicked aside. He was almost ready; he was ready. The sword—it was on. The hat—ah! how becoming.

Captain Vandeleur threw back his shoulders, raised high his head and strode to the door. He went through it and on to the landing, and had placed a foot on the stairs, when sounds from below made him pause. Creeping forward cautiously, he looked over into the hall below.

She was there! She was alone...for a moment. The young man had gone to the horseless carriage and was bringing it to the door; in the room behind were the parents. She was going—good! She was going with the young man, as was right.

But—she appeared to hesitate, and the Captain saw that she had stopped. She put her hands together and wrung them, and her glance went from the front door, with its glimpse of the drive, to the door through which she had just passed.

"Francesca!" called the doctor.

"Francesca!" called Mrs. Fleury.

Captain Vandeleur saw Francesca waver, and then, to his horror, saw her turn slowly back towards the door of the flat. She was turning her back on the young man, on life, on love....

Elizabeth Cadell

Captain Vandeleur knew nothing about the young man, but on life and love he was an authority. With swift steps he moved downstairs and through the hall. One more step, and he was between Francesca and the door.

She looked at him, and Captain Vandeleur experienced his final triumph. For there was no surprise in the blue eyes regarding him, and no fear. There was recognition, there was gratitude. There would have been more, but there was no time. Outside, the young man and the machine panted; there was no going back, for Captain Vandeleur barred the way.

With a faint, swift smile, Francesca turned, ran lightly out on to the drive and settled herself beside the doctor in his little open two-seater. The car moved towards the gate, gathering speed; Captain Vandeleur came to the entrance and stood watching it. As it reached the iron gates, Francesca turned and, kneeling on her seat, fluttered a small white handkerchief. There was an instantaneous response—a flash of steel as Captain Vandeleur drew his sword and, standing to attention, brought it up in salute.

At the same moment there came from Georgina's bedroom a cry. It rose to a pitch of rage and frustration that made the birds twitter in the trees and caused Grand-dad Robbins' pewter mug to roll agitatedly from its bracket.

The afternoon session of the Parade being over, Deepwood brought its young home in order to divest them of their fancy raiment and set them down to high tea; but the news

The Greenwood Shady

that met them was of an order to drive normal domestic routine from their minds. The gardener had made off, taking with him the valuable military outfit lent by Lord Cheddarborough to his daughter. Police were scouring the district; detectives were seeking an interview with Mrs. Fleury, who refused to see anyone.

Cousin Clarry heard the news without comment. So strange and so unusual was her silence that Elinor wondered whether she knew more of the matter than she cared to tell—she had been over at Georgina's flat that morning, and she had been behaving oddly for a day or two. She was about to question her, when she decided to ask Willy instead; Willy knew everything about Cousin Clarry, and could interpret her strangest actions.

Cousin Clarry walked slowly outside and stood staring thoughtfully at the pile of parcels which lay, wrapped and labelled, ready to be transported back to wherever they had come from. When she spoke, it was—to Elinor's surprise—on a subject entirely removed from absconding gardeners.

"That taxi from Armstrong's—" she began.

"Oh, I rang them up and ordered one," said Elinor. "He says he'll send one as soon as he's got through all his Parade journeys."

"Oh. Well, ring him up again," directed Cousin Clarry.

"Again? But—"

"Tell him," said Cousin Clarry, "that he won't be wanted.

And now come and help me put all these things back."

Mark Stirling got out of the train at Weston, left his luggage in charge of a porter and walked out into the street.

He stood for a few moments getting his bearings and, having placed the High Street and shops, walked in their direction, looking with some astonishment at the extraordinary costumes to be seen on every side. He dodged two children dressed in Welsh national dress, tripped over a boy in a kilt and stopped to let a panniered Polly Peachum pass. Then, reaching the end of the High Street, he looked along it until he found the sign he was looking for: Weston Car Hire: Drive Yourself.

His business did not take long. He chose a four-seater, four-doored saloon, backed expertly into the road and drove to the station to collect his luggage. Tipping the porter, he settled himself comfortably in the driving-seat, lit a cigarette and looked at his watch. Almost five; he would be at the Lodge in time for a late tea.

He had cleared the outskirts of Weston and was preparing to put on speed, when a figure stepped into the middle of the road and held up a hand. There was nothing to do but stop; Mark put on his brakes with an oath and prepared to speak his mind and leave the traveller less optimistic about lifts than he had found him.

The car stopped. Before Mark could speak, the man, moving with a curious swiftness for so large a figure, had opened the car door and was sitting beside him.

The Greenwood Shady

"You're Mark Stirling?"

It was less a question than a statement. Mark found himself driving on and, as he did so, he had the curious idea that both the back doors of the car were closed firmly. He was about to glance over his shoulder, but concentrated instead on the road before him. He felt confused, and had an uneasy feeling that he had been driving for some hours. He glanced at the clock on the dashboard and noticed that the hands were almost at five o'clock. Staring out at the road once more, he saw that the sun was glinting on the radiator with a brightness that made his eyes smart. He wanted to address his passenger, but something prevented him—-a curious tightness in his throat.

Above the quiet hum of the car, he heard the chimes begin to strike on the Easton clock. Making a last effort, he addressed his passenger in a hoarse voice.

"Look—who the devil are you?"

There was no reply. Mark, his fingers gripping the wheel, turned and glanced sideways and, as he did so, Frobisher put up a hand and pushed his hat back from his eyes....

The crash, coming, Deepwood remembered afterwards, exactly as the last chime of five o'clock struck, caused general mourning in the village, for it sent Grand-dad Robbins' pewter mug hurtling off its bracket and through a hole in the wainscoting, from which it was never afterwards recovered.

There was some conjecture as to why Curzon's shirt

should have been found in Georgina's room, but Deepwood finally decided that he had sorted the laundry carelessly and that it had been there all the time. As to Colonel Fleury's brown trousers, there was no need for conjecture. Deepwood knew only too well what *they* were doing there.

THE END

Iris in Winter
by
Elizabeth Cadell

Iris Drake added a few lines to the sketch on which she was working and studied them critically, her head on one side. The result did not appear to please her for, with an impatient movement, she left her sketch-board and, walking to the window of the small, bare room, stared out moodily at the uninspiring view.

It was the beginning of September, but there was nothing outside to remind the watcher of the passing of summer. A heavy sky, a steady drizzle, and fallen leaves on the pavements seemed rather to lay undue stress on the more unpleasant aspects of autumn.

Iris turned away. It was not a sight to cheer anybody, and her spirits were already low. With a recollection of the tonic effect attributed to the counting of blessings, she leaned against the table and proceeded to enumerate her own.

There seemed to be, she admitted, a lot of blessings: youth—some people thought twenty-two quite young—and beauty. Everybody said that she was beautiful and, on days when her hair didn't give trouble and when she couldn't detect any lurking blemishes on her skin, she thought so herself. It counted, she thought, for very little—her beauty hadn't really done much beyond insuring her escorts for everything that went on. Talents? Oh well, she could sketch hats and she could write a pointless and vapid daily column in—well, it was, in a way—a leading newspaper. She had a well-paid job and a pleasant flat at Knightsbridge. But who, reflected Iris dismally, forgetting her blessings and concentrating on her woes, who wanted to sketch hats? She didn't. Here she was, with half her ambitions realized and the other half as far away as ever. She was in Fleet Street; but she hadn't wanted a job sketching hats. She had expected...

Her gloomy meditations were interrupted by the cautious opening of the door. A head appeared round it and the owner, finding Iris alone, stepped into the room. Iris looked at the newcomer without any perceptible brightening of her expression.

"Hello, Ted," she greeted him.

The young man dropped into a chair, crossed his legs comfortably on the table, and looked at her with pleasant brown eyes.

"I say, Iris," he said, "I popped in to ask whether you'd marry me."

Iris, back at her sketch-board, gave the hat a slightly larger brim and answered absently, "No, Ted. Thanks awfully, all the same."

"You had your whole mind on that answer, did you?" questioned Ted Harris anxiously.

Iris looked up. "My mind, my whole mind and nothing—I say," she broke off to inquire, "I thought you told me you had an important session with the Chief this morning."

"I did. I had," answered Ted. "I've had half of it, but there was an interruption. I saw it coming—at least, I didn't exactly see it—but I heard the scraping of chairs outside as flustered junior reporters leapt to their feet; I heard the creaking as elderly reporters bowed from the waist. Then the door was thrown open and there he was."

"Who was?" inquired Iris.

Ted smiled at her indulgently.

"Dear Iris," he said, "sometimes you don't quite merit the brilliance and the wit I shower upon you. Who, think you, would throw the main body of this organization into confusion? Think, now. It couldn't have been old Ernest, because he was with me—that is, I was with him. So that—"

"Oh—you mean Sir Kenneth Harfield? What did he want?" asked Iris.

"I can only guess," said Ted. "He owns this newspaper, but he doesn't tell me anything. Never confides in me. Ernest gave me a look which I could only interpret as one of dismissal, and told me to shut the door after me. And so here I am....did you really mean what you said about not marrying me?"

"Yes. And the look on my face," Iris informed him, "is one of dismissal. If Ernest finds you here—"

"Why should he come here?" asked Ted. "I mean, I know this room's the setting for one of Nature's brightest jewels and so on et cetera, but you also happen to be a very junior member of the staff. If Ernest wanted you, he'd have you fetched, wouldn't he?...What's making you so pensive?" He inquired.

Iris threw a glance of distaste round the room. "It's this rathole," she said gloomily. "And look at the view."

Ted looked.

"It's pretty bleak," he said sympathetically, "but you won't be looking at it long. When's the second bit of your vacation coming up?"

"End of the month," said Iris. "But my Swiss tour's fallen through."

"So one of the boys told me," said Ted. "What're you going to do?"

"Dunno," said Iris listlessly. "I keep looking at the Travel section but I can't work up any enthusiasm about any of the offers. I' 'm going to wait and see what my sister's doing. She's just taken a cottage in a place I've never heard of, and when I can find out where it is, and whether it's in a nice spot with all the amenities—"

"Meaning three cinemas and a pier?" put in Ted.

"Something like that. It doesn't sound promising."

"What's it called?" asked Ted.

"High something—yes, High Ambo," said Iris. "As far as I can—"

"Half a minute," broke in Ted. He was looking at her intently, a puzzled frown on his forehead.

"High—?" He paused.

"—Ambo," supplied Iris. "Know it?"

Ted spoke musingly. "Funny," he said. "That's the second time I've heard that name this morning. Ernest mentioned it. It's the scene of the rumpus—the site of—"

"What rumpus?" inquired Iris.

"The rumpus that my session with Ernest was about. The rumpus that's brought our Chief's Chief up from his landed estate. What *is* a landed estate, can you tell me?" he asked.

"Who cares?" asked Iris. "We can't be talking about the same High Ambo. The one Caroline, my sister's, going to is about six hours' journey from London and—"

"Well, this one's God-forsaken, too," said Ted. "Cumberland or Westmorland or one of those bleak outposts. Must be the same place. What's your sister going there for?"

"Well, to escape, in a way," said Iris. "It's a long story."

Ted arranged himself more comfortably and tilted his chair back at a dangerous angle.

But just then the door of the room burst open and the Chief, Ernest Reed, an ominous frown on his forehead, stood on the threshold. Ted swung himself to his feet in a lightning movement and, straightening his tie, turned to face his employer. Ernest Reed pulled a watch from his waistcoat pocket, studied it, and looked up at the young man towering above him.

"Half-past eleven," he informed him. "Your day's work, I presume, is over?"

"Er—not quite, sir," said Ted.

Mr. Reed spoke with rasping finality. "If you want to put your feet up and talk to young women," he said, "you can do it at your own expense. Get out of this room and stay out of it."

He moved aside. Ted walked past him and, with a backward glance at Iris behind Mr. Reed's back, closed the door quietly.

"You," said Mr. Reed, opening it again and glaring at Iris, "you come along and see me. Got something to say to you."

Leaving the door wide, he turned and walked away and Iris stared after him moodily. Perhaps, she reflected, he was going to sack her, and in her present mood she didn't care. If this was Fleet Street, they could have it.

Well, the sooner it was over, the better. With a glance at herself in the mirror behind the door, she went through the maze of offices which led to Ernest Reed's room. She knocked on the door and, entering, confronted the stout, irritable man at the desk.

Though unmarried and leading a bachelor existence, Earnest Reed nevertheless gave the impression of being a man oppressed by numerous family cares. He had a harassed, almost a haunted expression which gave strangers a feeling that he was being bullied.

Any bullying that went on, however, was done by Ernest. He disliked women and had never—until he met Iris's sister, Caroline Drake—felt the smallest desire to take one to his bosom. He had met Caroline too late—she was already engaged to be married to his neighbour, Jeffry West. But four years later, she was back—a widow, free and making arrangements to live in the big house standing next to his own. Ernest had been uncertain as to what length of time should elapse before widows could, with propriety, receive fresh advances. He waited six months and then began to call regularly, but he was dismayed to find that his visits were made, not only to Caroline West, but to several of her late husband's relations who seemed to have attached themselves to the household.

The wooing seemed to be making very little progress. Caroline was not, he told himself, quite like other women; she had a quiet aloofness—elusiveness—Ernest could hardly find a name for the quality which gave her an almost absent-minded air and made him feel that she scarcely knew, sometimes, who he was.

She had asked him to give her sister a position on the paper, and Ernest had done so—reluctantly, grudgingly, but still, he had done it. His kindness, he reflected bitterly, had done him little good. Caroline was as elusive as ever, and he was stuck with one of the kind of young women he hated most—the kind he considered pert, modern, made-up, overdressed hussies.

He studied the hussy before him and spoke abruptly.

"This Harris fellow," he said. "I suppose he's told you about the visit from Sir Kenneth Harfield?"

Iris felt a little surprise, but her air was composed.

"Yes, Mr. Reed."

"He told you where the trouble was?"

"Trouble?" Iris echoed.

"Don't be stupid," said Ernest testily.

"Yes, Mr. Reed."

"Place called High Ambo," said Ernest. "Know anything about it?"

Iris hesitated. He lived next door to Caroline, but she had no means of knowing whether her sister had told him of her plans. She decided that it would be better to know nothing.

"No, Mr. Reed."

Earnest directed a keen glance at her, and Iris met it calmly.

He toyed irritably with the papers on his desk and then leaned forward and addressed her.

"Listen to me," he said. "I'm going to give you a job."

A curious expression flitted across Iris's face. She had come into the room prepared to lose one; instead she was being offered one. She waited warily.

"When you joined this paper," Ernest continued, "you wanted to be a reporter—a damn silly idea that a lot of girls have nowadays. In my day they wanted to go on the stage; now they want to be reporters—pah! But that's neither here no' there. You wanted to be a reporter," he went on. "If you'd made as good a reporter as you did a columnist, then God help the paper—but that's beside the point. I'm going to—" He broke off, gave a shiver, and looked malignantly around the room. "Where's the damn draught coming from?" he demanded.

Iris wondered. Every window in the room was hermetically sealed. Mr. Reed, having ascertained this, directed her attention to the door.

"Push that mat under there," he directed. "No, not that one, not that one—the big one. That's it. Right against the bottom of the door—that's it. Nothing but draughts," he fumed under his breath. "Whistling all round me and getting on m'chest." He settled himself in his chair and came back to the subject in hand. "Now listen t'me," he said. "Listen carefully, because I don't go over anything twice. If you don't get it first time, then you can't follow good plain English. Now," He pointed a fat forefinger at his listener. "Up at a place called High Ambo there's a school—a prep school and a good one. I know, because I was there m'self once, when it was even better than it is now. They've got fine grounds, but near them there's a large property belonging to Lord Fellmount—a bit of an eccentric who lives by himself with an old manservant and likes privacy. There's a lake in his grounds, and he has a good bit of trouble keeping the schoolboys away from it. He complains to the School, and the authorities do their best, I take it, to keep the boys off. But they won't keep off, and so the old man—Fellmount—takes the law into his own hands and deals with offenders as and when he catches 'em. Well, he caught Sir Kenneth Harfield's son, and he threw him into the lake—to teach him. He didn't know who the boy was, and he didn't care—he threw him in. I suppose you've got all that?"

"Yes, Mr. Reed."

"Very well. Now comes the trouble—blast that draught!

Get up," he ordered, "and see if that window fastener's properly shut. That's better. Now, this boy Harfield was thrown in on the last day of the summer term; he fished himself out and nobody—so he says—knew anything about the incident except himself and the man who threw him in. He didn't want to be seen at the School, so he hung about until he was dry and then went back. The other boys had gone—the train contingent, that is. Harfield was to go home by car with his parents.

"Well, they came to fetch him. They took him home, and the next thing, he's down with a serious chill and misses pneumonia by a hair. They make inquiries when he's better, and it all comes out and his parents don't like what they hear. In fact, Sir Kenneth liked it so little that he wants me to print the story—delicate boy, large fees, school guilty of gross neglect and breach of contract. He wouldn't have a case in court, of course, because the boy was out of bounds, but the parents feel that no boy ought to be left in the position being able to run himself into serious trouble in that way. And he insists that the School—somebody in the school, anybody in the School—had a good idea of what happened but said nothing because they were frightened they would have to give up a bit of their summer holiday to keep the boy at school for a few days to see if any trouble developed. They let him—the father says—they let him do the long drive home and said nothing. Those are all the facts, have you got 'em?"

"Yes, Mr. Reed," said Iris.

"All right. Now I'll tell you what I'm going to do. I've

seen Sir Kenneth this morning and we've had it out. He's got the story and he'd like to see it in print—but I wouldn't. I was well looked after when I was at school there and I've got a feeling for the place. Print a story of this kind and bang goes the School. If the School doesn't face up to its responsibilities, if they've got people on their staff capable of neglecting their duty to the boys, then I'll print the story and be glad to. But I want to give the School a chance—and I've got Sir Kenneth round to agreeing to let me do it my own way. My own way is to send somebody down there to keep their ears open. I want somebody there who will get to know the school and who could do a little discreet questioning. Then I we'd get at the root of the trouble. If we found that the school wasn't to blame, Sir Kenneth's prepared to drop the matter; the boy's all right and clamouring to go back. But we've got to do a little investigating. And—" Ernest Reed leaned forward and glared at Iris—"and I'm going to send you to do it."

"Me?" In spite of herself, Iris spoke in a squeak of surprise.

"You. Don't imagine," Mr. Reed warned her, "that I've any confidence in your intelligence or in your discretion. Far from it—but that's neither here no' there. But High Ambo is a hamlet of—well, apart from the school, which is some distance above the village, there's a mere handful of people. No stranger could go there without having every eye fixed on him and every yokel asking questions about him. Nobody'll ask any questions about you. You're merely going to spend your holiday with your sister—that's all."

"With—"

"—your sister. Don't try," directed Mr. Reed, "to look as though you hadn't any idea she was going there. If you don't know now—which I'm convinced you do—then you'll know pretty soon, because she *is* going there. I saw her last Friday and, when I heard where she was going, I was naturally interested. Now I've an even greater interest. I want you to get her up to Town for a talk with you. Tell her what I've told you and make arrangements for going to stay with her at High Ambo. You'll get an increase in salary and your expenses, and you'll send me a report every week—understand?"

"Yes, Mr. Reed."

"And don't sit there and say, 'Yes, Mr. Reed,' 'No, Mr. Reed.' Get back to your work and think about what I've told you. When you've seen Ca—when you've seen your sister—let me know the date you're joining her. Now out and shut the door properly behind you and draw that rug back as you go out—closer now, closer—that's it."

The door closed behind Iris.

End of preview.
To continue reading, look for the book entitled
"Iris in Winter" by Elizabeth Cadell

About the Author

Elizabeth Vandyke was born in British India at the beginning of the 20th century. She married a young Scotsman and became Elizabeth Cadell, remaining in India until the illness and death of her much-loved husband found her in England, with a son and a daughter to bring up, at the beginning of World War 2. At the end of the war she published her first book, a light-hearted depiction of the family life she loved. Humour and optimism conquered sorrow and widowhood, and the many books she wrote won her a wide public, besides enabling her to educate her children (her son joined the British Navy and became an Admiral), and allowing her to travel, which she loved. Spain, France and Portugal provide a background to many of her books, although England and India were not forgotten. She finally settled in Portugal, where her married daughter still lives, and died when well into her 80s, much missed by her 7 grandchildren, who had all benefitted from her humour, wisdom and gentle teaching. British India is now only a memory, and the quiet English village life that Elizabeth Cadell wrote about has changed a great deal, but her vivid characters, their love affairs and the tears and laughter they provoke, still attract many readers, young and not-so-young, in this twenty-first century. Reprinting these books will please her fans and it is hoped will win her new ones.

Also by Elizabeth Cadell

My Dear Aunt Flora
Fishy, Said the Admiral
River Lodge
Family Gathering
Iris in Winter
Sun in the Morning
The Greenwood Shady
The Frenchman & the Lady
Men & Angels
Journey's Eve
Spring Green
The Gentlemen Go By
The Cuckoo in Spring
Money to Burn
The Lark Shall Sing
Consider The Lilies
The Blue Sky of Spring
Bridal Array
Shadow on the Water
Sugar Candy Cottage
The Green Empress
Alice Where Art Thou?
The Yellow Brick Road
Six Impossible Things
Honey For Tea
The Language of the Heart
Mixed Marriage

Letter to My Love
Death Among Friends
Be My Guest
Canary Yellow
The Fox From His Lair
The Corner Shop
The Stratton Story
The Golden Collar
The Past Tense of Love
The Friendly Air
Home for the Wedding
The Haymaker
Deck With Flowers
The Fledgling
Game in Diamonds
Parson's House
Round Dozen
Return Match
The Marrying Kind
Any Two Can Play
A Lion in the Way
Remains to be Seen
The Waiting Game
The Empty Nest
Out of the Rain
Death and Miss Dane

Introduction

Deepwood is no ordinary village, the flat dwellers at the Lodge are no ordinary tenants, and there is the matter of two extraordinary gentlemen not of this world at all.

Young love was doing badly in Deepwood as this story begins. But, let's face it, who can talk of love before talking of Cousin Clarry? Empires might crumble, food be rationed, romance be replaced by glands, but Cousin Clarry could triumph over all!

Six years earlier she came to the little English Village of Deepwood to spend a week. Now no one in the village could imagine life without her. No one could be funnier than Cousin Clarry on the subject of sex (and she was so right!); no one could be worse than Cousin Clarry on the cello. In short, no one could replace her and so she stayed.

It all had to happen in six of the hottest summer weeks Deepwood had ever known. The eccentric new gardener let the flowers scorch and talked to people nobody else could see. The gallant captain came back into his own as he stole the clothes of a lovely lady. The hardened hearts of the young nearly broke the hopeful hearts of the not-so-young...until the devil himself stepped in. As always, nothing could be more pleasing. Mrs. Cadell brings to real life a wide variety of people you will take to your own heart—shocking, misguided, importunate, surprising as they may be. She writes with a verve and fancy that is sheer enchantment and—unless you are prepared to be enchanted—there is no point at all in starting her wise and delightful novel.

Printed in Great Britain
by Amazon